A Discovery in the Cotswolds

a&b

A Discovery in the Cotswolds

REBECCA TOPE

Allison & Busby Limited
11 Wardour Mews
London W1F 8AN
allisonandbusby.com

First published in Great Britain by Allison & Busby in 2023.

A CIP catalogue record for this book is available from
the British Library.

First Edition

ISBN 978-0-7490-3037-7

Typeset in 11/16 pt Sabon LT Pro by
Allison & Busby Ltd.

By choosing this product, you help take care of the world's forests.
Learn more: www.fsc.org.

Printed and bound by CPI Group (UK) Ltd, Croydon, CR0 4YY

This one is dedicated to my dear friend Paula Brackston, who has been a staunch confidante for a long time now.

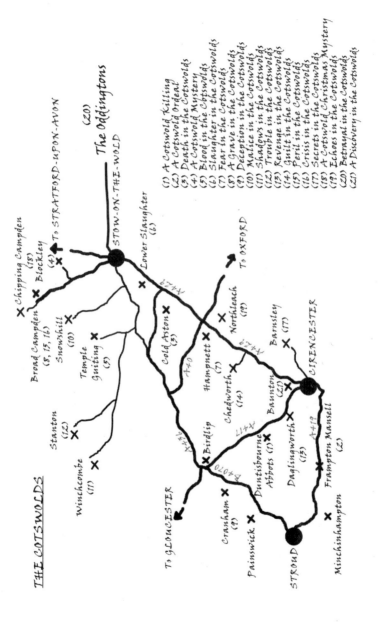

THE COTSWOLDS

Winchcombe (11)

Stanton (12)

Broad Campden (8, 15, 16)

Chipping Campden

Blockley (18)

→ TO STRATFORD-UPON-AVON

Snowshill (10)

Temple Guiting (5)

STOW-ON-THE-WOLD

The Oddingtons (20)

Lower Slaughter (6)

A429

Cold Aston (3)

A40

Hampnett (7)

Northleach (19)

→ TO OXFORD

A429

Birdlip

A436

Chedworth (14)

Barnsley (17)

B4070

Duntisbourne Abbots (1)

A417

Daglingworth (13)

Braunton (21)

CIRENCESTER

A419

Cranham (9)

Painswick

Frampton Mansell (2)

TO GLOUCESTER

STROUD

Minchinhampton

(1) A Cotswold Killing
(2) A Cotswold Ordeal
(3) Death in the Cotswolds
(4) A Cotswold Mystery
(5) Blood in the Cotswolds
(6) Slaughter in the Cotswolds
(7) Fear in the Cotswolds
(8) A Grave in the Cotswolds
(9) Deception in the Cotswolds
(10) Malice in the Cotswolds
(11) Shadows in the Cotswolds
(12) Trouble in the Cotswolds
(13) Revenge in the Cotswolds
(14) Guilt in the Cotswolds
(15) Peril in the Cotswolds
(16) Crisis in the Cotswolds
(17) Secrets in the Cotswolds
(18) A Cotswold Christmas Mystery
(19) Echoes in the Cotswolds
(20) Betrayal in the Cotswolds
(21) A Discovery in the Cotswolds

Author's Note

As with other titles in this series, the story is set in a real Cotswold village. Baunton is almost exactly as described, including the tumbledown sheds. But the Weavers' farm is an invention.

Chapter One

'I've discovered something,' Timmy announced over Sunday lunch.

'What?' asked Stephanie, with minimal interest.

'Tomato soup tastes nothing like tomatoes. It's not even the right *colour*.'

The whole family paused and looked at him. Thea had made two cans of soup stretch between four people as a first course before the roast chicken. First courses were unusual, but the chicken wasn't very big. Besides, it was half-term, which they all thought called for something a bit special.

'I tried making it with real tomatoes once,' she said. 'And it was revolting.'

'They add a lot of sugar,' said Stephanie in a helpful big-sisterly tone. 'And other stuff, I suppose.'

Drew was sipping soup thoughtfully. 'Makes you

think of Andy Warhol,' he said. 'And Coca Cola. Icons. Secret ingredients. You could do a PhD on it.'

'It's like the emperor's new clothes,' Timmy went on. 'Everybody pretending it's actually something it's not.'

'But it really is made of tomatoes,' Stephanie pointed out. 'Like ninety-five per cent of it is, or something like that. It must be to do with the processing.'

'Hurry up and finish,' said Thea. 'The next course is ready.'

'What's a PhD?' asked Timmy.

'The phone's quiet,' noticed Thea, an hour or two later.

'It's Sunday,' Drew reminded her.

'I know, but it's been quiet for a week now.'

Stephanie gave her a look. 'More than that,' she said. 'There's only one funeral this week – and only one last week, too.'

'Oh.' Thea cast her mind back, wondering how long it had been since she took a proper interest in her husband's schedule. 'It's one of those phases, is it? You can do some catching up, then.' *You could even go and see your mother*, she added silently. Drew's mother had turned out to be a very mixed blessing since she had re-entered their lives the previous year. Encounters with her were dutiful and strained, the lengthy estrangement too deep and damaging to overcome in any meaningful way. Drew had driven up to her distant northern home once, and never again. Talk of her moving to the Cotswolds to be near them had withered away as unfeasible.

'It's a bit more than that,' said Drew with a sigh. 'Those new people in Cirencester are turning into

10

real competition. They make me feel very stale by comparison.'

'Um . . ?' said Thea, slightly alarmed. She had evidently missed something.

'That new undertaker business, all run by women. Bespoke funerals, low prices, flexible in every way. Fresh, young, ground-breaking. Overturning all the old practices. You know what I mean.'

'Oh. I thought you were all those things.'

'I might have been ten years ago. The world appears to have changed quite a lot without me properly noticing.'

'Maggs would have made sure that didn't happen,' Thea acknowledged in all humility. Drew's original assistant had handled a substantial portion of the work, subtly educating Drew in countless ways and nudging him in the right direction when it came to public tastes and expectations. Nobody – certainly not Thea – had filled her shoes, and the initial novelty value he had enjoyed in the Cotswolds was rapidly fading away. Alternative burials were almost mainstream now, and providers were proliferating.

'I know,' sighed Drew.

Implications were legion. And familiar. Thea had put up a very poor showing as the undertaker's wife, distancing herself from the details of the work with little or no apology. Not – as many people probably supposed – because she had any difficulties with death, but more because she lacked the subtle sensitivities that her husband seemed to have been born with. The complicated realities of bereavement baffled her at times. She wholeheartedly endorsed the simple burials that were Drew's stock-in-trade: the absence of any religious ritual; the close involvement of the families in decorating the coffin and speaking over it before it was interred – it was all completely right, in her view. But there were more layers to it than that. The enormity of death had to be handled in small bites, seasoned with humour and tears, and sometimes openly defied. Whilst deploring the often-used passage written by Henry Scott Holland and subsequently turned into a poem, Thea accepted that it reflected what people wanted to believe at the moment of losing a loved one. 'Death is nothing at all. It does not count,' it said. 'I have only slipped away into the next room. Nothing has happened.' '*Nonsense!*' Thea had wanted to shout, the first time she heard it at the age of thirty-two. Her feelings had only grown stronger since then.

When her first husband had died, a friend had rashly suggested the reading, causing a painful meltdown on Thea's part, which evolved into a dark period of anguish and confusion. Grief had been subsumed under the heading of rage for a while, morphing into a grim phase of self-harming, as the jargon characterised it. She had pulled herself out of it with the help of her spaniel and a whole new way of life working as a house-sitter. There had been a new relationship which she had come to see as 'transitional', before meeting dear Drew Slocombe. Even then, it had been a long time before she'd found the courage to disclose all the details of her recent past to Drew. Her main worry was that he would overreact and offer an excessive level of retrospective sympathy. In the event, he had pitched it perfectly and firmly packed it away as long dealt with and finished. 'A normal part of the grieving process,' he said.

She knew she would never be able to match his

expertise when it came to managing the minefield of bereavement, and she was going to have to tread carefully when considering Drew's current predicament. 'So what are we going to do about it?' she said.

'Good question. I'm wondering whether I should get Maggs down here and see if she has any ideas.'

'She might not want to, you know. She's got plenty of other things to think about these days.' Maggs was married, with two small children, not much money and some worrying health issues.

'I could go there, maybe?'

Thea grimaced. *Going there* entailed revisiting the area where Drew had lived with his first wife and run a thriving alternative burial service. His children had been born there and his wife was buried close by. Maggs and Den Cooper lived in a neighbouring village, but had moved out of the funeral business. Den worked as a security officer at Bristol airport, and Maggs had become a full-time mother. Her second daughter, Imogen, was only five months old. Two months earlier, Maggs had suddenly become breathless and light-headed. An embolism was discovered on a lung, and everything had plunged into panic and uncertainty. The echoes of Karen Slocombe's experience were impossible to ignore.

'You know her best,' said Thea, 'but I'm not sure the timing is terribly good.'

'I'll phone her and see how things are, then.'

'The obvious answer is for me to earn some proper money,' said Thea, returning to a perennial topic that was never entirely resolved. Thea had sold a house in Witney when she married Drew, which gave them a large amount of savings which easily tided them over the quiet spells. Bearing this in mind, she felt she might be excused the annoyance of having to find a job, and Drew had agreed with her. However, there was a new tone to this latest analysis of their finances, which threatened to give rise to a new line of thought. If Drew's business failed, everything would be thrown up in the air. 'I should sit down and write a CV.'

'We're not very employable, either of us,' he pointed out. 'I can't just let everything fall apart – not with Andrew and Fiona relying on me, and after we've made all the alterations to the house and got the hearse . . .' He ground to a halt, looking miserable. 'I just have to pull myself together and keep up with the times. I thought I knew what people wanted, but I can see I've been lazy. Maybe I need to invest in another burial field if I can find one, with a different sort of ambience that might appeal to a whole new group of people.'

The conversation rambled on for a few more minutes, with Thea finding less and less to offer by way of helpful suggestions. The spectre of Maggs Cooper hovered at the back of her mind; Maggs who knew how to handle the bereaved and understood what was wanted from a genuine funeral. She had been Drew's assistant for years, seeing him through the loss of his wife and effectively carrying the business for a while. It would look as if Thea had failed him if Maggs were to be shipped in now.

'I'll just check a few things on Facebook and whatnot – see if anybody wants a house-sitter around here, then,' she concluded. 'After all, it's what I do.'

* * *

14

'There's a rather peculiar thing about Baunton,' Thea reported, later in the day. 'You know – that little place right beside Cirencester.'

'Never been there,' said Drew. 'Peculiar in what way?'

'I was just noodling around and got onto something about church paintings. You know – like the one in Oddington, where I was back in the summer. I'd got it in my favourites or something and it popped up, along with stuff about another one in Baunton. And that led me to a post somebody put up saying there was goings-on in a corner of the churchyard and there should be a rota of people to watch it in the night, to see what it was.'

'Goings-on, eh? Amongst the graves? Sounds pretty normal to me.'

'You're thinking of that woman who was killed and buried in Peaceful Repose before you'd even opened up,' she accused. He had told her the story several times, boasting of his own brief prowess as an amateur detective. 'Not that there was anything normal about that, of course.'

'I wasn't thinking about her,' he said, with a little frown that struck Thea as mildly irritated. 'It's more that most teenagers go through a phase of mucking about in churchyards. I think it has to do with confronting death for the first time. Trying to belittle it, or put it in its place. Do you know what I mean?'

'Sort of. Maybe that's what's happened in Baunton. Unless it's lovers looking for a quiet spot. Except it's serious enough to make the news, even if it's only local Facebook stuff.'

'Black magic, then?'

'Might be. I can't find anything else about it, but there's something up. A man's been complaining that his granny's grave has had a fire started on top of it. More than once, apparently.'

'I'm confused as to why you find this interesting. I thought you were looking for a house-sitting job.'

'I got side-tracked. One thing leads to another,' she defended vaguely.

'I have to say if you're looking for regular work, I'm not sure house-sitting is the best option. Not that I'm objecting or anything, but it does take you away from the bosom of your family, and that can be awkward. Stephanie doesn't like it, for one thing. And the dog's always a complication.'

He had neatly summarised the tensions that arose when Thea did accept a commission to watch over someone's Cotswold house for a week or so. She had done it for a few years before she met Drew, finding herself in surprising demand, in spite of the succession of calamities that followed her around. She had acquired a level of notoriety that actually appealed to some people. Her very presence sometimes overturned the daily routines of a small village and led to violence. The fact that house-sitting was essentially boring ensured that Thea took it upon herself to tackle the mysteries of local behaviour, generally with the encouragement – or at least concurrence – of the police.

'You think I should stack supermarket shelves?' she challenged.

'It's steady money and we'd get a handy discount on groceries.'

'While you just sit at home waiting for the phone to ring.'

'It's a hard job, but someone has to do it,' he twinkled. 'But as we said already, it looks as if I'm going to have to be more proactive than that. Winter is coming, people will be dying and I want to bury them.'

'You could make a banner saying just that,' she teased.

They both laughed, happy in the banter that might have sounded sharper to an outsider than it was meant. Stephanie and Timmy had long ago learnt to take it calmly, and only started to worry if Thea wept or Drew stormed out of the room. That hardly ever happened.

'Winters aren't so cold these days,' Thea reminded him. 'And nursing homes are suffocatingly hot.'

'Even so,' he muttered.

'I think I might go and have a look at Baunton tomorrow. Stephanie can come with me. Tim's got that Pokemon thing to go to.'

'Okay,' said Drew.

Which had not actually solved anything, of course. Drew pointed this out later in the day. 'We're just avoiding the issue,' he said.

'Ah,' said Thea, reaching for her metaphorical counsellor's hat. 'Well, let's be methodical about it. First of all – how much do you seriously want to carry on as you are? I mean, doing the same sort of burials at the same sort of prices. Are you actively committed to that or would a change appeal to you?'

'I'm not at all resistant to change, if a viable one offered itself. Have you anything particular in mind?'

'Not really. We should probably go over what it is

people most want from a funeral. Has that changed? If there's a sudden preference for quick cremations with nobody there, then we might be in trouble.'

Drew winced. 'Surely that can't really be what they want? It's so cold and callous. Such a waste of a life.'

'That's a bit strong.'

'No, but the funeral's where everyone gets a chance to recognise that a life has stopped, that there's a lifeless body that ought to be respected for who that person was. I must have watched thousands of people put that body into the ground, throw soil onto it and walk away knowing they've done everything properly. Somebody once said nobody should leave a funeral more miserable than they were before it. Something like that. And that's what I want to give them. The release of emotion and permission for life to go on. There's nothing more they can actually *do*. That's a good feeling.'

Thea laughed. 'Good Lord, you've still got it, haven't you! Just show up at all the WIs in Gloucestershire and say that and you'll have queues around the block.'

'Like I did ten years ago,' he agreed. 'But I get the impression that it's all going the other way now. Death is seen as morbid, ugly, frightening. Watching a flimsy coffin get covered in earth is too much for them. With a cremation it all goes on out of sight, and is a lot easier – or so they like to think. They've still got the satisfaction of getting it accomplished, without too much of the reality. Maybe that's okay. Maybe it's me that's got it wrong.'

'It's not,' she assured him. 'You need to save people

18

from themselves. They're only doing these horrible cremations because they think it's the cheapest way. People never believe that a burial can be cheaper.'

'Not just "can be". It *always* is, even in a churchyard or a municipal cemetery. Unless they have one of those really simple cremations with nobody there,' he finished with a sigh.

'Right. So tell them that. You have to get out there and spread the word.'

'Yes, dear.' He stared at a spot on the wall, processing his feelings. 'I just wish I didn't have to, that's all. People use such peculiar language these days. Everything's "cherished" or "precious". I like to use plainer words.'

'Says the man who ran "Peaceful Repose Burial Ground",' she taunted. 'I almost went off you on the spot when I heard that's what you'd called your place.'

He bridled. 'It *was* peaceful,' he protested. 'And besides, I was more idealistic then.'

She patted his hand. 'You're still idealistic. And quaint. And traditional. I mean – you don't even like it when people request brightly coloured clothes at the funeral, because that's what the dead person said they wanted.'

'That's true,' he admitted with a bowed head. 'It always feels like a sort of false modesty on the part of the deceased. As if they don't want their friends and family to really care that they've gone. Because it's usually at their request that people don't wear black.'

'I know. You explained it before. But that's how people are these days.'

'I always let them do what they want,' he defended.

'You do. And it'll be all right, honestly. Meanwhile Stephanie and I are still going to Baunton tomorrow. We'll do some shopping in Cirencester as well, to make it worth it. That's what half-term's for – replacing school stuff. She needs new trainers.'

Chapter Two

Thea parked close to the very large church that was one of Cirencester's main features. 'Do you want to go in?' she asked Stephanie, who had been taking considerable interest in religion for some time now.

'Not really,' shrugged the girl. 'We're looking at the one in Baunton, aren't we? Two in one day might be a bit much.'

Thea laughed. 'It's a handsome building, all the same. Look at it! It's like Northleach only more so.'

'Yeah, but it's not symmetrical, look. That extra bit is all wrong. And it's really much too big.'

Thea gave an obedient glance but found herself resisting any proper scrutiny. She had mixed feelings about churches in general, very aware of their declining relevance and the cost of preserving them. 'I agree with you about the size. It's just showing off.'

Stephanie opened her mouth to correct this calumny when her attention was caught by a figure leaning against one of the buttresses at the foot of the tower barely fifteen yards away. 'Look at that woman!' she whispered. 'Is she drunk or something?'

Thea tried not to stare, even though the person in question was in no state to notice or even care. 'I think she must be,' she said. 'But you can't always be sure. She might have brain damage or something.'

As they watched, the woman slid down the stonework until she was squatting on the pavement. Her head was shaking from side to side, and she patted the ground by her feet with both hands. 'Gosh!' breathed Stephanie. 'Shouldn't somebody help her?'

'Probably. But she's not causing any harm, is she? She might well not want any help.'

'Everyone's just ignoring her. They're embarrassed, aren't they?'

'Look, here's somebody. She seems to know her.'

Another woman was approaching with obvious purpose. 'Oh, Alice,' she said loudly. 'I've been looking for you. Get up, you fool.'

Alice did not move or speak. The newcomer stood over her, arms folded. Thea and Stephanie shamelessly watched the proceedings, each consumed with curiosity.

'They look just like each other,' said Stephanie. 'Don't they?'

It was true. Both aged about sixty, with fair hair gone grey and long chins, they might have been twins. 'The new one's quite a lot fatter, and a bit taller,' Thea murmured. 'But I bet they're sisters.'

'They look – unusual,' judged the girl. 'Not like most people round here.'

It was obvious what she meant. Cotswolds women had good clothes, expensive shoes, tidy hairstyles and always seemed to be in a hurry. They drove big cars and often had a big dog to match. The few remaining farm women were no exception, although their hair might sometimes be disorderly. Alice and her putative sister were both wearing grubby trainers, and Alice actually had a dry leaf and a small twig sticking to her jumper.

'Get up,' came the repeated instruction. Alice slowly complied, pushing herself upright with the help of the stonework behind her. 'Why are you here, anyway?' barked the vocal one. Alice merely shrugged.

'We should go,' muttered Thea. 'They won't want us watching like this.' As she spoke, the second woman met her gaze and held it. *She'll know me again*, thought Thea, turning away with a faint smile.

Stephanie was quick to agree, and they walked past the church into the main shopping street. 'Was she drunk, do you think?' Stephanie wondered, unable to drop the subject.

'Probably. We'll never know now, so let's just forget about it. She's got somebody looking after her, which is the main thing.'

By force of habit, Thea was heading for the Oxfam bookshop until her stepdaughter queried this. 'We don't need any more books,' she said. 'I thought we'd come to get me some trainers.'

'Sorry. You're right – although it's always fun to have a browse through a lot of books, and they're cheaper here.'

'We haven't got time,' said the sensible girl. 'You know you always take ages when you go in there.'

'You exaggerate,' Thea argued mildly. 'We've only been here once before, to my certain knowledge. Together, I mean.'

Even so, Stephanie prevailed and the trainers were purchased after careful comparisons between several pairs. 'Tim needs more socks,' Thea was reminded. 'And you did say Hepzie could do with a new collar.'

'Drew thinks he ought to get another tie or two, as well,' said Thea with an effort. 'He got a greasy mark on the best one he uses for funerals.' She was not enjoying this part of the expedition, with the mundane necessities that had no direct connection with her own priorities.

It was well past eleven when they finished. 'Let's get to Baunton now,' Stephanie urged.

'Right,' said Thea, resisting the urge to point out that none of the shopping had been for her benefit.

The village was approached via Baunton Lane, which led through a part of Stratton. 'Look at these houses!' Thea exclaimed as they passed a number of very big, very handsome Cotswold residences. 'Every one of them must be worth nearly a million,' she sighed.

'Really?' Stephanie sounded sceptical. 'That's a lot.'

'Maybe only the really huge ones. Oh, here we are, look.' They had crossed the A435 and were immediately in Baunton where the houses were still handsome but not quite as large. 'Now where's the church?'

They followed the little road around a bend, past houses that often had no barrier between themselves and the street, and which gave an instant impression of approachability and friendliness. 'How very different from Oddington!' said Thea. 'Everything's got big gates and electronic keypads there.'

'I remember,' said Stephanie. 'Horrible!'

They spotted a sign saying 'To the Church' and found a place to park. A woman in a garden opposite gave them a little wave as she cut the dead heads off a clump of dahlias. 'Wow – a real live person!' said Thea. 'That's a rare sight in most of these villages.'

Standing beside the car they both became aware of a constant noise, loud enough to force itself onto their attention. 'Cars?' said Thea.

'Must be.'

'They sound so close. And such a big road.' She was bewildered by the geography, remembering the quiet little lane they had used to get there. 'We'll have to go and look after we've seen the church.'

Stephanie just nodded and opened the little gate into the churchyard.

They could see nothing immediately worthy of note. Yew trees, gravestones, a wall and the church itself. They stood back and regarded it for a moment. 'Not like the one in Cirencester,' said Stephanie. 'This one's more like a house.'

She was right, Thea realised. No spire or tower, just a basic plain building with a large porch in the middle. 'It's really old,' she said. 'We should have done some homework on it before we came.'

'I did,' said Stephanie. 'It dates back to 1150, with some extras added in the fifteenth century.'

'Oh,' said Thea.

'Let's go in.'

The wall painting confronted them the moment they were inside. Most of it was visible, with St Christopher's red cloak the most vivid part. 'But where's the Christ Child?' wondered Stephanie. Little by little they detected the outline of a small figure perched on the saint's shoulder, marred by a modern beam-end that had presumably been inserted at a time when the painted had been obscured by Victorian whitewash. Stephanie recounted the legend of St Christopher for her stepmother's benefit, since her knowledge of such subjects was much greater than Thea's. 'Hmm,' said Thea, looking round at the rest of the interior. 'I bet that's not in the Bible.'

'Hardly any of the saints are,' said Stephanie. 'But that doesn't mean they're not good stories.'

Thea had found a curtain, which she opened to reveal a very old embroidery. She inspected it closely. 'This is lovely,' she called to the girl who had moved up towards the altar.

'So is this.' Stephanie was looking at the cloth hanging over the front of the altar. 'All done by hand.'

'That must be the replacement for this one, when it got too fragile. Now it's kept over here with a curtain to stop it fading.'

'Everything's so *old*. It makes my head hurt. Do you think people then were the same as us now?'

'Who knows? Lots of people say they were, that nothing has really changed since Neolithic times. The basic intelligence level of human beings is still the same as then, apparently.'

'They were good at embroidery, anyway,' smiled Stephanie. 'But I don't think they can have been anything like us. What about religion? They put all these pictures on the walls because people couldn't read. And they can't have been very clever, can they? They didn't invent stuff like we do now.'

'It's a big question. I think the main difference is in what people were most frightened of.'

'Dying,' said Stephanie readily. 'And that hasn't changed, has it?'

Which reminded them of Drew and funerals and murder. 'We haven't had a proper look round the graveyard,' Thea said. 'What about the strange goings-on we came to investigate?'

With a long backward glance, Stephanie followed her outside and they again examined the churchyard. 'It's very small,' Thea remarked.

'There's another bit round the corner, look.' The girl started towards the wall at the bottom of the short path and veered around the end of the building. 'They've got a lovely new shed,' she pointed out. 'Do you think the vicar hides out here if he doesn't want to talk to someone?'

'Bound to,' Thea agreed. The shed was an anomaly in itself, and she felt very tempted to see if she could look inside it. The door was not obviously locked. But she restrained herself and went to look at the additional collection of graves. On her left, the ground dropped away into a wide field several feet below the level of the church. A wall and a fence barred the way down.

'Look at this!' Stephanie was standing by an old headstone. 'What's happened here?'

A large earthy mound was lying at right angles to the stone, giving the whole thing a disjointed appearance. At first glance it appeared that there had been a recent burial, but looking again, Thea saw that it was not the work of any human hand. 'Ants?' she said. 'It looks like one of those big anthills you get on land that nobody's touched for a while.' She kicked it gently.

'Don't!' Stephanie stepped back. 'It's scary. There's a *body* down there.'

The mound was indeed roughly coffin-shaped, but somewhat smaller. 'No, there's isn't. I mean – not right here. The stone's facing the other way – see? But it's very odd, all the same. Why have they allowed it?'

'Conservation,' said Stephanie, as if that was obvious.

'Really? Do ants need conserving? I thought there were trillions and zillions of them.' She kicked again and a small number of insects made an appearance. 'I was right!' she said. 'They've made a proper ant city right beside this grave. I hope the person wasn't scared of them!'

'This isn't what you read about, though. That said something about a fire.'

'Right,' Thea remembered. 'They must have cleared it all up. I can't see anything. It was probably months ago now.'

They went back to the older section, Thea's attention constantly drawn to the field below them. 'It probably floods sometimes,' she muttered. 'The River Churn is over there somewhere.'

'I bet it's where they have the summer show and all that sort of thing,' said Stephanie, who had helped run a stall at the Chipping Campden Show and thought every village should have one.

'Baunton isn't big enough for its own show. But I do see what you mean.' She let her imagination run free. 'Maybe they had jousting and pig roasts and competitions for who owned the best sheep, back in the fifteenth century. The church was here then, so there must have been a settlement.'

'Hog roasts, not pig,' Stephanie corrected her. 'But otherwise, yes. Those woods look interesting over on the other side as well.'

'They do. And I can see people by them – look.'

She pointed to a group of three or four figures at the edge of the line of trees. They seemed to be consulting each other, before spreading out and pushing into the woodland in one or two places. Thea and Stephanie watched for a full minute, before Thea said, 'They must be walkers who've got lost, looking for a footpath.'

Stephanie shook her head. 'I think they're looking for a dog or somebody who's gone missing. You can't really go wrong if you're walking a footpath. There are signs everywhere. We're on the Monarch's Way here, you know.'

'Are we?'

'It goes right past this church. You can walk it from here all the way to our house.'

'And the rest,' said Thea, who had heard a great deal about the Monarch's Way from Timmy, and how it was 625 miles long, stretching in a crazy zigzag from Worcester to Shoreham in Sussex. Timmy had made his own comprehensive map of it, marking spots he had seen for himself, along with points of interest adjoining it. He had acquired a book about it, too, and never missed a chance to go and look at a new stretch. 'He'll be cross that we've seen this bit without him.'

'We'll have to come again. I like this village.'

'We've hardly seen any of it yet.'

The never-ending rush of traffic somewhere close by formed a backing to everything they said and saw. In every lull in the conversation it obtruded itself. 'I guess you'd get used to it,' said Thea. 'The traffic, I mean. It must be like having tinnitus.'

Stephanie requested an explanation. 'Oh,' she said, when it had been briefly delivered. 'So let's go and see how close we are to the noisy road, shall we?'

'Aren't you hungry? It must be lunchtime. I should be at home making something to eat.'

'Dad won't mind. He's got one of those pies he likes. He'll have it all to himself. Oliver's mum is making something for the Pokemon club.'

'Just twenty minutes max, then. Come on.'

They turned left at the church gate and followed the track past the last house in the lane, and onto a path that took them into a whole different world. On one side the ground dropped down to the small river, which was not always visible through rushes and low vegetation. On the other side there was a thin line of trees on a rising bank. Ahead, the noise grew louder until suddenly they found the road itself soaring above them. The footpath ran right underneath it. 'Wow!' breathed Stephanie.

The noise seemed to lessen as they stood directly below the road, with its supports perfectly aligned so there was a sense of being in a kind of cathedral. The underside of the roadway was clean and new-looking. There was no vibration and nothing visibly moving. 'It doesn't even smell of exhaust,' said Thea, trying to reconcile the monstrous intrusion with the ancient little village.

'It's awful. But weirdly wonderful as well.'

'That's exactly right,' said Thea. 'Now, come on. We've been here long enough.'

They hurried back towards the car, both aware that they would not be home before half past one at this rate, and hunger was an increasingly urgent issue. But Thea could not help slowing as they passed a short row of denser trees on the rising ground beside the path. She peered through them and noticed a wooden building perched at the top of the slope, half covered with ivy and other vegetation. 'Somebody's got a nice big garden shed,' she said. 'But they've let it go to pieces by the look of it.'

Stephanie barely glanced at the object of Thea's interest. She was still looking back at the road so high above them. 'Hmm,' she said.

Thea was still trying to get a better view of the shed. 'It might be a summer house,' she mused. 'I've always wanted a summer house. But I can't see any windows.'

'We should probably go,' Stephanie reminded her. 'You said twenty minutes max, remember?'

There were often times like this, when Thea felt she was actually the child in this relationship, and she reacted accordingly. 'But it doesn't really matter, does it? Apart from being hungry, we don't actually have to dash home for anything.'

'I've got homework. Hepzie needs a walk. Dad might have to go out. Did you bring your phone?' The last question was fired at Thea with a fierce look.

'No, because I knew you'd have yours.'

'It's out of battery,' the girl admitted crossly. 'I left it on all night and didn't have time to charge it this morning.'

As a family, the Slocombes had an ambivalent attitude towards telephones. They formed a crucial part of Drew's work, summoning him to collect bodies or meet with families, at short notice. Timmy and Stephanie used tablets for games and information, but Stephanie now had her own mobile, with the numbers of innumerable other teenagers stored in it, and membership of social groups that Thea struggled to keep track of. Stephanie used it very much less than others of her generation, but it was still a constant presence.

'Drew wouldn't phone us, anyway,' said Thea. 'Timmy's not due back until about four.'

'I just want to get back,' said Stephanie.

The car was just as they'd left it, except for a very obvious sheet of white paper clipped behind one of the windscreen wipers. Thea's first reaction was that it was a complaint at the spot she'd parked in. 'Did I block someone's driveway?' she asked herself, looking around.

'Read it,' said Stephanie superfluously.

'Listen to this. "Am I right that this is Thea Slocombe's car? I remember it from the time you were in Chedworth, three years ago or so. Maybe it belongs to someone else now. But just in case, this is Emmy Wilshire – remember? Or was I still calling myself Millie, then? The thing is, I need somebody like you, here in Baunton. I live here now. Here's my phone number. Can you call me?

"P.S. If the car isn't Thea's, then please destroy this note."'

Thea stared helplessly at her stepdaughter. 'Millie Wilshire,' she said. 'Of all people.'

'Who is she? What's she like?' Stephanie was torn between curiosity and her wish to get home.

'Young. A bit ditzy. I don't really remember her very well, to be honest. I wonder why she changed her name. Millie to Emmy seems rather odd.'

'Not if she's officially *Emily*,' said Stephanie.

Thea smiled. 'You are so clever sometimes,' she said. 'I never would have thought of that.'

Stephanie smirked and shrugged, and said, 'Chedworth's really near here.'

'Is it?' Thea frowned. 'I'll never get the hang of the way all these little places connect up. Although I know you're going to tell me it's on the Monarch's Way as well.'

'I'm not sure, but I think it might be.'

'Get in the car and let's go home. I'll phone Millie-stroke-Emmy from there.'

Chapter Three

Drew remembered Millie Wilshire with a wince. 'That was an awful business,' he said. 'What can she possibly want from you now?'

'I'm going to find out this very minute.' And Thea made the call. Five minutes later, she had plenty to convey to her husband and stepdaughter. 'She's married to a man called Nick Weaver, living on a farm just outside Baunton, not far from that big road, and her husband's got a niece who's gone missing.'

'None of which surprises me,' sighed Drew.

'No. Well, she wants me to go and stay in a sort of annex they use for visitors and see if I can ferret out what's happened. There's been funny goings-on in the village, as we already knew. It's also a sort of house-sit, because they've got nobody to help on the farm and so there's a domestic crisis as well.'

'Did the niece live with them?'

'Temporarily, apparently. She's supposed to be at university, but never went back at the start of the second year, for some reason. Emmy hasn't got a father, as you know, and her mother's not in the picture for some reason. Now this niece has foisted herself on Emmy and Nick. And after a few weeks with them she just vanished.'

Drew nodded to indicate that he well recalled the demise of the girl's father. Not only had the poor man been murdered in a barn, but Thea and Drew had found the body. 'Have they reported it to the police?'

'Oh yes – they say they can't see any real cause for concern because there are no suspicious circumstances. They're not very good at missing persons, as we've discovered before.'

'You make it sound as if we're experts on every sort of crime in the Cotswolds.'

Thea smiled. 'Well, we *are*, pretty much.'

'And we can always consult Gladwin or Caz if we get stuck,' said Stephanie, who had been listening quietly. 'It sounds like our sort of thing, all right. Can we go back there and see what we can find?'

'We?' echoed Thea. 'What makes you think you can go?'

'It's half-term,' Stephanie reminded her. 'I've got nothing else to do. I can stay in the annex thing with you, and do the washing-up for Emmy, or whatever. They might have calves to feed, or pigs, or—'

'Lord help us!' cried Drew. 'All my women are deserting me!'

'I haven't got anywhere near deciding to do it,' Thea soothed him. 'But can I just say that Baunton is a lovely little place, and we only saw a bit of it today, and it would be interesting to have a proper look round, maybe with the dog. Emmy remembers her and says she can come as well. She'd love sniffing round those little lanes.'

'What about Stephanie?' He glared at his daughter. 'Who has been altogether too closely involved in the more unsavoury aspects of life over the past months, if you ask me.'

'Says the undertaker with bodies in the back room,' Thea mocked him, in a style she had recently adopted, and which nobody else found very amusing. 'What is it exactly that you want to shield her from?'

'And what about Timmy?' said Stephanie abruptly changing tack. Her brother was missing this conversation, being in his bedroom at the time.

Everyone took a breath and Thea even managed a laugh. 'Let's not decide anything yet. I'll go over and see Emmy tomorrow, and try to get a proper story out of her. She might have got it all wrong about the niece. You know what families are like,' she finished vaguely.

'You've got a few nieces yourself,' said Drew. 'Jocelyn's Toni, for one.'

'Indeed. And it's probably a small miracle that she's never gone missing.'

'Oh, I *love* Toni,' cried Stephanie. 'Why haven't we seen her again? It's absolutely *ages* since she stayed here with us.'

'She's at university. Maybe we'll try and see her and the others at Christmas. Don't change the subject. You're both doing it.'

'Sorry,' said Drew, giving his daughter a more friendly look. 'I like Toni as well.'

* * *

Thea drove back to Baunton next morning, leaving Drew sitting beside his silent telephone, making scrappy little lists of ways in which he might enhance his business. Stephanie was reading something on her tablet and Timmy was waiting to be collected and delivered to his friend's house for another day of Pokemon. 'I won't take the dog,' Thea decided. 'It won't be very interesting for her if all I'm doing is talking.'

Drew merely grunted and Stephanie made no promises to Hepzie about walks.

It was easily twenty miles from door to door, effectively from one end of the Cotswolds to the other, north to south on fast straight roads that were very familiar. But at Calmsden she dived off to the right and approached Baunton down small lanes that passed through North Cerney, following the River Churn. Close by were Bagendon and Daglingworth and several other villages she had got to know through her house-sitting. Her mental map was full of these small settlements, each one entirely individual and only very loosely connected to each other. In Baunton she had no sense of the nearby Daglingworth, and even less of Sapperton where she had been with her sister Jocelyn several years earlier. However many times she ventured off the main roads into the various deserted little places, she never lost the sense of mystery and other-worldliness. Except in Oddington, where something important had been lost; something you might be tempted to call a soul.

Emmy had given her directions to a farm that was situated roughly north-east of the village, and she found it with little trouble. The house was of the usual solid stone construction, crouching heavily on a flat area of ground, with a barn, sheds, a yard, and scattered clumps of trees on all sides. Thea saw little sign of any of the usual farm animals, except for some hens scratching about. The yard was clean and the open-fronted barn was empty of hay or straw, or even fodder beet or sacks of cattle cake.

The fact was, Thea had seldom visited an actual working farm anywhere in the Cotswolds. She was ignorant of the daily practices of animal husbandry or field-based agriculture. Tractors or other large machines ploughed the land, sowed seeds on it, gathered in the crops. People like TV farmer Adam Henson had huge barns full of rare beasts, but more than that she scarcely knew. She knew about dogs, pet rabbits, garden birds and house plants. None of them very rural, she admitted to herself. As with other aspects of the area, there was a lot that was illusory. Almost all the properties she had taken care of could have been in the middle of a large town for all they taught her about the muck and mayhem of farming.

Emmy's farm had an aura of putting on an act of some sort, deviating from expectation in subtle ways. There was land and hedges, a pick-up truck and the picturesque brown hens. But the more Thea gazed around, as she stood beside her car for a moment, the stronger the impression of neglect and abandonment became. There were thistles in the nearest field, dried up on long stalks. The hedges had a fuzzy untrimmed look, entirely out of character in the tidy Cotswolds. And yet there *were* areas like this – pockets of untended land where rushes and brambles flourished, along with hogweed and docks. There had been a short stretch like that alongside the Monarch's Way, which she had walked the previous day with Stephanie. Perhaps things had been changing without her noticing.

Giving herself a shake, she went to the door of the farmhouse, which had a small porch around it, and knocked. There was no front garden, just an old table standing beside the door, which had empty plant pots stacked up on it.

'Oh, damn it!' she heard a voice from behind the door. 'Can you go round the side? We don't use this door much and it sticks.'

Thea obeyed and found another door which was standing open. Emmy was waiting for her. 'Sorry,' said Thea. 'I should have realised.'

'The path's the clue. Most people figure it out.'

'Sorry,' said Thea again. 'I can be very thick sometimes.' She looked at the young woman, trying to reconcile the person in front of her with the one she remembered from Chedworth. There were several very obvious differences, not least the name. Thea was still mentally using *Millie*.

But the main one was that Emmy-formerly-Wilshire was heavily pregnant.

'Come and meet Nick,' she said. 'This was really his idea.'

Nick Weaver was in his mid-thirties, with rosy cheeks and thick dark brown hair. He was standing in the kitchen holding a full mug of coffee in one hand and fondling the head of an extremely large and shaggy black dog with the other. It was definitely not the sort of dog you normally encountered on a farm. 'Newfoundland,' he said, 'before you ask. His name's Joshua.'

Thea was thankful she had left Hepzie at home. This creature might crush her with a single careless movement.

'Gosh!' she said faintly. 'Hello, Joshua.'

The dog wagged its heavy tail and gave her a slight nudge.

'He's only a puppy, really,' said Farmer Nick. 'Fully grown, though – we hope.'

'Get on with it, Nick,' said Emmy. 'This is Thea – obviously. It's nice of you to come,' she told the visitor. 'Do you want some coffee?'

'Um . . .' said Thea. 'Yes, all right. Thanks.'

'Sit down. It's warmest in here. We only got the stove going last week, and now we're hooked. An oak tree blew down two years ago, and it's keeping us in firewood.'

Thea was aware of a faint sweetish smell that reminded her of late summer and wasps and her mother's kitchen when she was small. 'How long have you been here?'

'Just two years. Well, Nick's been here all his life. I came when we got married.'

'When's the baby due?'

'Christmas Eve,' Emmy laughed. 'My mother-in-law was furious about it when we told her. You'd think we'd done it on purpose.'

'Does she live here?' Thea had in mind various scenarios in which generations lived together in big old farmhouses, which she assumed still pertained.

'Not any more!' said Emmy with feeling. 'That's why we've got the annex available for you.' She drew breath to say more, but was interrupted by her husband.

'Never mind all that, Em,' he said. 'Let's stick to the point.'

'We haven't even *got* to the point yet,' Emmy pointed out.

Thea waited patiently while the tangled tale of Miss Ginny Chambers emerged. Aged twenty, peripherally involved with climate activists based in Bristol over the summer and scared by the violence and public opprobrium, she had shown up at the farm a month before and offered her services either indoors or out. 'As a better use of her time than finishing her degree,' said Nick with a scowl.

'We told her we thought she was making a mistake,' said Emmy defensively. 'But she was badly shaken by some of the things that happened in Bristol. I think she just wanted to get right away and give herself a bit of time to think.'

'And now she's done it again. My gran would have called her a "bolter". A woman who runs away,' Nick explained.

Thea was jumping to a series of conclusions. 'Can we assume that this disappearance has something to do with what happened in the summer, then?'

Nick and Emmy both shook their heads. 'We wondered about that,' said Emmy, 'but it doesn't feel right. Things have gone quiet again in Bristol – all the students have gone back to college. Ginny was only ever on the sidelines. And we've got her thinking through some of the more extreme claims of the activists. She admitted it was all fairly mindless and hysterical.'

'She's a sensible girl,' said Nick. 'She soon saw our point. And she was very useful when we had a course running,' said Nick. 'She was here for the last two,' he added, as if this would make perfect sense to Thea.

'Course?' she queried.

'Oh – haven't we told you? We run courses on conservation and rewilding and all that. Some of them are for writers, some for painters and some are just about the way everything works, ecologically,' Emmy explained, leaving Thea only slightly the wiser.

'And very lucrative they are too,' said Nick, his eyes wide. 'I still can't believe how much people are willing to pay. It's playing havoc with my tax returns.'

Emmy slapped his arm. 'Don't start that,' she said before addressing Thea again. 'No, but it's true. There's always a waiting list – we could do twice as many as we do. As it is, we run three a month, five days each, and we made a clear profit of twelve thousand pounds every month since last April. It's like having a magic money tree in the garden. There's another one starting at the weekend.'

Thea was tempted to ask for details, with Drew and his burials in mind. Could *he* run courses about how to conduct a funeral, or how to give death its due regard? The idea seemed suddenly highly appealing.

'The trouble is there are far too many people involved,' Emmy went on. 'It makes it horribly complicated because they don't always get on, and they have incredible *fads*. Ginny was here for four courses altogether, which means she met thirty-two new people – some of them fairly crackpot, I have to say. They even fall in love with each other quite often, after about two days' acquaintance.'

'None of that concerns Ginny at all,' her husband corrected her. 'I still think she'll have gone off with bloody Joe Twelvetrees. You could see what he was thinking, from the minute he got here and bumped into her in the yard.'

'Except he says she hasn't, and I believe him.' Emmy looked helplessly at Thea. 'I phoned him on Friday, and he swears he's got no idea where she is. He's got a partner and a bunch of foster children and all kinds of commitments.

Ginny's not with him. I know she's not. Nick's got it all wrong, but he won't listen.' She threw a less than friendly look at the man.

Thea quailed as she became increasingly aware that these people expected her to act as a fully-fledged private detective. 'Well . . .' she began. 'I'm really not sure . . .'

'We're making an awful mess of explaining, aren't we?' Emmy moaned. 'Nick knows quite well that Ginny's not with Joe. That would be too easy. I mean – too *obvious*.'

'So who is Joe exactly?' Thea asked.

'He comes as tutor on some of the courses. He and Nick don't always agree about things. Like buttercups.' She giggled. 'That sounds mad, doesn't it? It's amazing what funny things people argue about.'

Thea cocked her head, trying to appear interested and open-minded. 'It's hard to see how anyone could argue over buttercups,' she said.

'You obviously didn't grow up on a farm,' growled Nick. 'I did, and try as I might, I can't shake off some pretty deep convictions. One of them is that the buttercup is a pernicious useless weed. Nothing eats it. It spreads like wildfire. I know it's taboo to use weedkiller, but I still itch to spray the damned things into extinction.'

'And Joe says his mother used to make a wonderful ointment with the flowers,' said Emmy. 'Although we could never find any proof that it's good for anything. A few people think it soothes sore throats if you make it into a syrup, that's all.'

'Drifting off the point, love,' warned Nick.

'Whose side was Ginny on?' asked Thea, hoping to steer things back on track.

'Oh – Joe's mostly,' said Emmy. 'But you need to know that our whole purpose, our *philosophy*, is to avoid extremes. We want to convince people that it's actually quite normal to give wildlife more space and to let all kinds of plants and insects thrive, while living a proper life with all the modern comforts. Well – not *all* – but we have no intention of going back to the Dark Ages. We do try to persuade people not to waste so much – especially food.'

'You can see where my PR comes from, can't you?' said Nick, proudly.

'You make a great team,' Thea told him. 'So is there any more I should know about Ginny?'

There was a short silence, then Nick slowly started speaking. 'You should know that she's easily led. She takes enthusiasms. She's not very thoughtful . . .'

'And she didn't like Joshua,' Emmy put in. 'He can be rather scary, we admit. There's always somebody on every course who won't go near him. It's a shame, because he picks up on their fear and acts up because of it.'

'He can be shut in the yard at the back,' Nick defended. 'He's never any danger to anybody.'

Thea was regretting not having brought pad and pencil to take notes. 'There was no row or anything, then, before Ginny went off?'

Emmy shook her head. 'We don't remember exactly when we last saw her. We think she just walked off, around five o'clock last Wednesday. But we didn't actually start to worry until halfway through Thursday. Nick was busy somewhere and I stayed in bed until nearly ten. The last course had finished and we were just relaxing. The weather was lovely.'

'But it was out of character for her not to say anything?'

'Absolutely. She could have phoned or texted. And she isn't a sneaky girl; she wouldn't just disappear deliberately and leave everybody in such a panic for no reason. Somebody must have forced her. And that's what the police won't listen to. They keep saying there's no evidence and she's an adult, free to go where she likes.'

'Insofar as anybody is,' said Nick darkly. Thea began to wonder what he really thought. The theory about the Joe man carried very little credibility if he had willingly spoken to Emmy and assured her that Ginny was not with him.

'Nick thinks we're living in a police state,' said Emmy with a weak little laugh. 'And I must admit it didn't help us at all when they found Ginny's name on the police computer in Bristol. They've got her marked as a troublemaker, and probably assume she's off on a protest somewhere. We were stupid, really, to ever go to the police in the first place.'

'Ah!' said Thea doubtfully.

Nick had not finished. 'Never mind that – the fact is they've been bloody useless when it comes to finding my niece. She's my sister's daughter, by the way. She's just a nice ordinary girl, very excited about her new baby cousin, likes being outside getting her hands dirty. She got sucked into the climate change business without thinking. She's not really like those characters at all. Not glued to devices like the rest of them. She can tell a rook from a crow, which is more than most people can, of any age.'

He was leaning earnestly towards Thea, his eyes fixed on her face. 'All we really want from you is to be here for a day or two, just gathering up all the bits of the story and seeing what you make of it. I've got this very strong feeling that she's not far away and that she's been forced into something against her will. I hate to think of her locked up somewhere, scared and lonely.' He shook his head impatiently. 'And I understand that it might all be a fuss about nothing. That doesn't help.'

'There's not a shred of evidence,' added Emmy, spreading her hands in a gesture of helplessness. 'And there's another thing – we don't want to raise too big a noise about it, because of the courses. Do you see? We can't have any bad publicity. There's another lot due next weekend, and everything's got to look calm and normal by then.'

'Which must have hampered the police?' said Thea, thinking of her friend Detective Superintendent Gladwin and her colleagues.

'We didn't say that to *them*,' said Emmy, with scorn in her voice. 'When it became obvious that they weren't interested, we just left them out and kept quiet. I guess they might give us a phone call one day and ask if we found Ginny – but they probably won't. Nobody seems to do what they say they'll do these days. Have you noticed that?'

Thea smiled, thinking this young woman sounded about seventy years old. She was still trying to match the person in front of her with the girl she remembered from Chedworth as Millie. So much had happened since that time that she found most of the details had faded from her memory. A house with an attic, a man dead in a barn. Dogs and cars and a few interesting characters. Drew had been with her, and his reactions had dominated a lot of her attention.

'She's right,' said Nick. 'And even if it's not nice to feel you're just being fobbed off, it suits us, in a way, for them just to forget all about it. We didn't make a very good impression on them, and that's not helpful. They've got no idea about wildlife and all that. They took one look at this place and decided we were little better than gypsies.'

'They've got absolutely no idea,' echoed Emmy, shaking her head.

Chapter Four

Negotiations took a while, despite Nick's evident restlessness. 'I've got things I should be doing outside,' he said, more than once.

'So go,' said his wife. 'I can manage without you.'

But he stayed, and after a few more minutes he took the role of leader of the little tour of the farmstead that Thea was treated to. The dog followed along behind like a great bear. Thea's initial disjointed impressions coalesced into a more coherent picture of the main house, flanked by an annex and a large barn, which maintained most of its external appearance. Across the yard was a long low building that had perhaps once been a cattle shed, with freshly painted woodwork and a new-looking roof. 'That's where the punters sleep,' said Nick. 'We spent a fair bit on converting it. Had to put in loos and showers and any number of power points. It's divided into four double rooms. Everybody has to share, whether they like it or not.'

'It is a bit like a barracks, in some people's eyes,' Emmy admitted. 'But it's warm and quiet. The annex isn't any better.'

They then showed her the annex. 'This was actually the milking parlour until two years ago,' said Emmy. 'We had to pretty well tear it down and start again. The layout's a bit weird, even now.'

The only door led directly into a living area that served as kitchen, sitting room and dining room all in one. The kitchen was on a higher level, accessed by a long step running the whole length of one end of the room. A shower room contained a lavatory and washbasin and no bath. 'This was the tank room,' said Emmy, to Thea's confusion. 'We had to extend a bit to fit the bedroom in.'

'It only had stands for six cows at a time,' Nick explained. 'We never did modernise. This was built about 1950, when milking got more mechanised. Before then it was done by hand in the shippon – the place over the yard.'

Thea was trying to visualise a working dairy farm. 'So, the cows came from over there, across the yard, to be milked here? Is that right?'

Nick nodded. 'There was a system of gates, and a gathering yard. My mother always said it was much too close to the house. You could smell the muck in every room. Not that anybody minded that, except her.'

'When did it all stop?' asked Thea.

'Five or six years ago now. It was impossible to carry

on as we were. The herd was too small to be commercially viable and it would have been extortionately expensive to expand and upgrade effectively. And it was all on me. I didn't feel capable of shouldering it all. But I still miss the cows,' he added sadly.

'Do you have the courses all year round?'

Emmy answered. 'No – people wouldn't feel they were getting proper value if the weather stopped them getting out all day. Everybody's got so *soft*, even the ones who claim to be living in a state of nature. They won't go out in pouring rain, and they'd never cope with the mud.'

'I don't blame them,' said Thea.

'Well, don't worry – you'll be fine in here. The forecast's not too bad, and it's got perfectly good heating. We're only asking you to stay a couple of days, as it stands.'

Thea resisted asking what fuel was used. There had been no sign of solar panels, and she wouldn't know a heat pump if it snorted beside her. 'Okay,' she said, taking a deep breath. 'Although, I'm still not sure . . .'

'Honestly – we know what we're doing. I think it was a brilliant idea to ask you to help,' said Emmy, smiling at her husband.

'She's told me all about how you were over the trouble in Chedworth,' said Nick. 'And I just thought you'd be the ideal person for the job. It's not as if we're asking you to do very much. If you can just walk your dog out and about, all round the village, chat to anybody you meet – check out any little corners.' His face became drawn. 'Because I just *know* something dreadful's happened, and somebody's got to get to the bottom of it. I can't rest until we've found her.'

Thea had a sudden flash of memory. 'You know I was here in the village yesterday,' she began.

'Yes, because I left the note on your car,' said Emmy patiently.

'Yes. Well, we'd just seen some people in the field below the church – right the other side of it. They seemed to be looking for something, in the trees. Would that have anything to do with Ginny? How much do the locals know about her going missing?'

'Hardly anything. That won't have had anything to do with us. They were probably hunting for a lost sheep or something. They keep pheasants down there somewhere, as well. Maybe they were checking on them. I don't imagine it was anything suspicious.'

'What about that stuff online – about sinister goings-on in the churchyard?'

'What?' Emmy looked utterly bemused.

'I found it at the weekend. That's why Stephanie and I came for a look.'

'Oh – right. I did hear something. It must have been Abby who was talking about it. She thinks it was a Samhain thing – you know?'

Thea was transported back to Cold Aston, some years earlier, when she met a woman committed to pagan celebrations. 'Ah,' she said. 'That's next week, isn't it?'

'Apparently. It all came to nothing, anyway. Just a few local kids experimenting. Of course, there's always some annoying busybody making a fuss about anything like that. Then somebody puts it on Facebook and it becomes a big thing, out of all proportion. Honestly – some people are so *silly*. '

'We don't have much to do with the locals,' Nick explained. 'Some of them opposed our planning application for converting the buildings when we got the project started, and the farmers are twitchy about the rewilding. Hogweed seeds blowing over the hedge and so forth. Although they've calmed down lately. History's on our side, for once. And we're not at all proselytising about it. We haven't even got solar panels!'

Thea had a sense of being deliberately diverted but did not put up any resistance. Emmy was following her husband's lead and added some remarks about public opinion concerning their activities on the farm. 'We got landed with some real extremists who told us we shouldn't use anything that wasn't "sustainable". We thought that was perfectly rational to start with, until we drilled down for details and realised they've got no idea about where things actually come from. They got hysterical when we asked them for some hard facts.' She shuddered. 'I was quite scared once or twice. So we changed the titles of the courses, and focused on vague words like "discussions" and "creativity" and concentrated on stuff like self-sufficiency and how to tell one butterfly from another. We've got loads of butterflies,' she finished proudly.

Thea tried to extract the salient points from this, with some difficulty. As far as she could understand it, she was in no danger of running into any of the people attending the courses. 'Sounds a bit of a minefield,' she remarked.

'It's that all right,' said Nick. 'The basic ideas have plenty of merit – obviously, since we're trying to live by them ourselves – but the simplistic headlines and half-baked science can be terrifying. People believe the most idiotic things.'

'And we're trying to set them right, fools that we are,' laughed Emmy. 'As gently as we can. Our next course is called "Doubts and Questions" – which is quite revolutionary in itself, believe it or not. Asking questions is frowned on these days.'

'So is having doubts,' said Nick. Then he frowned. 'And Ginny was really looking forward to that one.'

Thea resigned herself to hearing a whole new lot of information, wondering whether she would ever get away, but Nick interrupted. 'I really have to get on,' he said. 'And Thea's probably had enough for now. When can you come and settle in?' he asked her, very directly. 'Today would be good.'

'Well . . .' When had she actually agreed to do what they wanted, she wondered. 'First, I have to double-check with you that it's really all right to bring my dog. And even worse than that, my stepdaughter wants to come with me. She's thirteen and very sensible. She's free because it's half-term. But I think we might want to leave it until tomorrow, and come in the morning. Is that all right?'

'That's wasting a day,' Emmy sighed.

Thea waited, saying nothing.

'It'll be exactly a week since she vanished,' Nick pointed out what Emmy had told Thea over the phone. 'We last saw her on Wednesday.'

This was going over the same ground again, Thea thought, but conceded that it might be useful. 'That's quite a long time,' she said. 'I'm surprised the police aren't a bit more bothered.'

'Well, to be fair, we didn't contact them until Friday. They insisted she's low risk. I get the feeling they wouldn't know where to start even if they did decide to worry about her.' Nick shrugged, softening his earlier diatribe against the forces of the law. 'I have to say their attitude wasn't ideal, but basically I'm not sure we can really blame them too severely in this instance. All the same, you can understand why we wanted some extra help, can't you?'

'But I'm just one person,' Thea almost wailed. 'How am I expected to find her on my own?'

'I thought you said your daughter was coming as well. And your dog,' said Emmy. 'Which we always assumed would come, by the way.'

'What about Joshua?' Thea fixed her gaze on the massive animal and wondered what would become of anyone – man or beast – who got the wrong side of him. 'Won't he object? Hepzie does sometimes annoy other dogs.'

'He doesn't go out much, to be honest. They're lazy things, you know.' Emmy patted the huge head and the dog gave a slobbery grin.

'What do your customers think of him? The ones who aren't scared of him, that is.'

'You mean – where does he fit with all this environmental stuff?' Emmy gave a dramatic groan. 'The fact is, he doesn't. He breaks every rule in the book. But Nick loves him, and he loves Nick and there's no more to be said.'

But what about the baby? Thea suddenly wondered. However well-meaning, you wouldn't want something the size and weight of a small grizzly to be romping with your toddler, never mind a newborn. Thea didn't fancy romping with him herself, come to that.

'He was rather a mistake,' said Nick. 'But he's a fixture now.'

'How old is he?'

'Just over a year. We still have to give him time to learn some sense.'

They had been standing in the yard for the past few minutes, Thea trying to drift towards her car, with scant success. 'So – is tomorrow morning okay, then?' she asked. 'We might manage to be here by about ten, if that's any good. We'd only be able to stay two nights at most. We should be able to comb every inch of the village and beyond in that time.'

'Well . . .' said Emmy doubtfully. 'I suppose it's better than nothing. We thought you might do some searches on the computer as well. We're hopeless at that sort of thing. We even have to get help with the basic promotional stuff. And before you go today, could you maybe just have a quick look around the village? Let me get you a photo of Ginny, and then you can go and get the lie of the land, at least.' Before Thea could speak, she had trotted back into the house. Two minutes later she came back, holding a picture of the lost niece. Thea gave it a careful look. It showed a fair-headed young woman, with a wide smile and dimples. 'She looks nice,' she said fatuously.

The others said nothing and Thea went on, 'I do hope she's all right.'

'So do we,' said Emmy. 'You will help us, won't you? Have a bit of a snoop around, even if you already did that yesterday.'

'We only went to the church, and along the footpath to where the big road goes overhead. What an amazing thing that is!'

'It's an abomination,' said Nick and Emmy in unison, and all three of them laughed.

It was well past eleven-thirty when Thea drove into the centre of Baunton and left her car in a similar spot to the one she had used the day before. She sat for a minute or two just looking around, assessing the atmosphere. She had a flask of squash and a bag of crisps on the passenger seat and she gave herself a little snack while she went over the conversation with the Weavers. There were no residents to be seen in any direction. There seemed to be very little point in following Emmy's suggestion that she 'have a bit of a snoop round' in such an open and innocent-looking village. The longer she sat there, the less enthusiastic she felt about the task. Prolonging the moment, she turned the car radio on and listened idly to the midday news, letting more minutes pass by. At last she could delay no longer. Getting out of the car, she turned her back to the lane containing the church, and went slowly down a slight incline and looked around. There was an open gate leading roughly eastwards with a picture of a cow attached to it on a metal plate. The roadway grew narrower beyond it, but did not resemble a farm track as might be expected. Feeling naked without her spaniel, she approached it for a better look.

Just past the gate there was a footpath sign pointing to her left, up a scrabbly little path that looked as if no one ever used it. There were good-sized trees shielding it, and more on a scrap of land extending to the east that looked very neglected. She realised that the Weavers' farm must be in that direction, perhaps not very far away across the fields. The small roads had taken her on a convoluted route from farm gate to village centre. Within a few yards was a stile leading into an open field, with the path heading back towards the big noisy road, as far as she could tell. She went as far as the stile and turned to look back.

The main part of the village lay clustered just below her, settled into a hollow. The jumbled roofs presented an ageless picture that echoed small villages all across Europe. Certainly she could be in France or Italy, with only minor differences. The early builders had sensibly chosen a spot far enough above the river to minimise risk of flooding. They had put their church safely on even higher ground to the north. And now, the residents invisibly conducted their lives against the constant background noise of traffic.

She found herself once again making comparisons with other Cotswolds settlements. Bigger than Hampnett, smaller than Stanton, as old as any of them, and almost as deserted. Timmy had asked her recently, as part of a school project, 'What's the economy of the Cotswolds based on?'

Stephanie had interrupted, saying, 'Wool.'

'That hasn't been true for about a hundred years,' Thea corrected her. 'Two hundred, even. They made nails or needles around Winchcombe, at that sort of time, but hardly anything since then.'

'So what do they produce now?'

'Nothing,' said Thea, after some thought. 'They go to work in towns or business parks, or sit at their computers all day at home. They don't *produce* anything at all.'

'There are some farms. They've got sheep. So, there *is* wool,' argued the girl.

'Which they use for making roads or insulating houses,' said Drew, who had come in halfway.

The conversation had fizzled out, leaving Thea with a familiar sense that the whole area was clinging to ancient memories of long-gone glory days, typified by the lovely stone buildings and very little else. Its appeal to tourists had dwindled to a handful of places where people could pause and take pictures – places such as Bibury, Bourton-on-the-Water, Broadway or Winchcombe. They fantasised about royal connections and spent an hour in Stow-on-the-Wold looking in the shops.

She gave herself a little shake and decided she was definitely wasting time. Ginny Chambers was hardly going to pop up from behind a hedge and pretend that nothing had happened to her since Wednesday. The commission given to her by Emmy and Nick Weaver was already feeling flimsy and foolish. It would take anybody a scant couple of hours to search every inch of Baunton itself – there was very little scope for concealment or intrigue. Except she then remembered the odd group of people peering into the woods below the church and wondered if she might be fooling herself. After all, even if Emmy brushed it away as unimportant, *something* had been going on in recent times, because she had read about it on the computer.

But then there was an odd sound a little way to her left, as she stood facing the village roofs. A chittering little voice that most people would assume was a bird, but which Thea had learnt was made by a squirrel. They could keep it up for long minutes at a time, sitting high in a tree or on a roof. It was like a song, thrown defiantly into the air just for the sake of it. Slowly she turned to look, hoping not to alarm the creature.

She found it instantly, sitting on top of a wooden construction that had perhaps been a summer house, or elaborate home for a lot of hens. It was leaning slightly, but looked basically sound – though she wouldn't trust the roof to keep much weather out. Frowning, Thea groped for the recollection of something very similar seen very recently. It came to her after a few seconds – the rickety shed she and Stephanie had noticed near the new road when they had walked a short stretch of the Monarch's Way the previous day. What was it with this place, she asked herself, that they put up these rustic buildings and then let them disintegrate? Were there more of them scattered about? Had some highly persuasive salesman come along sometime in the 1980s and sold everybody a lavish hideaway that was bigger and better than a normal garden shed but which soon proved surplus to requirements?

Because it *was* a hideaway. There was no sign of a house to which this thing belonged. What had it been used for? And what went on in it now? Quite possibly, it was inhabited by squirrels, hedgehogs and big black spiders. Incurably curious, Thea Slocombe went for a closer look.

Chapter Five

It was relatively easy to get over the fence, despite having short legs and the whole thing being on a slope. Two strands of wire sagged somewhat between wooden posts that must have been there for fifty years at least. Holding a post, which wobbled, she swung a leg over the wire and, with a little jump, followed with the rest of her, putting most of her weight on the post. The post was not equal to the responsibility and tilted sideways. Thea landed inelegantly but unharmed on a soft bed of leaves, on the required side of the fence.

She laughed out loud at her lack of gymnastic prowess and brushed a few leaves off her legs. The shack, or cabin, or whatever it was, seemed to lean towards her, ten yards further up the slope.

The ramshackle building was in the shadow of the trees that grew close by, dominated by a tall dark green yew.

Brambles and ivy added further concealment. But Thea pushed through, looking for a doorway of some kind. On the side away from her, she discovered a sort of rustic verandah, with a window and a door behind it. Although somewhat tilted, with no glass in the window, the whole edifice was more robust than she had first thought. And it was big enough for someone to live in, at a squeeze. She was minded of the shanties in Soweto she had seen in films, where a whole family occupied something not much bigger than this. In fact, there was more space here than in the average caravan or canal boat.

Had this, then, been the home of a farmworker, or a shepherd, or even some sort of forest ranger?

The squirrel had disappeared and there were no signs of any sort of life. In the lane below her, nothing stirred. A small group of young cattle stood on the far side of the field she could just glimpse through the trees.

She stepped onto the verandah and peered through the window. It was almost without surprise that she saw, in the shadows, a pair of human legs lying on the floor, in a tableau that included an easy chair, a small table and a large pool of blood.

'Oh!' she breathed. 'Ginny?'

Because surely it had to be the missing Ginny Chambers. For a fleeting second, Thea congratulated herself on such quick work. Barely an hour after leaving Emmy and Nick, she had concluded her assignment. But then she went closer, entering the building on tiptoe, knowing instinctively that she must not do anything to disrupt the probable evidence that the police would have to gather. She kept her hands close to her side and breathed a silent thanks that Hepzie wasn't with her.

'Ginny?' she said again, trying to persuade herself that there was a slim chance that this was a live person who had simply decided to lie on the floor because she had a nosebleed. But there was no answer, and when she finally managed to position herself so as to see the face, she knew it was all in vain.

The blood had come from the victim's torso, it seemed – probably the heart, as it had become punctured by a weapon that was lying on the floor in full view. A short knife that you might use for cutting up vegetables, with a very sharp point. The person was female, grey-haired, shabbily dressed and definitely not Ginny Chambers.

Thea had left her phone in the car and had to run back for it. The notion of knocking on the door of the nearest house was quickly dismissed, for many excellent reasons. She keyed 999 first, while badly wanting to call Detective Superintendent Sonia Gladwin on the privileged direct line Thea had been permitted to use for quite a time now. She would not be thanked for doing that before all the required processes had been undergone. Police doctor, due paperwork, ambulance or undertaker, depending on the situation. Police tape, identification, call for witnesses. Thea was very familiar with the whole well-rehearsed business.

Cirencester was no distance away and there was a very quick response. The sudden influx of official vehicles in a very small village attracted a degree of attention, and people gathered near the gate with the cow on it. Five people, when Thea got round to counting them. Again, there was an odd familiarity about it. In Duntisbourne Abbots, on her very first house-sitting job, something quite similar had happened. It was a good idea to take careful note of who these people were, because they tended to show up again over ensuing days. But her main focus was still on the body in the hut – or whatever it was – and what it meant for her personally. She had been sent by Emmy Weaver on a deliberate search of the nooks and crannies of the village, and within moments had found something terrible. Wasn't that all a bit too neat? She stood in the lane and tried to gather her thoughts. Police officers had arrived, one to view the remains and the other to question Thea. There were phone calls and manoeuvrings and anxious frowns.

'Is the deceased known to you?' asked the constable, who was armed with a tablet containing a great many questions to be answered.

Thea shook her head slowly. 'It isn't the person I was looking for,' she said stupidly.

'And who might that be?'

'Well – a girl called Ginny – Virginia, I suppose. She was reported missing a few days ago. But this isn't her.'

Activity was swirling around them. Since Thea had first encountered a suspicious death, technology had escalated considerably. Cameras flashed, very small keyboards were tapped, and Thea half expected a drone to appear overhead. Instead, there were two more cars, following closely on the ambulance. 'Coroner's Officer and the DI,' muttered one constable to another.

There were audible remarks coming from all sides. 'Still warm,' was one. 'Looks like she was *living* here,' was another. And then the unmistakeable word '*Suicide*' could be heard. The little group of villagers showed no sign of dispersing, so Thea went to speak to them.

'Are you with the police?' a man asked her.

'No. It was me who found her,' she said.

'"Her"? A woman, then?'

Thea nodded. She knew better than to give much away, but it might make sense to engage these locals in conversation. 'Do you live close by?' she asked, addressing the whole group of five people.

'I'm right here,' said a youngish woman, waving vaguely at the nearby houses. She looked nervous, glancing all around as if looking for a particular person. 'It's definitely a woman, then?'

Thea merely nodded.

'We're just round the corner,' said an older woman, who was standing an inch away from a man who could only be her husband.

The man who had spoken to her first made no reply. He was about fifty with wiry grey hair and wellington boots.

'Why do you want to know?' said a person standing slightly apart from the others. Thea turned round for a look. She saw someone hardly more than her own diminutive height, dressed in a green padded anorak and a felt hat. The voice had been that of a man, but Thea's judgement was inconclusive where the person's gender was concerned.

'Just curious,' she shrugged. 'And while I'm at it – who owns that shed?' *Might as well go the whole hog*, she thought wryly. Asking questions was what she did, and somewhere there was an echo of Emmy's remark about it being frowned on in recent times. That only made her more inclined to break the rules.

Nobody responded but everyone looked at the man in the boots. Finally, he nodded, and said, 'I suppose that would be me, technically. But it's more a quirk of history than anything else. I actually live a mile away.'

'So do I,' said the small person.

'Not that much,' said the husband who lived round the corner.

And then Gladwin materialised, with a man at her side who Thea did not recognise. 'Thea,' she nodded as if not the slightest bit surprised. 'What have we here, then?' Her glance swept the knot of villagers, eyebrows raised. They edged back in unison.

'I was looking for a missing person,' said Thea apologetically.

'And found her? It is a her, I'm told.'

'No, actually. This is someone else.' In a sudden flash, the nagging sense of having seen the face of the dead woman before became certain. 'And I've seen her before. Only yesterday,' she said, not caring that the assembled group of onlookers must have heard her. 'She's called Alice,' she went on, describing the scene in Cirencester to Gladwin with a piercing pang of sadness.

Gladwin sent Thea to sit in her car while she spent twenty minutes on the minutiae of her work. 'Where's your dog?' she had asked, and Thea started to explain. 'No, don't tell me now. I just wanted to know it wasn't ferreting about under that shed.'

As she waited, Thea sat back and tried to let ideas form of their own accord. *Suicide*, someone had said, and she could see that this was a probable conclusion. The woman could have thrust that short knife into her own heart and then dropped it as she fell and bled to death. There were plenty of small hints to reinforce the theory. Living alone in a state of dereliction; patently obvious mental trouble or alcoholism; winter coming – it all pointed to depression and despair. Images from the day before in Cirencester, where Alice had sunk to the ground and given every impression of never wanting to get up again, filled Thea's mind, along with the sister – if that was what she was. A sister who was impatient, brisk and perhaps unkind.

It was well past lunchtime and she realised she was hungry. And Drew would be wondering where she'd got to. As far as she could recall, she had told him she was only going for a preliminary chat to the Weavers and was unlikely to be away for long. The chances were that he would be in his office, trying to think of ways to increase his business, so she rummaged for her phone, which she had dropped carelessly into her bag, and called him.

He answered swiftly but calmly. 'Got held up?' he asked.

'Very much so. You're not going to believe this . . .'

'Okay. I expect I am. Just tell me you aren't sitting in a pub somewhere with DS Gladwin.'

'Not quite. But you're very warm.'

'The dog hasn't been out all day,' he reminded her. 'And I think you told Timmy you'd collect him from his friend's house.'

'I said only if nobody else could do it. I expect one of the mothers will take pity on him. Call me if nothing's happened by four o'clock. I'll probably be back long before that, so I can get him if necessary.'

'I hope you will be back, because Andrew and I have a removal in a minute. I don't know how long we'll be. It's in Evesham.'

'Oh. No problem. Stephanie'll be all right on her own for a bit, if necessary. But I will try not to be long. You don't want the story, then?'

'The story can wait,' he said, with a sigh.

Poor old Drew, she thought fondly. Even though he could hardly claim not to have known what he was getting when he married her, the reality was often quite a challenge. But they were old enough to roll with most of the knocks and face them honestly. Thea insisted that she was the problem, the flawed character who could not resist pursuing killers and taking outrageous risks. 'I was born without fear,' she said. 'It's a sort of brain damage, I suppose.' Despite involvement in numerous violent crimes, she herself had never been attacked – at least not physically. Quite a lot of people had shouted at her and called her names, which was wounding – and even frightening, in a way – but she saw no reason to 'stay safe' as everyone adjured her to these days. Safety was not something she particularly valued.

When Gladwin came back, Thea whined about being hungry and the detective produced a miraculous ham sandwich and thermos of coffee. 'This is a first,' said Thea. 'We've always gone to a pub before.'

'Cost cutting,' said Gladwin shortly. 'So who's this dead woman, then?'

'I told you. Her name's Alice, and I think she's got a sister. Was it suicide?'

'Too soon to say. We're hoping so.'

'Sad.'

'True – but less ghastly than murder, in the scheme of things. Not that the scheme of things is usually straightforward, of course. A person can be driven to kill themselves by other people. Neglected, abused, tormented – until life's not worth living.'

'Which is what you think here?'

'Don't you? Living like this – it has to be the end of the line, rock bottom. The place doesn't even have any glass in the windows.'

'Was she actually *living* there, then?'

'It's hard to say. You must have seen what was there – a little bag of clothes – just pants and a jumper. A towel and toothbrush. Binoculars. Bottle of water. Candles. All the basics for survival for a night or two.'

'I didn't notice,' said Thea.

'No – well, I suppose that's not surprising. How long were you in there?'

'No idea. It felt quite long, but might have been hardly more than a minute. I had to go back to the car for my phone, and I stayed there until the first lot of police arrived. They were very quick.'

'I saw you talking to those locals. True to form. Any observations you might like to share?'

Thea laughed. Gladwin was her own age, tall and slim with a Tyneside accent. Thea had first met her when she was new to the Gloucestershire Constabulary, implementing practices that were sometimes unorthodox. The existence of a profoundly inquisitive house-sitter who fearlessly knocked on doors and mingled with suspects had come as a delightful surprise and the two quickly became friends.

'They were a good mixture,' she ventured. 'The man with the boots seemed a bit arrogant. You'll be wanting to talk to him because he owns the shed. And there was a small person who seemed a bit hostile. Might have been a birdwatcher, although I didn't see any binoculars.'

'Wait, wait,' Gladwin begged. 'You know the name of the deceased. You know who owns the place she died. What else? Did you say something about a sister?'

'A woman of a similar age who looks like her. I could be jumping to a conclusion that they're related. Stephanie and I saw them in Cirencester yesterday.'

'If they were so similar, how can you be sure this is the one called Alice?'

Thea paused. 'That's a good question. I just assumed it must be, because . . . well, because the woman we saw first looked as if she might be living rough. And more than that . . .' She stopped, feeling slightly sick. 'It sounds awful, but I'm somehow not terribly surprised that she's dead. I mean – she seemed on the edge. Desperate. And mentally unbalanced.'

'Vagrants don't usually have sisters watching out for them,' said Gladwin. 'If she really was a vagrant. Nothing's sure yet. We don't even know it *is* a sister. Might have been a social worker or something.'

'I don't think so. And I bet there are lots of destitute people who have relatives keeping tabs on them.' Thea could think of a number of novels containing characters who ended up homeless because their families couldn't abide them any longer, and yet didn't lose touch entirely. 'Maybe this Alice was violent, or demented or impossibly noisy. Nobody would want someone like that living with them, but they wouldn't give up on them completely.' For some reason, she was finding it important that the dead woman should have had somebody who cared about her.

'We're speculating,' said Gladwin. 'And I've got to get moving. They'll all be waiting for instructions.'

Most of the vehicles had left the scene, with one police car remaining. 'Is he waiting for you?' asked Thea.

'He is. That's my newest detective constable. Caz can't stand him, which is unfortunate. He isn't so bad, really – just needs to experience a bit more real life.'

'Which Caz has experienced rather too much of,' said Thea. The detective sergeant under discussion had grown up in the care system, and knew more than was healthy about the appalling behaviour that parents were capable of.

'Right. And he doesn't take that on board when he's talking to her.'

'What's his name?'

'Erik. With a "k". His mother's Norwegian or something. He's very bright,' said Gladwin with a sigh. 'Full of theories about human potential and stuff like that.'

'And that's him patiently waiting for you?'

'I told him you were a regular participant in Cotswolds cases and had to be treated with respect.'

'Oh God! He'll hate me, then,' laughed Thea.

There were too many calls on her time for comfort. Despite the shared sandwiches and coffee, Thea still felt hungry. She had not told Gladwin about the Weavers and their missing niece, vaguely and very briefly thinking it might muddy the water. Now, thinking back and wondering about her motives, she concluded that Ginny and her caprices could surely have nothing to do with the rough-sleeping Alice. She could imagine scenarios where the two came into contact, but nothing more sinister than a casual conversation seemed feasible. It probably wasn't even a crime anyway. If Alice had killed herself, then there was no more to be said. There would be no murder investigation; no need to question everybody in Baunton or delve into the affairs of people like the Weavers and be forced to consider far more unpalatable possibilities concerning Ginny Chambers. Suicide would be almost welcome if it avoided all that. She could almost hear Gladwin thinking the exact same thing.

Chapter Six

Half-term brought its own complications, of course. Although the children could be left untended in the house for short periods, it was something to be avoided if possible. Most of Drew's work was done in the office – formerly dining room – in their Broad Campden home, but now he had told her he was going out on a removal – as he always called the collection of a body – with the implication that it would be good if she could cover for him, especially as Stephanie was there on her own.

Furthermore, Stephanie would be wanting to hear all about Emmy and Ginny, even before the additional news about Alice. Not to mention poor Hepzibah, abandoned that morning for no good reason. And last but by no means least, she might have to collect Timmy at some point during the afternoon. So she headed home with a lengthy list of obligations weighing on her shoulders.

During part of the drive, Thea rehearsed what she would say to the Weavers in a phone call she would have to make before much longer. They were unlikely to regard the discovery of a dead woman barely half a mile from their home as of any relevance to the search for their niece. At least, they would try their best to keep the two things separate, because any hint that there was an association could only bring very disagreeable implications with it. And Thea had some sympathy with that approach. However, there was an alternative possibility, whereby the police began to take a much bigger interest in Ginny Chambers – as well as vague tales of odd happenings in Baunton. Somebody would eventually make a connection – which was not as common an occurrence in the police mind as might have been expected. It could take a while, unless Thea Slocombe herself drew their attention to it. Which she supposed she ought to have done already, while sitting in the car with Gladwin. As it was, all she'd done was to briefly mention Ginny's name to the constable with the ProntoForm.

So – she would phone Emmy and warn her that Baunton was going to be under much more scrutiny than before, and that any search for Ginny would be superfluous. Even if it became unarguable that Alice had killed herself, there would still be a degree of investigation into her unorthodox circumstances.

Home life went more or less as expected for the rest of the day. Stephanie was annoyed to have missed the latest excitement in Baunton, and Timmy was tetchy about some disagreement he had had with his friend. Drew came back from his removal in a mood of some frustration. 'They want to do almost everything themselves,' he reported. 'Decorating the coffin, digging the grave, printing the leaflet. All they want from me is transport, basically. And storage.'

'You don't print the leaflets, anyway,' Thea pointed out. 'Not that there is one, usually.'

Drew had opted to designate the customary Order of Service that was generally provided at funerals as a 'leaflet', because he said it wasn't a 'service', the way his funerals were conducted. Accurate terminology was important to Drew.

'That's true,' he admitted. 'But it does leave me feeling a bit redundant.'

'I'm probably going to be redundant as well,' she sympathised. 'With this new turn of events in Baunton, I can't see myself being of much use to Emmy, after all. Not that I ever thought I was likely to find their dratted Ginny. The whole thing's a bit silly, really.'

'But what did they *say*?' demanded Stephanie who had absorbed the account of Thea's grim discovery with a very calm interest, before showing a delayed excitement when she realised she had actually seen the victim alive. 'Are we going there or not? I don't expect the Weavers care about the Alice person, do they? They'll say she's got nothing to do with anything.'

'I know. I mean – I thought that as well, but it might not be right. Everything's terribly close together, if you see what I mean. The villagers probably know exactly what everyone's doing at any given moment. Look how Emmy found my car about five minutes after I parked it.'

'It was there for at least an hour,' Stephanie corrected her pedantically.

'So phone her,' sighed Drew. 'And get it sorted one way or the other.'

Which she did.

'We know Alice,' came the not entirely surprising news from Emmy. 'She did a bit of work for us earlier this year. There are lots of people like her, you know. They live off the grid and keep a low profile. We liked her, even though she could be awfully flaky at times – and she liked a drink. Joshua couldn't stand her, which made things awkward. She had that in common with Ginny, although she kept trying to be his friend. She would never believe he meant it when he growled at her. We worried that he might kill her one day. And now she's dead. That's so awful.'

'You heard, then?' said Thea, thinking that Emmy sounded genuinely sad.

'Hours ago, yes. The whole place is buzzing with it. Killed herself, apparently, poor thing. I keep thinking that Nick and I should have been nicer to her. I don't follow the stuff they're saying about her living in a garden shed, though. I thought she had somewhere in Cirencester.'

'Oh,' said Thea. 'I suppose all that will be explained before long.'

'And we sent you out to nose around the village – I'm guessing it was you that found her, from what they're saying.'

'You sent me to explore the village,' Thea confirmed rather snappily. 'So I did.'

'Don't blame me! What does it matter who finds her, anyway, if she was already dead?' The tone was mutating from sad to bitter, which Thea supposed wasn't entirely surprising. Emmy – even in her former incarnation as Millie – did not relish unpleasantness or discomfort.

'It wasn't very nice,' said Thea mildly.

'Just as well it was you, then, seeing as how you're fairly used to that sort of thing.' Emmy's laugh was almost painfully heartless, but she had a point, Thea was forced to admit. She gave a matching laugh. 'You could say that, I suppose. But I expect you would have coped all right if it had been you instead of me.'

'I like to think so,' said Emmy. 'I've grown up a lot since that business in Chedworth. Probably thanks to you, a little bit.'

'Ahh,' crooned Thea, feeling more friendly. 'That's nice of you to say.'

'Well . . . what about Ginny? Are you still going to come tomorrow?'

'I don't know. It seems a bit pointless when Baunton's got so much police attention. If she's hiding away somewhere close by, they'll probably find her.'

'They won't, though. They're not going to take much notice of a suicide, are they? They'll be gone again before we know it.'

'I think you're wrong there. Alice's lifestyle is going to make them start ferreting about and asking questions. They don't like that kind of thing. They think it's untidy.'

'And you should know,' said Emmy, her tone growing sharper. 'You being such good mates with all those detectives.'

'Is that a problem?'

'Not exactly. It just makes you . . . unpredictable. Nick

thinks it's worrying. What if—?' she stopped. Thea had an idea that Emmy might have been about to reveal more about Ginny and her activities. If not that, then there was certainly something unsaid, to do with the missing girl and the police.

'What if what?' she asked.

'Oh, nothing. We still want to find her, and Nick says this business with Alice is probably more bad news than good. It's going to attract the wrong sort of attention. I'm not entirely sure what that means.'

'Hmm,' said Thea, feeling a decision solidifying inside her. 'I think I probably should come back tomorrow, on balance. And if I do, Stephanie and Hepzie are going to be with me.'

'Good,' said Emmy Weaver.

Stephanie was in two minds about the plan. 'It's all much more complicated now,' she pointed out. 'What are we actually going to *do*? The police won't like it if we keep getting in their way.'

'I really have no idea,' Thea admitted. 'I get the feeling there's more that Emmy wants to tell us, for one thing. There's a man called Joe, who sounds as if he might be important. And you'll like the farm. It's got all sorts of wildlife and the Weavers strike me as quite sensible about that stuff. They don't just choose one species to encourage and destroy all the rest, like some places. Although Nick really hates buttercups.'

'They're like that in Australia,' nodded Stephanie. 'They choose one species to hate and do all they can to exterminate it.'

'Closer to home than that. I keep hearing awful stories about the Lake District and what they're doing to grey squirrels.'

'People are stupid,' said Timmy, who had been listening. 'Why can't I go as well? To Baunton, I mean.'

'I didn't think you wanted to.' Thea gave him a long look. 'Are you feeling neglected?'

'A bit. It'll be boring here with just Dad.'

'Oh dear.' Thea felt a familiar flick of resentment that Drew had not already organised something for his own child instead of leaving it up to her. It could be argued that she was causing the problem by going off, but her riposte to that was that even if she had stayed at home, the task of entertaining the kids would fall to her. 'I think I assumed you'd be Pokemonning all week.'

Timmy shook his head. 'I've got a bit of homework, that's all.'

Thea sighed. The boy was ten years old, but often behaved much younger. The death of his mother had injured him in some deep place that nobody could quite locate. Drew was fully aware of his failings as Tim's father and tried to rectify them, but never quite succeeded. Thea could remember her own brother at the same age, and believed there was no need for much attention so long as his parents displayed regular approval and offered some suitable outings. But then Damien had been blessed with three younger sisters, which gave him a strong motive for finding his own amusement. When Timmy retreated to his room with his games and tablet, it felt as if it was because nobody could offer him anything better and he was making the best of a disappointing situation.

'Dad might need some help with things,' said Stephanie. 'Tidying up the office maybe. You could do a bit of filing. I did that when I was eight. It's fun, actually.'

Timmy gave a lethargic shrug, which both Thea and Stephanie found exasperating. 'Don't make suggestions,' said Thea. 'It never works.'

'It'll be okay,' said Timmy with an effort. 'I can do some cooking – can I? I know how to make Welsh cakes, and scrambled eggs, and other things.'

'Good idea,' said Thea. 'Just don't touch the deep fat fryer. And make sure Dad's in the house before you start.'

Thea did not sleep well that night. On all sides business was unfinished and questions were proliferating. Gladwin would surely update her the next day about Alice and how she died. Emmy, Nick and Ginny were all anticipating some sort of miracle from her – though perhaps not Ginny, who was unlikely to know that Thea Slocombe existed. Timmy was being abandoned, and there could be uncomfortable clashes between dogs. When she did fall asleep, her dreams were about money and Drew searching for some in cupboards. She woke up, saying to herself – *I forgot to ask Emmy if I'm going to be paid.*

She turned to Drew, who was still asleep. Outside it was dark and she could hear rain falling. On cloudy days at the end of October it might not get light until eight in the morning and was then dark again by six p.m. When the clocks went back, the evenings would be much worse. Thea sometimes wondered how to bear the prospect of sunless winter days, but somehow they always passed. Christmas helped, of course.

She was tempted to wake Drew and dump all her worries on him. Some of them were his worries as well, or so she told herself. Timmy definitely was. Poor boy – he was taking such a long time to grow up compared to his sister. The prospect of having Stephanie at her side when she went to Baunton was a warm one. Any notion of taking Tim as well was firmly rejected. He would ask too many questions and pay insufficient attention to the answers. He would disappear at a crucial moment, or make a noise, or panic. Besides, there was no way Drew would permit such a thing. It was bad enough that his daughter had been seduced by Thea's amateur detective activities and the enticing presence of police professionals. It had clearly never crossed his mind even a year ago that this might happen, despite his experience of Stephanie as seriously intelligent, inquisitive and fearless – just like her stepmother.

What time was it? Somewhere between seven and eight, she supposed. It was half-term – no need to scramble through breakfast and school things and catching the bus. But it was a weekday, and lying about in bed like Emmy Weaver evidently did was decadent and shameful and they should all get up and face the day.

The time was soon announced by Stephanie who came into the room cautiously, after knocking on the door. Adolescence bred such wary behaviour, Thea remembered from her own daughter Jessica. Gone were the uninhibited days when children would burst into the parental bedroom regardless of what marital activity might be underway. Timmy, of course, had never lost his inhibitions towards his replacement mother. He liked her well enough, but her presence was at root a perpetual puzzle to him. Some cosmic mistake had been made – or perhaps a cruel trick had been played on him. Either way, it gave the universe a precarious aspect for him.

'It's ten to eight,' said Stephanie. 'What time are we going?'

'Somewhere around half past nine,' said Thea at random. 'Have you let the dog out?'

The girl nodded. 'It's raining,' she said.

'Oh joy,' said Thea.

'Errggh,' said Drew, from under the duvet. 'Is somebody going somewhere?'

His women said nothing, waiting for him to come to his senses. If the phone rang in the small hours, he would leap into full competence in seconds to take details of a new customer for his burial ground, but in any other circumstances he was slow and muzzy for far too many minutes.

Thea threw back her half of the duvet and headed for the bathroom. 'Is it cold?' she asked Stephanie as she went.

'Not at all. A bit windy. The leaves are flying off the trees. It's like a brown snowstorm. With rain.'

'Lovely,' said Thea.

Chapter Seven

Breakfast was as sketchy and disorganised as always. Timmy came down in pyjamas, as a celebration of half-term. Thea gave Drew a meaningful look, hoping to convey that he needed to take an interest in his son and offer suggestions as to what the day might hold for them both. The hint was partially taken. 'Well, Tim – what's the plan?' he asked.

The child shrugged. 'Dunno.'

'Hm. You could go and help Fiona, if you like. She's planting a whole lot of new things in the field. And digging up thistles and stuff. She could do with an assistant.'

'It's raining,' Timmy pointed out.

'I know, but it's going to stop soon. The ground's going to be nice and soft. Perfect for new planting, apparently. She's got some actual trees to put in up at the northern end.'

'Mum would be doing it now, wouldn't she? Planting things, I mean,' said Stephanie unself-consciously. She referred to Karen with no hesitation, at odd moments when nobody else was giving the first Mrs Slocombe a thought.

Timmy flinched, and Drew said, 'She would. She knew the exact right moment to do garden things. I never really got the hang of it all myself.'

'Maybe Tim has her green fingers as well,' said Thea with a smile.

'Green fingers?' repeated the boy.

'It means being good with plants. I think it's time we found out, if that's all right with you?' said Drew. 'Fiona can give you lunch as well, if you like. I don't know whether I'll be here all day.'

Fiona Emerson was the wife of Andrew, assistant in Drew's funeral business. The couple had abandoned farming and moved to a small house in Broad Campden, less than half a mile from the Slocombes. Fiona had gradually developed a concern for young Timmy, and had recently started to suggest activities for him, as well as collecting Stephanie from school once in a while. Her own son was twenty-five and living in Kent.

'Okay,' said Timmy neutrally.

At least he wasn't actively resistant, thought Thea. 'Good old Fiona,' she said heartily.

Timmy sighed and looked at the spaniel sitting near him. 'Are you taking Hepzie with you?'

'Yes,' said Thea. 'Although I'm a bit worried about the Weavers' dog. They've got a massive thing like a bear. It could eat her in two bites.'

'Is it friendly?'

'Fairly. I didn't much like the look in its eye, though.'

'Dogs don't eat each other,' said Drew irritably. 'Don't tease.'

'Apparently it hardly ever leaves the house. Big dogs are terribly lazy. So I guess we'll be all right. They're putting us in a sort of annex that they made for Nick's mother. She changed her mind about wanting it – or something.'

Stephanie's eyes were sparkling. 'This is going to be so exciting!' she trilled. 'A proper farm! And a mystery to solve.' She bent down and grabbed the dog's forequarters. 'Hey, Heps – we're going to have an adventure.'

'More likely the missing niece'll show up ten minutes after we get there and we'll just have to come home again,' said Thea.

'No, but what about the Alice person? That's a big mystery as well. They called *Mrs Gladwin*, remember. That means it's suspicious.'

Thea frowned at this. 'I have a feeling they only called her because it was me.'

'Why? Did you call her?'

Thea shook her head. 'I wanted to, but resisted the temptation. She showed up all of her own accord. Pretty quickly, actually. But I doubt if she knew I was there, now I think about it.'

Stephanie considered this for a moment. 'Isn't that a bit funny – calling her so soon? She's a superintendent, after all.'

'Sudden violent death – she'd automatically be brought in. And I dare say it was unusual enough for her to want to be there out of interest, if not strictly needed.'

'Not because of you at all, then,' said Drew, a trifle sourly.

'Well, we won't know anything until we get there,' said Thea. 'Just let me wash these things up and pack a bag and we can be off. Do you want me to help with your packing?' she asked the girl.

'Already done,' said Stephanie.

Her stepdaughter's enthusiasm was infectious, ensuring a holiday mood when the three of them finally drove off. The rain had stopped as Drew predicted and the dog was sitting upright on Stephanie's lap, looking eagerly out of the window. 'Poor old Tim,' said Stephanie. 'Missing all the fun.'

'We could hardly bring him as well. There's only one bedroom, for a start, with only two beds in it.'

'He doesn't really want to come, anyway. Fiona's always nice to him. But he didn't want us to bring Hepzie. She sleeps on his bed when you're not there.'

'Does she indeed? Nobody ever told me that.'

'He makes sure he brushes all the hair off the duvet before you come back.'

Thea decided she had no objections, given that it was very rare for her to go away without the dog in any case.

'It's sad about the Alice person,' Stephanie changed the subject. 'Quite a coincidence that we saw her on Monday, as well.'

'A bit of a one, I agree. But half the people in Cirencester probably saw her as well. She was quite noticeable.'

'Did you tell Emmy about it? I mean – there *might* be some connection, don't you think? What if the niece killed her?'

Thea's breath caught halfway down her throat. Why had that idea not occurred to her already? It had been nudging gently, somewhere in a corner of her mind, she realised, but been firmly crushed. It was both too neat and too horrible at the same time. She decided to treat it lightly. 'That would be stretching things much too far,' she said. 'Besides, the police are thinking it was probably suicide.'

'They should know for sure by now. What do you think it was?'

'I don't know. I didn't look hard enough to make any sort of judgement. All I saw was blood and a knife on the floor. And her face, which I recognised after a few minutes.'

'Were her eyes open?'

'God, Steph – you're being a bit ghoulish, aren't you?'

'Yes, but were they?'

'Actually, sort of half-open, I think.'

'Like this?' Stephanie fluttered her eyelids, tilting up her face.

Thea took a quick glance. 'Not really. It's something people almost never do when they're alive. I never thought of that before. The eyeballs roll up somehow.' She experimented briefly. 'It's quite difficult, in fact.'

'So that's how you knew she was dead, is it? Did you feel for a pulse?'

'No, I didn't. It was obvious without that. No blood flowing. No breathing movements. It's the *stillness* that tells you.'

'Right.'

Stephanie was the daughter of an undertaker, Thea reminded herself. She had been around dead people from infancy, asking questions and taking everything in her stride. She knew from experience that dead faces relaxed into a total absence of expression. She knew that mouths and eyes had to be glued shut if families wanted to view their dead relative. She had been allowed to brush hair and straighten clothes from the age of ten. To apply the word *ghoulish* had really not been appropriate at all.

'We didn't come this way before, did we?' Thea had turned off the A417 where a sign said 'Bagendon'.

'No – this avoids Cirencester. It's quicker and more interesting. And a bit convoluted. I hope we don't get lost. We're supposed to come to the A435 and turn right. Then it's just on the left somewhere, down a track. I came back through North Cerney yesterday, more or less by mistake.'

'I can get the map on my phone if we're lost,' said Stephanie reassuringly.

It turned out not to be necessary and the Weaver farm was readily located.

Emmy met them, looking tired and worried, holding a mobile phone. Nick was a little way behind her. 'I've just had a call from Joe,' she began without preamble. 'He's in Cirencester again.'

'Again?' queried Thea, trying to recall any scraps of information she had regarding Joe.

'Yes – he lived there for a bit, this time last year, then came here for the courses and met Ginny. But he went off a little while ago, without saying anything except that he's got the job he'd always wanted and couldn't stay.'

Nick joined in. 'Caused all kinds of nuisance. He's one of those people who won't make any kind of commitment. Knows his stuff, I admit, but is hopelessly unreliable.'

'Except he has stuck with Sunny and all those kids,' Emmy defended. 'She says he's amazing with them.'

'Easy to do when you don't have a job to go to,' muttered Nick. 'I still think he was a bad influence on Ginny.'

'You didn't tell me any of this yesterday,' Thea accused. 'Isn't it obvious that Ginny's gone to join him, wherever he is?' In which case, she and Stephanie and the dog may as well turn right round again and go home.

Emmy shook her head violently. 'No, that's not it at all. He's got no idea where she is. He's *worried* about her. He wouldn't risk going off with her or getting either of them into trouble. He's on the police record as an activist, even though I doubt if he does anything actually illegal. He's come back to Cirencester to see if Ginny has turned up because he really cares about her. And not in any nasty way either.'

'Or so he says,' Nick remarked. Emmy threw him an angry look and made a hissing sound.

Thea looked at her stepdaughter, wondering what she was making of this new data. Like anyone her age, she was at least theoretically up for some social disobedience if it was going to save rain forests or Alpine glaciers and the wildlife they harboured. Stephanie was still in the passenger seat of the car holding Hepzibah, watching Emmy's face. 'This is Stephanie,' said Thea belatedly. 'And you probably remember my dog. I hope we're not too early.'

It was a daft thing to say, but it conveyed something of her uncertainty. What exactly did Emmy want them to do, and when? Where was the big dog, and what exactly did they know about the dead Alice?

'Early for what?' said Emmy, understandably.

'Well, for whatever you want us to do. The more I think about it, the less I think we can be remotely helpful. I mean – the village is much too small for anybody to get lost in, for a start.' She looked again at Stephanie, wondering what the girl was thinking.

'Come in for a minute, and we'll talk it over properly. Hello, Stephanie, by the way. I met your dad in Chedworth, not so long ago. It's half-term, I understand?'

'Right,' nodded Stephanie. 'Can we bring the dog in? Where's yours? Thea says he's big.'

'Huge. Actually, he's safely penned up in the backyard. You'll meet him later on.'

Nick mumbled something about having things to do, and Emmy led the way into the kitchen, as before, and the three females sat round the table. Emmy slumped in her chair and put a hand to her lower back. 'Another eight weeks to go,' she moaned. 'It seems like a lifetime.'

Thea attempted some consolation. 'It'll soon pass,' she said. Then, not wanting to waste any more time, she asked, 'Have the police been to talk to you about Alice?'

'What? No – why should they?'

'Because you said she worked here. They'll want to construct a picture of who she was, what connections she had locally, all that sort of thing. You said you knew her, so . . .' she tailed off, observing Emmy's expression. It was not encouraging.

'I wish I hadn't said that. You'll be running off to tell the cops all about it now, I suppose. You've probably done it already.'

'No I haven't. But why would it matter if I did?'

'Because they'll jump to conclusions. They already know

Ginny's gone missing. We know they've got a file on her from the Bristol business – and us now as well, probably. Knowing how their minds work, they'll imagine some sort of fairy tale where Ginny and Alice got together somehow, and with Alice dead, they'll be suspicious of Ginny.'

'At least that means they might start looking for her properly,' said Thea. 'You should be pleased about that.'

'Not if they charge her with murder when they find her.'

'Who said anything about murder? You said everyone thought it was suicide yesterday.' Thea was rattled. She had assumed that the lack of any word from Gladwin meant that Alice had been proved to have killed herself. Sad, but no worse than that. 'What have you heard?'

'Just village gossip. The woman who lives just by the place you found her comes up here for eggs, and of course she couldn't stop talking about it.'

Thea had spent part of the previous two days recalling her earlier dealings with Emmy in Chedworth. The girl had been working for the BBC, best friends to a famous television actor and suddenly bereaved when her father died. She had begun by avoiding the less pleasant aspects of life, but over the course of a few days Thea had watched her grow up. Now, with another missing person, and Thea herself again on the scene, Emmy must surely be reliving that time much as Thea was.

'Nick must know most of the people around here,' she said. 'He's lived here most of his life, if I remember rightly.'

Emmy gave her a long look. 'Well, yes, he does, but I only know a handful of them. I was in Stratford before I came here to live – although I was often in the area visiting my grandmother, and my father worked with a lot of the local farmers, but I didn't *live* here.'

'Sorry,' said Thea. Then she had another thought. 'Do you remember Andrew Emerson, from Yanworth?'

'With the dairy herd? Oh yes. They had TB and he sold up. Why?'

'He works for us now. He and Fiona live in the same village. They'll be glad to know things are going so well for you, when I tell them.'

Emmy gave a cynical laugh. 'Things are going well, are they? I'm not sure Nick would agree with you about that.'

'Really?' Thea was also remembering how persuasive the young woman could be when she tried. She had foisted a pair of sheepdogs onto Thea with no notice, for one thing. The way she had so easily dragged Thea into a search for a lost niece was really quite in character, on reflection. Emmy had a knack of making people do what she wanted. And now, as before, she was obviously going to make a powerful case to support her demands.

'Oh, it's not so bad, I suppose. Farmers are always complaining, as my father used to say. And he can't believe how lucrative the courses are – thinks it can't possibly last.' She gave an unconvincing little laugh and changed the subject. 'I had a call from my friend last night, as well. You remember her – Judith? She's moved up to Durham now, so I hardly ever see her. It's all completely different from when all that stuff happened in Chedworth. It feels like another life. But it must only be about three years ago.'

'About that,' said Thea. 'Although I admit I'd forgotten all about it until you showed up again.'

'And Andrew's working for your husband? That's a surprise. What does he do?'

Stephanie had been listening to their talk with increasing impatience. 'Shouldn't we be *doing* something?' she finally burst out. 'Not just talking about old times.'

Emmy laughed. 'You're right – except it's not that easy. We really do have to talk quite a lot first.'

'Your phone's ringing,' Stephanie told Thea, having detected a jingle coming from Thea's bag, which was on the floor by her chair.

'Is it? I can't hear anything.'

The girl grabbed the bag and extracted the device. 'Here,' she said. It was still imperiously demanding some action.

Thea experienced her customary flicker of panic, not so much at the likely identity of the caller and what he or she might have to say, but at the phone itself and the need for instant response. She still wanted to tap when it required a swipe, or vice versa.

It was Gladwin, as the screen had already informed her. 'Can you talk?' she asked.

'Sort of. I'm at the Weavers' farm with Stephanie. We've just got here.'

'Where's that?' The detective sounded bemused.

'You know – I told you yesterday.'

'You didn't say a word about a farm. I would have remembered. In fact you didn't tell me anything about why you were in Baunton. I've been wondering.'

'Oh. Well, never mind – it's not important. Are you phoning about Alice?'

'I am. She is – was – Ms Alicia Ferguson. Everybody always called her Alice, evidently. She owns a house in Oxford, which is used as a holiday let. Why she decided to move out and live in a shed remains unexplained.'

'Alicia's a nice name,' said Thea absently.

'Stick to the point. I'm calling you to tell you it wasn't suicide.'

'Ah!' Thea took a deep breath. 'You're sure about that?'

'Absolutely certain,' said the detective. 'The woman was murdered.'

Chapter Eight

After a few minutes of very persuasive forensic details, Gladwin abruptly asked, 'Who are the Weavers, then?'

'Oh – I probably should have told you yesterday. I would have done if you'd asked me.'

'I get it. It's my fault. So tell me now.'

It was not easy to phrase the story in a way that made it sound unconnected to a matter that had suddenly become very much more serious than the suicide of a vagrant. Especially not with Emmy listening to every word. 'Well – they're Emmy and Nick. I met Emmy a few years ago in Chedworth. She's just got in touch again and wanted me to—'

Emmy was staring at her and flapping a hand in an obvious attempt to silence her. '*Is that the police?*' she mouthed, in a near-silent whisper.

Thea nodded, and said to Gladwin, 'Hang on a minute.

Actually, can I call you back? I've only just got here and it's rude to talk on the phone just now.'

'Oh, excuse *me*,' said Gladwin, sounding genuinely cross. 'It's fairly busy here, come to that. And this isn't just a call for a friendly chat – we need you to come in and give a proper statement. We'll need your fingerprints as well.'

'Bloody hell,' said Thea. 'When?'

'Now would be nice.'

Emmy was still flapping, while Stephanie watched her with a grin. 'I bet it's Gladwin,' she murmured, and moved a few steps away from Thea. Emmy followed her. 'Who?' she demanded.

'Thea can tell you. Give her a minute.'

Thea was trying to explain that she had her stepdaughter and her dog with her, and coming into Cirencester would be a nuisance, but she was making a feeble job of it, knowing she had to do as Gladwin asked. Half a minute later she ended the call and met Emmy's inquisitorial gaze.

'Alice was murdered,' she said starkly. 'I've got to go and give a statement about finding her. By the time I get there they might have connected your name to your report of Ginny being missing. I'll have to tell them all I know.'

'Can I come?' said Stephanie.

'I expect you'll have to. And the dog.'

'They can stay here,' Emmy offered. 'And I don't know why you think I should mind what you say to the police.'

'Because you were waving at me to stop talking,' said Thea.

'Only because I wanted to know who it was, and what they were telling you.'

'She was convincing me that it couldn't have been suicide.' She met Emmy's eyes. 'Do you really not care if I tell them all about Ginny?'

Emmy did not blink. 'What does it matter when they already know all about her? We reported her missing, remember?'

'I know, but if I start talking about her again now, they're more likely to get interested and connect her to this latest thing. I got the impression from Nick that he rather regretted calling in the police about her.'

Emmy wriggled her shoulders. 'It's complicated. Ginny's mother is his sister, and he feels responsible.'

'So why isn't she here herself, trying to find her daughter?'

'Because she was so disgusted about the business in Bristol that she more or less threw the girl out. But she didn't mean it seriously.'

'I expect Ginny thought she did,' said Stephanie, her eyes wide. 'She must have been really upset.'

Emmy shrugged this off. 'We played it down when Susie called us – about her being missing. Just said she'd gone off for a few days. Ginny hadn't been answering her phone. Obviously,' she added. 'That's what bothered Nick the most, actually. He had visions of some abductor destroying the phone and keeping her locked up somewhere. He's calmed down a lot since then. Since you turned up, he seems to have stopped worrying about her. I think he's got something else on his mind now – though I've no idea what. Probably hedgehogs or red kites or nightingales.'

Thea frowned, trying to follow the logic of the story.

'But the police must have asked for her parents' details. Isn't that the first place they'd look for her?'

'They took our word for it that Ginny wasn't with them. Her father's long gone, anyway. She'd never dream of going to him.'

'Okay. Which doesn't help much when it comes to deciding what to say to the police now.'

'I'd have thought it was fairly simple. Don't mention her if they don't.'

It probably would be that simple, Thea supposed. Then why did the idea make her feel so unhappy? 'Is that what Nick would say, as well?'

'Probably.' Emmy chewed her bottom lip for a moment. 'Does that bother you?'

'A bit,' Thea admitted.

'Well, take it from me – none of this has anything to do with Ginny. So, if you can keep her name out of this interview or whatever it is, that would be appreciated. No more than that. Don't tell any lies on our account. And who is this police person anyway? Somebody called Gladwin, right?' She looked to Stephanie for confirmation. 'Is he one of the same bunch that bullied me when my dad died?'

Thea answered the questions. 'She. Gladwin's a she. Detective superintendent, as it happens. And nobody bullied you. It was Jeremy Higgins you saw, and he's not remotely a bully.'

'He wasn't very nice,' Emmy insisted. 'He wouldn't believe anything I said.'

'Well, things have changed since then. *You've* changed, for a start.'

'I had to. So – what happens now?'

'I'll have to go. One more thing – what about this Joe person? Should I keep quiet about him as well?'

Emmy shook her head impatiently. 'You're raising all the wrong issues, but we can't get into all that now. You've got to go to Cirencester. Leave these two here – I'll keep them as hostages, to make sure you come back. You are staying overnight, aren't you? Did you bring food? We forgot to talk about that.'

Thea blinked. 'No. I suppose I thought we'd eat with you. Is that wrong?'

'I don't cook much, to be honest. You can have eggs, and that's about it. We don't milk, of course. It all comes from the supermarket, like it does for everybody else. I suggest you do some shopping while you're in Cirencester.' Which didn't explain anything, Thea thought. And what about *money*?

Thea was exchanging glances with Stephanie when a voice came from across the yard. 'Hello there! Better put your dog in the car for a minute. Just to be on the safe side.'

It was Nick Weaver and his gigantic animal. Thea hurriedly bundled Hepzie into the car and stood well back. Stephanie, made of sterner stuff, leapt forward, arms outstretched and threw herself at the animal. Nick made a strangled sound of alarm, but all was well. Joshua simply stood calmly while his neck was embraced, then his ears and his shaggy back. 'He's *gorgeous*,' trilled the girl. 'What's his name?'

'Lucky for you, he's worn out from walking half a mile. All he wants to do is lie down by the fire. He's called Joshua and he's a Newfoundland.'

'Is he usually aggressive, then?' asked Stephanie.

'No, not really. He just sort of *lunges* at people. Knocks them flying. Same with other dogs, especially small ones.'

'Alice was murdered,' said Emmy suddenly. 'Thea just had a call from a detective woman and she's got to go to Cirencester to answer questions. She should have gone by now.'

Her husband stood even more still than his dog, his face altering dramatically. 'No!' he said. 'Abigail said it was suicide.'

'That's the woman who comes for eggs,' Emmy explained to Thea. 'You saw her yesterday, apparently. She's the one who lives close to where Alice was.'

'Gladwin says she's officially called Alicia,' said Thea. 'That's really not the same name as Alice, is it?' She was surprised to find herself still harbouring a sliver of resentment at the change from Millie to Emmy – which was coming through in her voice.

'Who cares?' snapped Emmy, reverting to the impatient feckless girl Thea had known in Chedworth. 'All *we* care about is Ginny and finding out where she is.' She went to her husband and took hold of his arm. 'Isn't it? Unless this means there's a madman loose in the village and he's murdered her as well as Alice.'

'Hush now,' said Nick, patting her back. 'We'll find Ginny any time now, you'll see. She's a big girl. Nobody's going to murder her.' He looked at Thea. 'But don't say anything about her to the police, unless they ask you directly. Okay?'

'I'll do my best,' said Thea carelessly, while inwardly taking note. Nick evidently had an even clearer understanding of the implications than did his wife. And Thea found herself agreeing with him. At that particular moment it felt like an easy promise to make.

All three adults simultaneously remembered the presence of thirteen-year-old Stephanie, who was still fussing over the dog, but obviously listening avidly as well. 'What's your name again?' asked the farmer. 'I've forgotten.'

Stephanie told him, and then looked back at the car. 'Can Hepzie come out now? I'm sure it'll be all right.'

'Go on, then. I'm holding onto Joshua, but I warn you, when he really wants to move, nothing can stop him.'

On being released, the spaniel took one look at the monstrous creature and scuttled underneath the car. Everyone laughed except Thea, who said, 'She'll stay under there for ages now. How am I supposed to get to Cirencester if I'm scared of driving over her?'

'I'll shut him in the back. She'll come out then,' said Nick, and dragged his dog away.

'What a waste of time,' grumbled Emmy. 'The day's going to be half over at this rate, and nothing's been done.'

'Where do you want us to look for Ginny?' asked Stephanie, standing tall, with a responsible expression. She had captured the spaniel and was holding it to her chest. 'And should Thea really not say anything about her to the police?'

Emma chewed her lip, indecision plain on her face. 'They've had their chance, don't you think? And seeing they aren't bothered about her, you'd do better to stick to the Alice business. Every time I think about it, I get all jangled and worried that the police are going to jump to some horrible conclusions.'

'Like thinking Ginny killed Alice?' Thea suggested.

'Right. And Nick would be so upset if that idea got around. I know I shouldn't ask, but it would be really much better if you try to steer clear of the whole business of Ginny. I mean – not if it comes to telling actual lies or anything. After all, there's a police file somewhere about Ginny, anyway. They'll connect it up themselves eventually, I suppose. Just . . .'

'One thing at a time,' Thea nodded. 'I'll do my best. Besides, we can surely assume by now that Ginny's nowhere in Baunton. I dare say that's been true for a week now. Missing people leave the country, or hide on a tiny Scottish island. They don't hang about half a mile from the place they were last seen.'

'Unless they're dead,' said Stephanie brightly.

Nobody at all laughed at that.

It took barely more than five minutes to reach the police station, during which time Thea thought over the half-baked commission that Emmy and Nick had landed her with. It looked more and more ridiculous with every passing moment. So ridiculous, in fact, that it began to feel obvious that there was a hidden agenda, a very different motivation from the one she had been given. Emmy had freely acknowledged that her earlier encounter with Thea had led her to believe that here was a person with the time, the nerve, the wits and the experience to tackle whatever murky goings-on there might be in the Weaver household.

The question was – should she disclose any of this to Gladwin?

Her inclinations were entirely unclear. On one hand the Ginny business could prove to be an annoying distraction from the investigation into what happened to Alice/Alicia – which was complicated and intriguing enough without new elements that probably had no relevance. Except they *might*. The counter-argument was every bit as strong: the disappearance of Ginny was strangely coincidental, timewise. *Probably* was the operative word. Ginny, after all, just might have killed the peculiar woman who owned property but who behaved like a vagrant. A woman who sat on the pavement in Cirencester and demonstrated every sign of insanity or drunkenness.

She reached the police station, found an easy parking space and was walking in with her mind still in a ferment when Gladwin met her with a brief smile and took her into a small windowless room. She had been in the building before, but not this dispiriting little space. 'Sorry,' said Gladwin, glancing around. 'This is all that's available. The place is being rewired and there are workmen everywhere else.'

Thea merely nodded, and the detective pressed on. 'So – listen. This is a murder investigation, as I told you. There are details I can't tell you about, to do with angles and blood flow and so forth that prove she couldn't have stuck the knife in herself. Whoever did it was pretty clever, up to all the usual tricks with fingerprints, so we're having to mobilise some fancy forensics on it. That'll take a while. We'll do you in a bit.'

'Okay,' said Thea, aware that she was being given far more information than any average member of the public might expect. 'But you mean you might yet find some

DNA or something to show who did it?'

Gladwin laughed. 'In *theory*, possibly. We're having trouble explaining the knife. It doesn't appear to have been hers – but that's just speculation. An absence of any sign that she's had it in her bag or pocket. There's a footprint as well. And a few other snippets. But the thing's rather a mess, one way and another. We need to know a lot more about the woman before we can really get much of a picture.'

'I see,' said Thea.

Gladwin went on, speaking earnestly, leaning forward slightly. 'The thing is, she had only been dead a short time. A *very* short time, actually. Which makes it a bit awkward for you, in a way. I mean – you were pretty much at the scene while it was happening. Do you see?'

'Well, *I* didn't do it,' said Thea with a little laugh.

'I hope not. But in the interests of a thorough investigation I'll have to ask you to account for all your movements in the two hours before you phoned 999. Where you went, who you saw, who saw *you*. You know the drill. I don't expect it's the first time, is it?'

'Well . . . it feels different from anything I can remember. It's more like what happened to Drew, when I first met him. It never even *occurred* to me that I might end up as a suspect. I was sitting in my car round the corner for quite a long time, eating crisps. I wouldn't have seen anybody near the hut.'

'We don't think of you as a suspect, you know. Nor anybody else. We just gather up every scrap of testimony, evidence, and so forth, make connections, test theories. We say "person of interest" instead of "suspect" now.'

'And am I one of those?'

Gladwin sighed. 'Thea Slocombe – one way or another you're *always* one of those.'

Thea had no further wish to laugh – for the second time that morning. 'This isn't funny, is it?' she said. 'I hope you've got time, because I've got rather a long story to tell you.'

'That's good, because I still don't understand why you're here at all and certainly not how you came to see the victim hours before she was killed. You're not house-sitting in Baunton, are you?'

'Most of it is sheer coincidence,' Thea began.

'I doubt that,' Gladwin said. 'But just let me switch this on, okay?' She pressed a button on a small device that could only be a voice recorder. 'I might miss something otherwise.'

Thea repressed a flicker of resistance, promising herself to watch every word. She shook her head slightly, in a gesture that Gladwin took as acquiescence, and then began a careful exposition. 'I need to go back to that business in Chedworth, where the man died in a barn. You weren't directly involved, as far as I remember. It was all Higgins. The people were called Wilshire. One of them was Emmy, only she called herself Millie then. She's Mrs Weaver now and she lives in Baunton.' There was no longer much of a dilemma as to whether to include the quest for the missing Ginny – or so it seemed. If Gladwin needed all Thea's movements, then that had to be added in. And yet, Thea still found herself oddly resistant to doing any such thing. It would drag the Weavers into a murder investigation quite wrongly. The police mind would conflate the two distinct occurrences, if only on the grounds of geography. Nick Weaver in particular would not like that. She went on, 'Well, Stephanie and I came here on Monday for a look at the church in Baunton. But before that we went shopping in Cirencester and saw Alice behaving strangely by the big church. She seemed to be having a sort of breakdown.' She went on to briefly describe the woman's behaviour and the arrival of the second woman.

Gladwin jotted a few things downs and asked no questions while Thea reached the part about the note left on her windscreen. Getting the sequence right was harder than she'd anticipated, but Gladwin left her to sort it out without comment until she finished with a very expurgated account of her subsequent visit to the Weavers, in order to catch up with Emmy in her new life. 'It was nice to see her again,' she added at the end. 'I went for a little walk around the bit of the village we didn't see on Monday, and stumbled on poor dead Alice.' The decision had somehow made itself, to say nothing at that point about Ginny Chambers. It felt dishonest and uncomfortable, but somehow necessary.

'That took about seven minutes,' Gladwin said, looking at a digital clock that was part of the recorder.

Thea felt that was inordinately long. Had she deviated, added irrelevant anecdotes, left long silences? 'Did it make sense?' she asked. To her own mind, the deletion of Ginny had left a gaping hole.

'It's a basis for further investigation. Now tell me some of the less factual stuff. Impressions, connections – all your usual contributions.'

'That you find so incredibly helpful, you mean?'

'Exactly.'

'You'll have to prompt me. I feel as if I've told you everything that's relevant already.'

'Tell me more about these Weavers, who suddenly invited you to stay at a moment's notice.'

Gladwin had inevitably homed in on the unavoidable fact that Thea was actually planning to stay with the Weavers. Without an honest explanation, Thea knew it seemed suspiciously odd.

'I think it's mostly that they need a bit of help. She's very pregnant, and they have an awful lot of work to do. There's stuff going on in the family that's distracting them. They've had a bit of trouble.' She was closing in on the central point, finding it more and more difficult to avoid mentioning it. And yet she still couldn't quite do it. It would feel like a betrayal of Emmy and Nick, and even though they had no reason that Thea could see to conceal anything, it was hardly up to her to drag them into Gladwin's investigations. After all, there would be a police report about the missing Ginny on the computer in Cirencester anyway. It could not take much longer before somebody made the connection. *Why should I do all their work for them?* she asked herself. *Because without people like you, they'd never be able to do their job* came the obvious answer.

'What sort of farm is it?' asked Gladwin.

Thea cheerfully explained about the courses and all the work they involved. 'It's a great idea, you know. I'm going to suggest to Drew that he tries something like it. He might even think about offering to run a course for the Weavers.' The idea quivered with fresh opportunities and she smiled. 'I just thought of that.'

Gladwin was musing, sucking her upper lip. 'That must all involve a lot of people coming and going, forming relationships, keeping in touch. I wonder if Alice Ferguson ever went there? They must have needed some casual help, and she'd be usefully off the books.'

'Yes, she did,' said Thea, relieved to be telling the plain truth. 'They knew her vaguely. But they had no idea she was living in that shed. I think lots of people do casual work up there when the courses are on. Emmy doesn't like cooking, apparently. And there'll be all those beds to see to.'

Gladwin stared at her notepad for a long moment, tapping a fingernail on the table, 'That's all very interesting,' she concluded. 'If there are writers or painters, they'll all be in competition with each other. There'll be strong emotions all over the place, which might easily spill over to people working there as well. Then you factor in the eco-nuts. They won't all be there to spot a red squirrel or a rare orchid. They'll be looking for every sort of sinfulness – a drop of oil in the wrong place, or a careless word about red kites. Not everybody likes red kites,' she added darkly.

'I don't know,' said Thea again. 'I haven't seen any of that. There aren't any courses on this week. There's one starting at the weekend, though.'

'Why not during the week? It's half-term. You'd think it would be packed with families or teachers with time on their hands. People expect to go away and do something different when it's half-term.' She sighed again and Thea remembered that Gladwin had two sons who might well expect their mother to take them away somewhere different for the week.

'Well, maybe Emmy and Nick wanted a holiday as well. Honestly, I've only had about an hour to get to know her again. She's grown up a lot since Chedworth.'

Gladwin closed her eyes briefly, and then flipped back through her notes. 'There's something strange here, even for you. Everything's been so *quick*. And I'm not happy about the undeniable coincidence of you being on the spot when a woman's killed.'

'I know,' said Thea miserably. 'I think I was just so intrigued by Emmy showing up again like that, and the farm and everything . . . it's nice what they're doing. I didn't see any harm in having a walk round the village, just to show willing, and then finding Alice threw everything else into the background.'

'Everything else?'

'Oh, well – Drew's having conniptions about the business, and it's half-term, and the dog's getting fat and bored. Emmy seemed like a nice change. I think she rather took to me, back in Chedworth, and wants to be my friend. She always was a bit needy – that hasn't changed, even though she's got a much richer life now. She just persuaded me to come and listen to her troubles. I can't really explain it better than that.' Except she could have done, she admitted to herself. She could have supplied a whole additional mystery on top of what happened to Alice Ferguson, and before very long she knew she would have to. Gladwin would lose trust in her when she discovered the blatant omission of crucial information – as she inevitably would. But

Emmy and Nick deserved some consideration, too.

'Maybe she's a hypnotist,' smiled Gladwin, coming closer than she realised to Thea's thoughts.

'She's just pregnant,' said Thea and Gladwin laughed.

'I'm not really a suspect, am I?' Thea asked, after another two or three minutes.

'Pinning a motive on you would be tricky, I admit. But – God, Thea, your timing is little short of magical. If you hadn't come across her she might have been there for days. We haven't found a single person who knew she'd been living there.'

This was much safer ground. 'Not even that neighbour woman? And the man who owns the shed? They both showed up pretty promptly yesterday, as if they might have some idea about what was what.'

'Er . . .' said Gladwin. 'Names?'

'No idea. I spoke to them for barely a minute before you turned up. That group standing gawping over the police tape. A very short man. A woman who said she lived right there. A couple from round the corner and a landowner who said he lived a mile away. I did make sure I remembered all they said. That's surprising really, after what I'd just seen. Maybe all my senses were heightened. Maybe I subconsciously thought one of them was the killer and I should be on the alert.'

Gladwin shrugged. 'I think you and I need to go back there together and walk it all through. At least it's nice and local this time.'

Thea had a sensation of being balanced in the middle of a see-saw. The demands of the Weavers on one side and Gladwin on the other threatened to pull her in half. And each got in the way of the other, so she couldn't hope to give full attention to either of them. And not just that. 'What about Stephanie?' she asked.

'What about her?'

'I told you. She's with me at Emmy's, because she was bored at home. But now there's a definite murder, she's going to want to get involved with that as well.'

'She can't. She's much too young.'

'That's what Drew says. But she's very tough and sensible – and she knows her own limitations. She's quite capable of backing off, saying "I'm not old enough to cope with that". She said it in Northleach quite recently.'

'Even so,' said Gladwin sternly. 'It might be dangerous.'

Thea always reacted badly to remarks like that. 'I don't expect it is,' she said carelessly. 'After all, the person who killed Alice left the knife behind.'

There was a tap at the door and a young female came in with the fingerprinting kit. 'I'll leave you to it,' said Gladwin, getting up.

'Right,' said Thea.

They parted on a somewhat fractious note. Gladwin had duties at the police station, monitoring her team and devising strategies for the investigation, which meant she would not be free for another hour. Thea was keen to get back to Stephanie, and have a serious talk with Emmy. But first she had to pause at a supermarket and gather up cold meat, salad and bread.

The farm was still quiet when Thea got back. Again, the short drive had provided the opportunity for a concentrated think with no interruptions. The sudden switch from town centre to tiny village, achieved via narrow winding lanes, was so typical of the Cotswolds that Thea could not avoid memories of other situations in very similar settings. Perhaps, she acknowledged, there were clues to be gleaned from earlier investigations. But she quickly dismissed the temptation to overhaul every murder she had encountered since embarking on her career as a house-sitter. Every one was different, when it came to it. So many motives, so many surprises – and so many malicious deceitful individuals living apparently ordinary lives.

Emmy came to the door, holding Hepzie in her arms. Panic swept through Thea, even though she could see no blood and the dog's plumy tail was wagging. Spaniels were not naturally suited to being carried, the weight distribution making them top-heavy and Hepzie never enjoyed it. 'Put her down,' Thea ordered.

'We were just having a cuddle,' Emmy defended herself, ignoring the instruction. The pregnant bump was providing a sort of seat for the dog, Thea noticed. 'Are you ready for some coffee or did your detective friend give you some?' Emmy went on.

'I'm gasping,' said Thea. 'Thanks.'

They all went into the kitchen, where Joshua was slumped on a large woven rug at one end of the room and Stephanie was sitting at the table with a laptop. Emmy explained that she had already supervised a careful introduction of the two dogs, which had passed without incident. They were now amiable acquaintances, if not exactly friends. Hepzie was set down on the floor, and left to perform her usual self-abasement, showing the giant canine her pink underbelly. He sniffed it carelessly and put his head back between his huge paws as if completely unmoved. 'How rude!' giggled Stephanie. 'He doesn't fancy her at all.'

'Thank goodness,' said Thea.

'What did Gladwin say?' Stephanie asked impatiently. 'You were gone a long time. Did you say anything about Ginny?'

'She made me go through everything I could remember from Monday and yesterday. She didn't tell me anything much – just recorded what I said and asked some questions. And no, I didn't mention Ginny. I would have done if it had seemed important, but it just never did. She was interested in all the people I've spoken to – the ones who came to see what was going on when the police showed up in force. I don't really think I was terribly helpful.'

'Did she think it was a big coincidence that we saw Alice on Monday?'

Thea paused to think. 'She doesn't like coincidences. She's probably trying to find a rational explanation for it – as well as the way Emmy spotted the car by the church.' She looked at the pregnant woman. 'That's really quite hard to explain. I mean – who remembers an ordinary car after nearly three years?'

Emmy drew back as if under attack. 'Your car isn't ordinary to me. The registration number was burnt into my brain when my father died. I don't think you realised even then how much I was relying on you, and how passionately I wanted you to find out what happened. I spent days watching out for that car. The only surprising thing is that you've still got it.'

'Why were you walking past the church though?' asked Stephanie.

'I do it three times a week, regularly. It's a circular walk, two miles, down the Monarch's Way and back along White Way. It's supposed to be good for the baby and all that.'

Thea and Stephanie had little choice but to accept this explanation with good grace.

The question of lunch was beginning to raise its head by the time the coffee was finished. Gladwin had not set a time for 'walking through' the events of the previous day, but it was clearly not going to make any allowance for mealtimes. And what about Stephanie – what was she meant to do during that exercise? That question had not been resolved, either.

But Stephanie herself was on top of the whole thing. 'I'm going to use Nick's computer to see if I can find anything out about Ginny,' she announced. 'Emmy and Nick aren't really up to speed with Instagram and the other newer platforms. They haven't got further than Facebook, actually.'

'And you are? Up to speed, I mean?'

'More or less,' shrugged the girl. 'Emmy's given me a few hints, and I can easily follow them up. There's a lot of stuff about rewilding and all that. And Ginny had a thing about reintroducing lost species. Beavers and wolves and red kites. That narrows it down a bit. I might find something she's posted in the past week, and then we'd have a much better idea of how to find her.'

'If she's posting things, then why do we *need* to find

her? We'd know she's alive and well and doing her own thing,' said Thea.

'True,' said Stephanie with a smile. 'Although—'

'Not true at all,' snapped Emmy. 'We've *got* to find her, wherever she is.'

'Why?' asked Thea.

'Because she's gone off with something extremely precious to me and Nick, that's why.'

Chapter Nine

Many possibilities flowed through Thea's mind over the next ten seconds. Jewellery? An animal? Family papers? A treasure map? Seeds of a rare wild flower? Boring old money?

'What?' she asked.

'It's complicated and rather sensitive,' Emmy prevaricated. 'That's why I didn't tell you before. We didn't tell the police, either. I mean, it doesn't actually affect the fact that she's missing. Nobody knows where she is. We've tried at least a dozen people. And now there's somebody out there doing murders, we can see that it has all got much more serious than we thought. We don't know what to think now, or what to do for the best.' Her face screwed up in real distress. 'Nick seems to be at a complete loss, which is scary. He's never like that usually.'

'What did she take?' demanded Thea, slowly and loudly.

Her spaniel turned a startled look on her, as did Stephanie.

'Nick's mother's diary,' came the reply.

Right third time, thought Thea smugly. A diary definitely counted as family papers.

'Nick's mother is Ginny's granny – right? So it's going to mean something to her. Is she in it?'

'It's not really that sort of diary. It's more a notebook. Or a cashbook. And a lot more. It's got *everything* in it.'

'So why was it here? Does Nick's mother know it's gone?'

'Listen,' said Emmy, holding her unborn baby with two hands, as if to protect it. 'The Weavers are rich. Ginny's mother is the eldest in the family, but she's never been very competent and now she's gone all judgemental and beastly about Ginny we try not to talk to her if we can help it. Then there's Nick's mum – Ginny's grandmother, as you said – and Uncle Rupert, who's her younger brother. They're still in charge of the family business even though they're quite old now. I don't understand all the details, but it involves this farm and shareholders and trustees and all sorts. It's been the same for generations – they're all very clever with money – except Nick, I suppose. There's been a bit of a crisis this year, with my mother-in-law at the heart of it. She was keeping notes of who said what, and all the financial ins and outs, everything like that. The diary was a sort of bible, where she recorded it all as it happened. Then she got it onto the computer as well. It's not as if anything's really *lost*. Just that it's all so *confidential*.'

'Something is lost, though,' said Stephanie calmly, while Thea was still trying to get a handle on this new revelation.

117

'And that's Ginny. Why didn't you tell all this to the police or us before now?'

'Because they would have said it's obvious that Ginny has just gone into hiding, after stealing the book, and isn't in any danger. If she's planning some kind of fraud against the family, they're not going to be very interested, are they? At least not until the deed is done.'

'So you were hoping to use them to find her for you?'

Emmy nodded. 'But it didn't work, so I thought of you.'

'Does Nick's mother know it's gone?' Thea asked again, keeping a firm hold on the logical thread running through this new development. 'Does *she* think Ginny might be planning something like that? Whatever *that* is. How would a fraud work?'

'Nick's mother's in no position to know anything,' came a voice from the doorway. All the women jumped. Hepzie froze as the Newfoundland rose from his rug and gave a deep *woof* of welcome.

'Oh, hello,' said Emmy, looking worried. 'You've been gone a long time.'

'What have you been saying? You've told them more about Ginny, from the sound of it. Didn't we agree . . . ?' He stopped, fixing his wife with a stare more puzzled than angry. 'Has something else happened?' He looked round all three female faces. 'Did I miss something?'

'Not at all,' soothed Emmy. 'Thea kept quiet about Ginny in her police interview, but she and Stephanie both felt sure there was something more we hadn't told them, so I fessed up about your mother's notebook thing. It did seem wrong not to say anything about it.' She gave a big ingenuous smile. 'Don't you think?'

'I don't know. It goes against the grain to splurge private family matters.' His cheeks were red and his hair disarrayed. He rubbed his forehead distractedly.

'But we need to know why Ginny took it, and what she means to do with it,' Emmy persisted.

Her husband sat down at the table, and took a deep breath. 'Actually, I have been thinking about it quite a lot, and it seems to me it might be more a sort of act of sabotage than any kind of fraud. You know how she was always calling us capitalists and exploiters and that stuff – well, she might have thought it would give us a setback if she took the book. We did treat it as almost sacred, after all.'

Emmy gazed at him in frank admiration. 'Gosh!' she said. 'I bet that's right. So you think she burnt it or threw it in a ditch or something?'

'I wouldn't put it past her. I doubt very much if she's got the wits to make any real sense of it, or use it to do any harm.'

Thea and Stephanie were following this avidly. 'So, you think that's why she disappeared, do you?' asked Thea. 'As a sort of sabotage?'

Nick worked the fingers of one hand through his thick hair in a gesture that Thea suspected was habitual. 'I have a feeling we did something to annoy her, and this is her revenge. The trouble is, I can't think of anything we could have done.'

'And none of it has anything to do with Alice,' said Emmy, with an air of finality. 'Now, tell us what you've been doing for the past two hours,' she ordered her husband.

He smiled broadly at her, and readily complied. 'Had to go and look at the apples. And look what I found.'

He opened a large hand to reveal several bright shining chestnuts. 'The trees I planted less than ten years ago are laden with nuts. I only noticed them today. Look at them!'

Stephanie and Emmy both approached. 'Are they edible?' asked the girl.

'Oh yes. Sweet chestnuts, not conkers. They'll be delicious – better than the mouldy dried-up things you get in the shops.' He tipped the nuts onto the table and stood back. There seemed to be some sort of hiatus, suggestive of unfinished business.

'Did you tell them about Ginny's mother and the rest of the family?' Nick asked Emmy, after some moments of quiet.

Emmy nodded. 'A bit. Not the part about Anita.' She turned to Thea. 'She's Ginny's mum.'

'So what's wrong with your mother that she doesn't know anything?' asked Thea.

Nick answered, in a husky voice. 'She's in an induced coma. She had a car accident ten days ago,' he said. 'I dashed up there when it first happened, but they said there was no sense in hanging round her. She can't hear or see or anything.'

'But . . .' Thea spluttered. 'But why didn't you say anything about that sooner? Doesn't that explain why Ginny would behave strangely? She must be really worried. How many more secrets are there around here?'

He shook his head. 'It doesn't have anything to do with the business here. My mother and I never got on too well, even when we both lived here. We were always pulling in different directions. She's a very controlling person. When it came to explaining things to you, we tried to keep it simple. And relevant. The only point that matters is that we are desperately keen to find Ginny. The rest is just distraction. You have no need to know anything about the background.' He spoke with an intensity that was almost scary and threw a sudden angry look at Emmy.

Thea held up a hand to silence him, while she thought back over the previous twenty-four hours. 'So why did you tell me so much about your courses and the farm? How is any of that relevant?'

'Because it's what Ginny was involved in. The people she met – they've got to be in the picture somewhere. There's even a chance that she's ganged up with someone and she's doing her best to bring this family down – it's possible she's trying to ruin us. I haven't wanted to admit that to myself, but I can see it now.'

'So what about Joe?' asked Stephanie.

Everyone paused, frowning. Then Emmy burst out, 'For God's sake! What does he have to do with anything?'

'You'd been talking to him when we got here. It was the first thing you said to us – that he'd come back to Cirencester. You seemed to think it was important – so the police might be interested in him as well, don't you think?'

Nick turned to his wife, his face even redder. 'She's right. I knew it was a mistake to bring him into it.'

Emmy calmly met his glare. 'You make it sound as if we're riddled with secrets, and people not to be mentioned. I don't get it. We're perfectly ordinary people, running a business, falling out with our relations now and then. None of it needs to be hushed up – we've nothing to feel guilty about. Stop getting in such a state.' She turned to Thea. 'I already told you that Joe's got no idea where Ginny's got to. It's just a waste of time to bring him into it.'

Nick snorted. 'That's what I just said. He's not just a waste of time – he's a waste of space as well. The man's a walking disaster. I wouldn't be surprised if it was him who killed poor old Alice.'

'Nick! What a thing to say! I know you never liked him, but he's not a *murderer*.'

'You both knew that Alice was murdered, then – before I told you what Gladwin told me?' said Thea, focusing on Nick.

He gave her a long and rather patronising look. 'It seemed obvious to me. But I happened to meet Abby Seldon just now and she told me. The police are back, going door to door with their questions. They'll be here any time now. Of course *you'll* have been told personally by your chums in CID, won't you?'

'Who's Abby Seldon?' asked Stephanie.

Emmy laughed. 'There's only one person in this room with any real sense, it seems to me. This girl is a genius at sticking to the point.' She grinned at Stephanie, and explained, 'Abby lives very close to where Thea found Alice. She's the one who comes here for eggs. But she hasn't been today.' She looked at Nick. 'Where did you see her?'

'The top field. She was picking mushrooms. I told her she could have a few. She'd just found the most magnificent specimen. Must have been eight inches across, perfectly white. Too good to eat, really.' He laughed. 'Although it would just go rotten if you left it. After the slugs have had a nibble. I made sure she knew she should only take a few. That woman never knows where to stop,' he added with a theatrical sigh and a laugh.

Thea judged the laugh to be somewhat forced, but the image of the huge white mushroom was appealing. 'I haven't had a real wild mushroom since I was about ten,' she sighed.

'We have loads this year. I'll give you some,' said Emmy. 'Nick's family have always invited the whole village to help themselves – blackberries, sloes, hips – and now we're trying to stop them. Abby calls it foraging, which some people think makes it sound more respectable and green. But we think wild fruit and so forth belongs to the wild creatures. People already take far too much from the land, after all. But Nick finds it difficult to say no.'

'It makes sense to let them have something,' he argued. 'Keeps everybody on side. It's good PR.'

'Until you start throwing out accusations of murder,' Emmy said. 'Even if it is only Joe. Which reminds me – he said he was coming over this afternoon, so watch what you say to him.'

'I'll do my best to avoid him, if you like.'

Stephanie and Thea were concentrating on keeping up with what felt like a lot of new information, while at the same time becoming well aware that there was far more to learn. The vague hints that Thea had been given the day before were expanding and mutating out of all recognition. Emmy's boasts about the lucrative nature of the courses they ran were starting to look rather hollow, if the business was in jeopardy. Nick's mother sounded to be at death's door in hospital, and there was a sinister man called Joe about to materialise. Ginny was a thief, and at least one of the locals apparently had open access to the Weavers' land.

And Alice had been murdered. Thea clung to that point,

just as Stephanie was clinging to the quest for Ginny.

'Gladwin's only interested in Alice,' Thea reminded them all. 'But I did tell her that you knew her, and that she came here to do casual work sometimes. That's bound to need following up. Obviously, she must have met lots of people here on the courses—'

'She didn't,' said Emmy firmly. 'She did cleaning, collecting eggs – that sort of thing. She was kept right away from the clients, I promise you. She looked such a mess, we couldn't have her mixing with them.'

'Lowering the tone,' said Nick injudiciously, earning himself a frown from Stephanie.

Thea was wrestling with the inconsistencies. 'But she had a house in Oxford. She wasn't really a vagrant at all. Mentally ill, perhaps, with a drink problem. In genuine trouble, I suppose, living like that. But you must have known *something* about her, before you'd let her work here – didn't you?'

'Not really,' said Emmy. 'We don't ask many questions, to be honest. She turned up one day and asked if she could do a bit of casual work and we said yes.'

'That was nice of you.' Thea was rehearsing her own confused feelings about the murdered woman. 'She rented her house out, so she must have had some money.'

'You have no idea what was really going on with her,' said Emmy impatiently. 'You're just guessing and you've probably got it all completely wrong. I would be very surprised if she had any money at all. She was probably in terrible debt or something.'

'So tell me how it seems to you, then,' said Thea.

'Why should I? You're not here to solve a murder.

You're here to find Ginny, who has absolutely nothing to do with bloody Alice Ferguson. If the police come nosing about here because of what you've told them, you can just go home now. You're more trouble than you're worth.' She pressed her hands on her pregnant bump and clenched her jaw. Hepzie and Joshua both threw curious glances her way. Thea could see she was close to tears.

'Steady on!' protested Nick. 'That's not fair. Plenty of people knew Alice came up here when we were busy. Someone would have told the police regardless of what Thea said. It's no reason to give her the sack before she's even started.'

'Looks to me as if she's *never* going to get started, the way it's going,' Emmy mumbled.

Stephanie made a sound of protest. 'I'm *trying*, but everybody keeps talking. I can't concentrate.'

It was past twelve and Stephanie was clearly restless. 'I got some food on the way home,' Thea reassured her. 'We'll go and make ourselves some lunch, then I'll try to get hold of Gladwin and see if she wants us this afternoon. She's sure to be pretty busy.'

'Send her a text and say we'll be here until she tells us what she wants,' Stephanie advised.

'I will,' said Thea. 'Now, let's get a move on. Before anything else happens, we've got to eat.'

Emmy emitted a sort of moan, but then gave herself a visible shake. 'Take no notice of me. I was just having a wobble. But I know it's *awful* of me not giving you any food,' she said. 'But I never could cope with feeding people. Heaven knows how this poor baby will ever survive. When we have the course people here, I pay a caterer to bring all their meals. They'd have to pay for food anyway, so it doesn't make much of a hole in the profits. I've got some good people in Cirencester who do a wonderful job.'

'And it leaves you free to do some of the more interesting stuff,' said Nick. 'Instead of slaving in the kitchen.'

'Right,' said Emmy with a faint smile. 'We agreed about that from the start.'

'Come on, then,' said Thea decisively. 'Let's get some lunch. We can start again after we've seen Gladwin, if there's any point.' She stood up and then gave Emmy a searching look. 'I'm not sure there is, really. This is way beyond what I usually do. It was never likely to work, let's face it.'

'But I've hardly started,' wailed Stephanie. 'You don't mean we're just going home again, do you?' She was following her stepmother to the door, where they both paused and looked back.

'Leave the computer,' said Emmy. 'Nick doesn't like it to be taken out of the house. You could come and do some more after your lunch, maybe. I don't suppose the detective woman wants you tagging along, if she does take Thea off again.'

Thea answered Stephanie's question, once they were back in the annex. 'It might be the best thing if we just pack up and go home, actually. We might well be doing more harm than good hanging about here. Emmy just said as much. It's obviously very complicated here, and much as I'd like to have a look at this Joe person, I can't pretend that's anything more than idle curiosity. What we've just heard makes the whole thing a lot more serious, and I know Drew wouldn't want you involved if it gets too close to an actual killing.'

'I'm not *involved*. I'm just looking things up on the computer. How can that possibly hurt anything? Although Emmy's quite annoying. She never settles to anything and she keeps changing her mind. It was the same when you were out, talking all the time and not letting me get on with anything. I bet I could have found that Ginny by now if she'd given me a chance. Except she wouldn't give me any proper information.'

'Like what?'

'Oh – the names of Ginny's main friends. Facebook groups and all that. Where she was before coming here. She threw out a few ideas, all vague and probably wrong. Started going on about red kites – that happened twice.'

'What about Nick?'

'He was hardly there. The dog growled at Hepzie a bit, so he took it for a walk. When he came back he said it would be too tired to be any trouble – which it was. Then he went off again. He acts like a farmer, but it's not really much of a farm, is it?'

'I don't know. Just at the moment I feel as if I don't know anything at all. Nick and Emmy are obviously not much bothered about Alice, which is frustrating. And there's a lot more to Ginny's disappearance than they told me at the start. Quite honestly, I'd love to just pack up and go.'

Stephanie's main focus was on food. She emptied Thea's shopping bag onto the table and rapidly made herself a sandwich. 'I like it here,' she mumbled. 'And it would be bad to back out now. Emmy just wants to keep on talking about Nick's family, doesn't she? I'm still in a muddle about which is an aunt and which is a granny. It's like one of

Dad's funerals – having to sort out a whole lot of relatives.'

'I keep thinking it's Ginny's mother that's in hospital, but actually it's the granny. They don't seem to care very much, do they? Do you think they've made the whole thing up to gain our sympathy?'

Stephanie went on chewing, while she considered this idea. 'I can probably find out. Somebody's sure to have posted it on WhatsApp or somewhere.'

'But does it *matter*?' Thea sighed. 'If you ask me, we'd be better just sticking to the murder and abandoning the whole business of Ginny.' She busied herself making her own sandwich and two mugs of tea. Then she began to think aloud. 'I'm starting to feel I'm being used as a smokescreen or something. Nothing is how it looks on the surface.' She tailed off, hearing herself. Where had that come from? What had suddenly aroused her suspicions? How closely would the Weavers have collaborated on what could only be a very elaborate plan if any of her suspicions were valid? 'I don't think Emmy really wants us to go home – she was just cross with me for being so matey with Gladwin. She's never liked having to deal with the police. I have to admit she has good reason, after the horrible business in Chedworth.'

'I don't understand the part about a smokescreen,' said Stephanie.

'A diversion. Hiding the real facts. Have you noticed the way she drops a whole new subject in when things start to get awkward? Like that diary thing.'

Stephanie's eyebrows kinked in puzzlement. 'Well, maybe a bit. She seems quite . . . well, *innocent* to me. I don't think she's telling us any lies – is she? I suppose I might not spot a lie if it was clever enough. I thought she was just rather scatterbrained.'

'I always want to believe people as well. It's all part of living in a society, isn't it? You couldn't have any proper institutions or systems if everybody told lies all the time.'

'Mm,' said Stephanie uncertainly. 'But that isn't really what we're talking about, is it? We're just interested in Emmy and Ginny at the moment.'

'And Nick.'

'Yes. And Nick.'

As soon as their lunch was over, they went back to the farmhouse, Thea holding her phone in expectation of a call from Gladwin. 'Where is she?' she muttered. 'I thought I'd have heard from her by now.'

'Busy, presumably,' said Stephanie. 'Do you think Emmy will want to go on talking to us? Should we be bringing Hepzie?' The spaniel was following them closely, her ears and tail drooping in an unusual display of unease. 'She doesn't look very happy.'

'I can't think why. She and Joshua were getting along all right.'

'Atmosphere,' said Stephanie shortly, as they knocked on the side door and were invited in by a voice from the kitchen.

It was arranged that Stephanie would continue her computer searches, while Emmy pottered around on minor domestic matters. Nick was intending to spend the afternoon in his extensive apple orchard, with his dog at his side. 'I must take you on a proper guided tour sometime today,' he said to the visitors. Everyone looked questioningly at Thea, as if wondering what role she would adopt.

'I'm supposed to be going round the village with Gladwin,' she said. 'She'll call me soon, I expect.'

'Meanwhile, you can stay and chat,' said Emmy easily. 'It's nice to have you here. I'm sorry about this morning's little drama. I just get waves of panic about Ginny, and how it feels as if we've wasted so much time. She doesn't have any time for her mother, but Anita does care about her deep down, and she trusted us to watch out for her. I feel we've really let her down.'

Nick was pulling on a weathered browny-grey jacket with a tear in one sleeve. 'It's that useless Keith that's let her down, not us.' He faced Thea. 'That's Ginny's father. He's in South Korea, last I heard. Does something with computers. It's years since any of us saw him, although I gather he does send money now and then.'

'We're neither of us very good at families, are we?' said Emmy sadly, looking down at her pregnant bump. 'We shouldn't be allowed to have children.'

'Emmy!' Nick's voice was full of pain and alarm. 'Don't say that. We'll give this child everything our own parents failed to do. It's all I ever think about these days. Anything that threatens to spoil that needs to be kept right away. Everything we need as a family is right here – once we settle the business of Ginny.'

Emmy smiled sweetly at him. 'Gosh, Nick! It's nice to know you care so much. But we'll never be able to keep the world away completely – not if we keep letting all these people come to the courses. Besides, I wouldn't want to. I like all the different opinions and experiences they bring. Some of them have quite good advice about childrearing as well.' She smiled again and leant back in her chair. Hepzie went up to her, gazing at her face with liquid spaniel eyes. 'See – even the dog understands.'

Stephanie had opened the laptop and was giving most of her attention to it. Nick was in the small vestibule by the back door, lacing up some stout walking boots. 'Where's Joshua?' asked Thea.

'Out the back. I'll take him with me. Bye, all.'

'Bye!' called Emmy. She looked at Thea. 'I really don't deserve him, you know. I'm hopeless at anything practical, especially cooking. But he says I'm good with people – and money. The whole business of the courses was my idea, you know, and it's transformed the farm. In such a short time, as well!'

'He'd be lost without you,' said Thea. 'That's absolutely obvious.' She noticed a movement of her stepdaughter's head, and met her gaze. *So would my dad be without you,* she read the unspoken message.

'I think Joe might show up before long,' Emmy said. 'He can tell you more about Ginny, if you're interested. He's good to talk to, anyway. Nick doesn't like him much,' she added unnecessarily.

Thea experienced a brief flash of concern about Stephanie being exposed to a strange man, probably when she, Thea, was not present. 'You'll keep an eye on Stephanie, won't you?' she said. 'If I have to go off with Gladwin again.'

'Course I will,' said Emmy, and right on cue Thea's phone began to jingle.

'Gladwin,' Stephanie predicted accurately.

'Sorry to take so long,' the detective began. 'Where are you?'

Thea explained and it was arranged that they meet at the Plough Inn a mile or so away within the next few minutes. 'But don't expect me to feed you,' warned Gladwin.

'At last!' Thea said when the call was ended. 'Now I've got something to do. I'd better be off. I've got to find a pub called The Plough.'

'Go on, then,' said Emmy. 'But don't abandon looking for Ginny, will you? I didn't mean it about going home – what I said this morning. I know I'm a hopeless hostess. It's the same when the clients come for the courses – I never tell them all the things they need to know. Ginny was really good at all that stuff.'

Thea stood up and her dog automatically followed. 'No, Heps, you stay here with Stephanie,' Thea said.

'The Plough's a good pub,' said Emmy. 'You'll like it there. It's in Stratton. You can't miss it.'

There was little time for constructive thought on the short drive to the pub – which was very easy to find, as Emmy had predicted. She felt jaded and unfocused with the avalanche of events and conversations that had taken place over the past twenty-four hours. *This is exhausting* she thought to herself. *And the day's barely half over.* She parked and went into the pub, asking for coffee and sitting at a table at the back of the big open bar. Again she tried to order her thoughts, but the attempt was quickly interrupted by the arrival of DS Gladwin, sweeping into the pub, pausing to order a Coke and a packet of crisps and then plumping herself opposite Thea. 'Here we are again,' said Thea foolishly. 'Which is a relief, I must say.'

'What?' said Gladwin.

132

'In a pub, discussing a murder and figuring out the clues. How many times have we done this before?'

'Never with your stepdaughter in tow.' She looked round. 'You haven't brought her with you now, have you?'

'No, she's back at the farm. They think she might help to find Ginny – using the computer,' said Thea disastrously.

Chapter Ten

It took several minutes to unravel the implications of what Thea had disclosed. 'I wanted to tell you,' Thea insisted. 'But it seemed much less important than what happened to Alice. I kept getting diverted.'

'And you would have spelt it all out to me anyway this afternoon – I know,' said Gladwin cynically. 'Because you would never have withheld the highly important possibility that these two events in a very tiny village might be connected. After a very detailed and comprehensive interview only a few hours ago, in which you avoided any mention of this Ginny person.'

'Yes. I mean, no,' said Thea. 'Although . . .'

'What?' Gladwin was obviously trying to work out how angry she should be.

'You knew about Ginny already. The police, I mean. They'd have noticed eventually that Baunton had rather a lot going on. And not just concerning Ginny and Alice, actually. We only came here in the first place because it was in the paper.' She laughed. 'Good Lord – I'd forgotten that completely until now.' She faced the detective. 'If anybody's up to speed here, it's my clever stepdaughter. She keeps bringing everybody back to the main points. I should probably have brought her with me now, but she wants to be of use to Emmy.'

'I don't think you can rely on thirteen-year-old girls when it comes to detective work.'

'Emmy and Nick are really stressing about the missing niece,' said Thea. 'But they're hopeless at providing any real clues as to what might have happened. They throw out random facts and ideas, but there's not much of a consistent story. I honestly think it would be a waste of time to try and connect Ginny to the murder.' She explained about the recent revelation concerning the stolen diary. 'That seems to be pretty important to them, but it can't have anything to do with Alice.'

'It's all just a coincidence, you mean?' Gladwin was finally allowing herself a rare level of anger. 'By what conceivable piece of self-deluded logic can you say there's no connection? It looks to me as if both these women are squarely in the same picture – it's entirely possible that one killed the other – or that they've both been killed by the same person.' She was shaking with an emotion that Thea found hard to credit. She herself had barely stopped seeing the whole thing as a bit of a joke. 'And you've got it all very badly wrong,' Gladwin finished.

'What am I wrong about? I haven't even said anything.'

'You said Ginny isn't connected to the murder. But it

seems clear to me that she probably is. Don't you think it's obvious?'

'Emmy doesn't think so,' muttered Thea, aware of being severely wrong-footed.

'Your friend Emmy needs to be thoroughly interviewed as soon as can be arranged,' said Gladwin, already fingering her mobile. 'I'll send Barkley now, if she's free. She can take young Erik with her for good measure.'

It was all moving too fast, the whole affair being snatched out of Thea's hands – if it had ever been in them. 'Stephanie was going to look for Ginny through social media,' she said. 'If she's not the murderer and not dead, she might even be able to find her. It's often quite easy, you know.'

Thea was jumping from one agonised thought to another. 'Emmy's going to be so upset,' she wailed. 'And Nick. You need to tell Caz to be—'

But Gladwin ignored her, focusing on her phone, and getting up from the table when her call was answered.

The detective drained her Coke and bolted her crisps while standing beside the table. Then she straightened her shoulders as if making a decision. 'I've got to get back and log this business of the missing girl. What's her full name?'

Thea told her, trying not to sound sulky. 'Now what?' she asked.

'Look – it's just after two now. I'll be free again in an hour, with any luck. I've just had a text that I have to deal with. And listen – I suppose I'll have to tell you there's been a development.'

Thea smiled. 'You sound like Caz,' she said. 'She's always talking about "developments".'

'I'm warning you,' came the steely response. 'If I had my

way, you'd be ordered back to Broad Campden and told never to speak to me again. Ever.'

'So, whose way are we having?'

'Be quiet and listen. The woman you saw on Monday with Alice. We've been asking for the public's help, as usual, and a bloke came forward this morning, saying it must have been a certain Vanessa Ferguson, sister of the deceased.'

'I said I thought they were sisters,' said Thea. 'Couldn't you have checked that before now?'

'Alice has no less than three sisters, as it happens. We've been trying to find addresses for them. But now we've got more to go on and it would be useful if you could confirm her description.'

'So who's this bloke who came forward?'

'He says he rented Alice's house from her, back in the summer.' Gladwin took a deep breath. 'It's been very weird. While everyone in Baunton seemed to know the woman by sight, and that she was called Alice, none of them had a surname or address for her, which made things tricky when it came to identification. But we're there now. We've seen this Vanessa woman and she's been to confirm that the body is that of her sister. All done by midday, which is not bad going, given the situation.'

Thea knew better than to risk a comment. 'Oh,' she said.

'There's a whole lot I haven't told you. I didn't see any need to. But there's no logic at all to this case, and you seem to be a connection between most of the elements.'

'If there are three sisters, they probably all have some resemblance to Alice, and me describing the one I saw wouldn't have got us far, would it? If Alice had a house,

137

then why was she living like a vagrant in a shed?'

'Precisely. And for your information, two of the sisters have still not been located. They're like ghosts. For all I know, every one of them has been living off the grid in a shed.' Frustration came off the detective in audible waves. 'I'm starting to think it's not just your Ginny Chambers that's gone missing.'

'But now everything's all sorted because you've found the one I saw on Monday. Is that right?'

'Right. She lives locally. I thought you might be useful when I go to talk to her. She identified the body this morning and gave some basic facts.'

'She must be a suspect,' Thea said slowly.

'She's already been interviewed formally, just to ask where she was yesterday. I want to talk to her again, preferably in her own home.'

'And you want me to come?'

'I thought I did, but now I need to think about it again. I'll let you know. But I expect you would be useful.'

'What about Stephanie?'

'What about her?'

'I've been leaving her too much on her own. Can we do your Vanessa person tomorrow? We'll still be here.'

Gladwin pondered for a moment. 'If you like. That might be better, actually. I've got plenty else to do today. And by this time tomorrow you might have solved the whole thing for me.'

Thea winced at the sarcasm.

Gladwin went on, 'No, but it wouldn't be the first time, would it? Just do your thing for the rest of today and I'll catch you in the morning – all right?'

Thea nodded and Gladwin strode off without a backward glance.

Thea watched her go, in silence, reminding herself that the woman she regarded as a friend was also a senior police officer, constrained by protocols and procedures that Thea scarcely understood. If a murderer eluded capture because of something Thea did or did not do, it would be Gladwin who took the flak. All the same, the level of annoyance over Ginny still struck Thea as excessive. 'I think she overreacted,' she said to herself finally.

Feeling childishly defiant, she ordered another coffee and dug for her phone in her bag. 'Hey, it's me,' she said superfluously.

'Yes, I know,' said Stephanie. 'What's happening?'

Thea summarised the past half hour rather sheepishly. 'I really should watch what I say,' she concluded. 'Now Caz and Erik are on their way to question Emmy about Ginny, and she's not going to like it.'

'Who's Erik?'

'A new detective constable. I only caught a glimpse of him yesterday. I think Caz is meant to be training him or something.'

'Oh. Do you think we ought to get out of the way, then? I've got a bit stuck, anyway. There's nothing recent about Ginny anywhere.'

'Good question. It might be sensible to get lost for a bit until the police have gone. They'll probably be there any time now. I'll come back and get you and we can walk round the village again. We still haven't done it all properly. I'll only be five minutes.'

'I'll be ready. I'll tell Emmy, shall I?'

'Better not say anything about the police coming. Just mumble something about wanting some exercise.'

'All right. Can we go to the church again? I liked it there.'

'Okay,' said Thea, with the familiar flicker of unease that came whenever her stepdaughter manifested an interest in religion. It had begun over a year ago and showed no sign of abating. Drew insisted it was quite a normal phase, and no cause for concern. Thea had winced at the idea that they might find religion something to worry about – and yet it persisted. Christian values were fine and proper, of course. Several of the ten commandments made excellent social sense. But the rest of it – the ritual and dogma and arcane arguments – only made her impatient. Drew himself greatly preferred his funerals to be secular, with eulogies and readings at the graveside – but there were always a few who wanted a church element before the burial. The Broad Campden vicar was generally very accommodating when that happened.

Caz and Erik, in a police car, met Thea, Hepzibah and Stephanie in the road leading to the farm. The latter pair were on foot. They all waved, but the car did not stop.

'We'd better give them an hour or so,' said Thea. 'We'll head for the church first, shall we?'

'If that's okay. Actually, I suppose we should see if we can find some people to talk to, don't you think?' The girl looked around as if hoping to spot a small collection of villagers eager for a chat. 'But it's such a small place, isn't it? Even smaller than Broad Campden. They haven't even got a pub.'

'The Plough's only a mile away, or less. I suppose they treat that as their local.' They were standing at the junction of two small roads, from which well over half the properties in Baunton could be seen. To the right was the church, and to the left was Alice's hut, as Thea had started to think of it. A breeze was blowing from the direction of the bypass, making the traffic noise even louder than usual. 'We should probably have walked across the fields and had a look at Nick's rewilding. Maybe we'd see a hare or something. It would have been nicer for Hepzie.'

'Let's go down there.' Stephanie pointed to where the road curved round to the right, leading eventually into Cirencester. 'We can look at that war memorial or whatever it is.'

It was aimless, but Thea was happy to co-operate. Stephanie tried to take a picture of the modest memorial, but found her phone was still out of battery. 'It hardly lasts any time,' the girl complained. 'Can I use yours?' she asked Thea, who handed it over.

Seconds later the phone jingled and Stephanie automatically answered it. 'Yes, she's right here. Hold on,' and she thrust the phone at Thea. 'Mrs Gladwin wants to talk to you,' she said.

Thea took the phone, smiling at Stephanie's formality. 'Yes?' she said.

'I'm "Mrs Gladwin" am I? That's different.'

'What would you prefer?'

The detective ignored the question. 'Is Caz at the farm yet?'

'I assume so. We met them about ten minutes ago. We

decided we ought to get out of the way, so we're rambling round the village for a bit.'

'Good idea. But Thea . . .'

'What?'

'You will stick around, won't you – just for another day or two? I was out of order earlier. There's no way we'll figure all this out without you. And let Stephanie do her worst with Facebook and whatnot. I gave myself a little talking to just now, and reminded myself that you don't work for the police. You're free to do whatever you like, within reason. But I can't have you muddying the water of the investigation, and withholding information is obviously unacceptable. Even so, I can understand you might have divided loyalties – it wouldn't be the first time, after all. So – we're still friends, as Stephanie might say.'

Thea felt stricken. The detective had gone far beyond halfway in this rapid reconciliation. 'You're being much too nice to me,' she protested. 'I'd still be furious if I was you. But I'll keep trying with Emmy, if you think it'll help. It might be too late. When she and Nick realise that I've set Caz onto them, they might well never want to see us again.'

'Fingers crossed, then,' said Gladwin, sounding like her familiar unprofessional self for the first time that day.

Chapter Eleven

There was no need to explain anything to Stephanie. Before Thea could say anything, the girl was grinning cheerfully. 'She still wants us, then,' she said. 'I knew she would.'

'We need to be careful, though. Stick to what we know we can do and stay out of the way of the police.'

'We were doing that anyway. Finding Ginny isn't getting in their way, is it?'

'They might think it is. I wonder if it was daft of me to assume there was no connection. I mean – Alice knew the Weavers, so she probably met Ginny as well. I should have thought of that.'

'There hasn't been *time*,' Stephanie insisted. 'Everything's going too fast.'

Still attached to her lead, Hepzibah whined and both females instantly turned to her. 'Oh Heps – I forgot all about you,' said Thea. 'What a rubbish day you're having.'

'Let's take her for a proper walk, then,' said Stephanie. 'We can follow the Monarch's Way for a bit. Although . . .'

'What?'

'It feels a bit mean to do it without Timmy.'

'I know. I have a feeling it would be better to stay closer to the middle of the village and see what we can see here. We really should have a go at talking to some people. There's a woman called Abby, for a start.'

'Where does she live?'

'About fifty yards from where I found Alice, which is just over there. There's a gate with a cow on it. We'll see it if we go back to the corner.'

Despite the empty lanes and absence of visible people, Thea felt they were being observed. Did everyone who came here feel like that? Unlike Oddington, there was no sign of CCTV cameras or twitching curtains, but the sensation was undeniable. Had everyone in the place known full well what Alice Ferguson had been doing but pretended not to notice? Had Alice herself peeped out from her shed and watched everything going on in the village, in turn? She could have seen across a field or two, and down into a few gardens attached to the cluster of houses on the lower level. She might have observed something that put her in danger. And had the endless drone of traffic driven her to distraction? Surely there were a few hours of the night when it stopped? Clearly the wind direction made a difference. 'We need to know more about her,' she said aloud.

'Who?'

'Alice. She had a house, with a tenant in it. So why was she living like a tramp out here?'

'Did Gladwin tell you that?'

'She did. And that the woman we saw was probably her sister, as we thought. Vanessa. They couldn't find her until today, but now she's been interviewed, and Gladwin wants to go and see her tomorrow. I told you, didn't I?'

'No – you didn't say anything about tomorrow. We're staying here tonight, then, are we?' The girl had a wistful expression.

'Why? Don't you want to?'

Before Stephanie could reply, the dog yapped and Thea saw there was a man with a black and white collie eyeing them from the other side of the patch of green. 'I've seen him before,' she said. 'Let's go and say hello.'

'Okay,' said Stephanie bravely. 'Can Hepzie come as well?'

'Definitely. Although she doesn't always get on too well with sheepdogs. She thinks they're snooty.'

They walked towards the man, barely twenty yards away and Thea on a sudden whim decided to let Hepzie run free. There was no traffic and Thea liked to watch her enjoyment of sniffing everything around her. And it sent some kind of message to the autocratic-looking man watching her. 'Hello again,' she said, aiming for a friendly tone.

'I beg your pardon?' came a very frosty reply. 'Have we met?'

'Yesterday. Just over there.' She pointed. 'Not something you'd forget, surely?'

'Oh – *you*. The one asking all the questions and then snuggling up with the SIO in her car. Silly me. It's just that I wouldn't expect you to be back again so soon. Your dog's going to get run over if you're not careful.'

There was a big blue van approaching. The spaniel was fully aware of it, and at least ten feet away from the road. 'I think she'll be all right,' said Thea calmly.

'Stay there, Heps!' called Stephanie, for good measure. The dog gave her a patient glance and carried on with her sniffing. The van passed slowly and without incident.

The man was no longer watching them, but had his gaze directed upwards. When Thea looked up, she saw two birds circling overhead. 'Kites?' she asked.

He nodded. 'They follow the road mostly. I never get tired of watching them. One of the great conservation success stories. Even twenty years ago, it would be a rare sight.'

'Now you see them everywhere,' said Thea. 'Pity you can't say the same for hedgehogs or hares, or countless other sorts of birds.'

'It's out of balance,' said Stephanie. 'All because of human intervention.'

'You sound like Nick Weaver,' said the man. 'I sometimes think he'll only be happy when the whole of the human race is wiped out.'

'You can see his point,' said Thea. 'Think how wonderful it would be for all the other species. Except dogs, I suppose.'

'He can't be thinking that, though,' said Stephanie. 'Because he and his wife are having a baby.'

The man laughed in what sounded like genuine

amusement. 'He probably thinks his own child will have special powers of understanding and will save the world all by itself.'

It was only mildly spiteful, Thea judged. They were a long way from confronting the horrible event of the previous day, and Thea wondered if that was due to Stephanie's presence. Was this man being sensitive and tactful – or did he just want to avoid the whole subject? She chose just one of the many questions she wanted to ask him. 'You know the Weavers, then?'

'Their land borders mine. Their thistle seeds and brambles invade my pasture. Their *clients* or whatever they call them, leave gates open and frighten my heifers. Yes, I know the Weavers.'

'And Alice?' said Thea recklessly. 'Who was living on land that you own.'

'Ah – here we go. I was wondering when that was coming. Well, in the nicest possible way, I suggest you keep your nose out of that business. The police have their work to do, and I for one have every confidence that they'll do it properly. Why you should think you can serve any purpose by barging up to people you've never seen before and questioning them as if you have any such right is beyond my comprehension.'

'Gosh!' murmured Stephanie. 'And I thought for a minute he liked us.' She moved closer to her stepmother who gave her a wide smile and a wink.

The man had gone back to staring upwards. Two more kites had appeared, all of them circling slowly, coming lower with each circuit. 'They've seen something,' he said. 'Let's hope it's not your dog.'

'Very funny,' snapped Thea. 'I thought they only ate carrion.'

'Well you thought wrong,' said the man, before slapping his thigh and walking off with his dog at his heels.

Stephanie watched him go, with a small frown. 'Do you think he was cross or is he always like that?'

'It sounds as if he's got some beef with Emmy and Nick, and we've got associated with them in his mind.'

'He didn't answer the question about Alice, did he?'

'That was clever of him – and dim of me. I let him sidetrack me into all that nonsense about kites.'

'He didn't exactly do that,' Stephanie corrected her. 'He ranted about you playing detective and not leaving it all to the police.'

'Right. So he did. Do you think that means he's worried we might find something he'd rather we didn't?'

'Probably,' said Stephanie with a laugh. 'Let's hope so.'

The afternoon was eliciting very mixed feelings in Thea. Mostly it felt hopelessly unfocused, with nothing accomplished and no hint of a plan of action. Stephanie was wanting to get back to her searches. 'I can do it on my phone,' she had said at one point. 'But the laptop's better. Nick was kind to let me use his. It's really fast. I was just getting used to it when we had to go.'

'And your phone keeps running out of battery,' Thea reminded her. 'We haven't accomplished anything today, have we? Just run in useless circles.'

'Like the police,' said Stephanie. 'Unless there's a lot they're not telling us.'

'Which there probably is. I think they've done quite well, actually. They've identified Alice, found her sister and done the post mortem.'

'Can we go back to Emmy's now? It's ten to four – surely Caz will have gone by now?'

'No church, then?'

'That was only really to kill time. I think other things might be more important.'

'Very wise,' said Thea. 'Come on then. Hepzie's done a big poo on the village green, look. Do you think I'll have to scoop it up?'

'I think you should, but I don't suppose you're going to. Nobody walks there anyway.'

'Somebody might have seen.'

'Quick, then,' urged the girl. 'Come on, Heps. Time to go.'

Caz and her new sidekick had indeed left the farm by the time Thea and Stephanie got there. All seemed quiet, and there was no sign of the gigantic Joshua.

'Emmy might be having a rest,' Thea suggested. 'We don't want to disturb her if so.'

'She must be expecting us to come back,' Stephanie reminded her. 'Nick must be around somewhere.'

The two of them slowly crossed the yard, unsure as to whether to liberate Hepzie from her lead. 'Oh – there's a man,' said Stephanie softly. 'Over there, look.'

Sure enough, a figure was visible in the doorway of the biggest barn, which stood at right angles to the house. It moved very slightly forward out of the shadow and stared at them, eyebrows raised. Tall, bearded, late twenties, dressed in a colourful knitted jumper and jeans, with a kind of beret on his head, he was readily identified as a person from an urban background trying to fit into the countryside. 'Funny hat!' muttered Thea. 'And hopelessly clean shoes.'

Stephanie looked down at her own trainers, which were fairly clean, but old and scuffed.

'You're not the police, then?' the man said, with an accent that was much more Surrey than Gloucestershire.

'Not unless they've drastically reduced the age for entry,' said Thea. 'Is Emmy around?'

'Haven't seen her. Only just got here myself, actually.'

'Oh?' Thea looked for a car.

'By bike,' he informed her with a hint of superiority. 'I'm Joe, by the way.'

'Of course you are,' said Thea, with a laugh. 'I might have known.'

Stephanie threw her a startled look at what sounded like rudeness. Thea gave her a reassuring little pat. 'Emmy mentioned you, that's all. She might have said you'd be coming, as well. I don't remember exactly. It's been a busy day.'

'She texted me a little while ago and said there were police everywhere and everything was in a mess because a woman had been killed. I wasn't planning to come back here, as it happens. But she sounded in a bit of a state, so I thought maybe I should, especially given that Ginny still hasn't shown up. Last time I was here, Nick Weaver sent me packing, for no good reason. I'm not in any rush to see him again. He seemed to think I had designs on his niece.' He shook his head as if to say the idea was beyond ridiculous.

'And hadn't you?' said Thea.

'Not in the slightest. I have a perfectly fine woman already. What would I want with a child like Ginny? I liked a bit of a laugh with her, that's all. But Nick wouldn't take my word for it.' He sighed.

'Which is why you're hiding in the barn,' said Stephanie. 'It's no good, though – Nick's dog'll find you.'

'Oh God!' groaned Joe. 'I'd forgotten about the monstrous Joshua. Aren't you scared he'll eat your little thing?' He eyed Hepzie who was meandering around the yard, having also apparently forgotten about Joshua.

'A bit,' said Thea. 'But she can outrun him, if it comes to the crunch. So far, they seem to quite like each other.'

'Have you been looking for Ginny?' asked Stephanie, eager as ever to get to the point. 'Because that's why we're here. Or we were. The murder has put everything into a muddle and now we don't know what we should be doing. You do know Ginny, don't you? Have you any idea where she might have gone?'

'I do know her, yes. And no, I have no idea where she is. We worked here together on a couple of the Weavers' courses. She was fine last I saw her, earlier this month. Then Emmy phoned asking if I knew where she was and sounding in a proper stress, so I figured I should see if I could lend a hand somehow. I called her from Cirencester, but she wasn't making much sense. The thing is, I need to know where my next bed's coming from. It's a bit chilly for sleeping out and I can't get home until tomorrow.'

Which instantly reminded Thea of Alice Ferguson, thereby creating a connection which was most likely spurious, but felt as if it fitted somehow. Here in this not-so-quiet little village there were people living on the edge, in some kind of destitution and getting themselves killed. 'Did you know Alice?' she asked abruptly.

'Who?'

'The woman who was murdered. Sleeping rough in a tumbledown shed, down in the village. Emmy says she came here sometimes when it was busy, for a bit of ready cash. Someone killed her yesterday.'

Joe kept a vague expression for a few seconds too long. His eyes rolled up to the sky, his shoulders lifted in a shrug and his lower lip rose as if in unproductive thought. 'Was she the woman who came and did the washing-up sometimes?' he said. 'Never heard what her name was.'

'That probably was her, yes,' said Thea, matching his vagueness as a kind of tease. He had already admitted he knew there was a considerable police presence in the village, which almost certainly meant he also knew the reason for it. 'Emmy never explained what was going on, then?'

'Who *are* you?' he demanded. 'I still don't understand.'

'I knew Emmy a few years ago, when her father died, and this is my stepdaughter. Thea and Stephanie Slocombe. Pleased to meet you.' Again she spoke teasingly, taking him at less than face value, defusing his bluster and issuing what she hoped was a subtle warning. There had been something unsettling about her first sight of him, standing in the shadowy doorway, and she was determined to dispel any lurking notion he might have that he could intimidate her.

'Ah,' he said, clinging to the protective cloak of

elusiveness. 'Emmy's never mentioned you.'

'She wants us to help her find Ginny,' Stephanie broke in impatiently. The nuances of adult power games were far beyond her. 'But it's not going very well.'

'And I got in trouble for keeping that back from the police,' said Thea. 'They think there has to be a connection between Ginny going missing and Alice being murdered. It's all got alarmingly serious. I'm going to go and talk to Alice's sister tomorrow with the senior detective.' She wanted to shake him, to make him listen and be worried. It worked up to a point.

Joe stared at her, and said, 'Why tell me all that? None of it has anything to do with me.'

'I've learnt my lesson,' said Thea darkly. 'I'll have to tell them about you now, as well.'

Joe was saved the bother of replying by the appearance of Emmy Weaver at an upstairs window, overlooking the yard. 'What's all this noise?' she shouted. 'I'm trying to have a rest.' She was smiling and the words were correctly interpreted as friendly. There had, after all, been almost no noise at all. 'Joe!' she cried, then. 'What are you doing here?'

It all struck Thea as oddly false. Emmy had surely known that Joe was there before she started calling out of the window. She might even have been listening to what was being said. The distance from the house to where they were standing was only a few yards and the window had been open.

'Where's Nick? And his appalling dog?' asked Joe. 'I've been lying low in case he decides I'm not welcome.'

'Don't be silly,' chuckled Emmy. 'Anyway, you're

safe. They've gone to the top field or somewhere. He keeps going up there. I think there must be a badger or something that he likes to watch.'

'Wouldn't he tell you if there was?' asked Stephanie. 'Don't you want to go and watch it as well?'

'Lord, no! Look, come in and let's talk properly. All sorts of things have been happening. And it must be time for some tea by now.'

They assembled in the kitchen and Emmy made a pot of tea. Her movements were slow and effortful, and Thea tried in vain to remember what it was like to be seven months pregnant. The prospect of another eight weeks still to go had to be dispiriting.

In stark contrast, Stephanie was fidgety and impatient. Thea could almost hear her thinking *This is all just a waste of time*. Adult conversation tended to circle around invisible attempts to gain control or prove themselves right. Any exchange of hard information could get lost in the fog of game-playing, and logical threads quickly got broken. The appeal of a young mind in all its innocent clarity struck Thea with some force. She was reminded of a boy called Ben Harkness who she had met in the Cotswold village of Barnsley a year or so ago. Stephanie was showing many of the same characteristics, including a growing skill with computer searches,

'What do we know exactly about this Vanessa person?' the girl asked now, cutting through the banal issuing of tea and biscuits.

Thea sighed and glanced at Emmy. 'Nothing except she's Alice's sister. Bound to be the one we saw on Monday.'

The girl frowned. 'Shall I google her? What's her surname?'

'Gladwin did say, but I can't remember.'

'Ferguson,' said Emmy. 'That pair of detectives that came to question me just now asked me if I knew her.'

'Hang on,' said Stephanie, holding a finger in the air. 'Why are they both called Ferguson? Wasn't Alice married? Didn't DS Gladwin say she was *Mrs*?' Stephanie had grown up under the shadow of her father's undertaking work, where the details of family relationships and accuracy of names were of paramount importance. She had an instinctive grasp of the whole subject.

'Did she?' Thea wasn't sure. 'No – I think she said "Ms". But really, Steph, it absolutely doesn't matter.'

The girl nodded briefly, and went on regardless, 'It matters if she was married or not. There might be a nasty husband somewhere. He might even be the one who killed her.'

Emmy was standing behind Thea, holding the teapot and facing Joe. 'Of course Alice wasn't married,' she said. 'That would make no sense at all.' Thea was watching Joe's face across the table, and saw him kink an eyebrow in something that looked like a warning. 'Unless she was a widow or divorced, I suppose,' Emmy finished.

'How well did you know her?' Thea asked, twisting round to see the woman's face.

'Not well at all. I had no idea she was living rough, for a start. I thought maybe she had a caravan or something, but I never asked. She only came here about four or five times, when Nick took pity on her. Look – I've just told all this to the police. I don't want to say it all again.'

'Because you're here for Ginny, remember?' said Joe with a rather nasty smile.

'Did Ginny meet Alice, then?' It was Stephanie joining in the inquisition. 'Did the police ask you that as well? I suppose they must have done. I suppose they think that Ginny might be murdered as well. Or that she killed Alice. If you reported her missing last week and they didn't think it was worth worrying about, they might be feeling a bit bad about that now. They might think they should have taken it more seriously. Except that Ginny was a healthy adult, free to go where she liked, so they would do what they always do and wait for some sort of evidence that there was something bad going on. Isn't that right?' The girl looked at Thea for confirmation.

'Absolutely right in every detail,' said Thea. 'I'm very impressed.'

'Well, there's Jessica, you see . . .' Stephanie flushed. 'She told me quite a lot about police work, the last time she was here.'

'The plot is definitely thickening,' said Joe flippantly. 'All these wild theories and missing women. I'm completely out of my depth.' Nobody laughed, but he carried on. 'Nick took pity on this Alice person, then? I only got the odd brief glimpse of her. What was she like?'

'She was here when we did the course on birds and rewilding. We tried to keep her away from the punters, but there was a day when Nick asked her to keep an eye on the people who went off to the top field, where the bullfinches were nesting. There are hares up there as well. We had ten people on that course, and they were free to go off anywhere they liked, for part of each afternoon. We needed someone to make sure they didn't disturb things too much. I think she just lurked behind a hedge and watched them. I don't remember any trouble about it, so they must have behaved themselves. She was really useful in the kitchen, I must say – seemed to enjoy washing up. Oh, and there was another time, when there was an almighty fuss because a kite snatched a leveret, right in front of everyone and some daft girl had hysterics. Alice heard her and brought her back here and we mopped her up.' She stared at the floor for a moment. 'Now I come to think of it, Alice wasn't working here that day. She was just mooching about doing her own thing. I was surprised when she came into the yard with the weeping girl.'

'Bloody kites,' said Joe.

'Don't you start,' begged Emmy. 'You know perfectly well it's not for us to judge the ways of nature. That's the whole *point* . . .'

'Yeah, yeah, I know. The humans need to back off and let it all take its natural course. Just that sometimes it's not so easy, I can tell you. I had Sunny going on at me last week about weasels and the way they torture rabbits. It's not pretty.'

'Sunny's his partner,' Emmy explained to Thea as she circled the table with the heavy teapot. 'Top up, anyone?'

'Sit down,' said Thea. 'You look exhausted.'

'Sunny does her best,' said Joe, detecting a tone of criticism. 'She had a sheltered upbringing, that's all. She's doing a great job with the kids.'

157

'Her father's a QC,' murmured Emmy. 'They've got a mansion in Hampstead worth umpteen million.'

Stephanie was absorbing every word, ignoring the mug of tea in front of her. Unless it was made with about fifty per cent milk, she couldn't abide the stuff. Then she looked up sharply as she caught sight of something outside. 'There's Nick,' she said.

Emmy went to the window. 'And he's got bloody Abby with him. Again. As if we haven't got enough people here already.'

Thea tried not to take offence. Here was a woman who regularly ran courses for ten or twelve people at a time. She was surely used to large numbers around her kitchen table.

'Is Abby the one who lives by Alice's shed?' asked Stephanie.

'That's right,' said Thea, who was also peering out of the window. 'I've seen her before. She's the one I talked to yesterday, when I found Alice.'

'You found Alice?' Joe's voice was almost a squeak. 'Is that what you said?' He glared at Emmy. 'You never told me that.'

Emmy flapped a hand at him and went to meet her husband at the door.

Thea and Stephanie rapidly made their excuses and took the spaniel outside. 'Go and have a look round before it gets dark,' Emmy invited them. 'If you go up there by that fence you come out at the top field. It's worth seeing. There's a good view and you'll catch the sunset. Mind where you walk – and keep the dog on a lead, okay.'

Nick, Joshua and the woman referred to as 'bloody Abby' were jostling in the doorway leading to the kitchen, as Thea took her charges out of harm's way. The Newfoundland occupied almost all available space, standing his ground if anyone tried to push past him. 'That dog's a liability,' muttered Thea, as they headed across the yard. 'We'd better go and inspect this view, then.'

'What a day!' Stephanie exclaimed. 'Just one thing after another.'

Thea laughed. 'That's the way it goes sometimes. Don't forget it's only one day since Alice was killed. Everything's bound to seem tangled up and confusing for a while. And this time it's all mixed in with the Ginny business. That's why it seems so complicated.'

'I don't want her to have killed Alice,' wailed Stephanie, like a six-year-old. 'That would be awful.'

'I don't see why. What difference would it make?'

'She's Nick's *niece*. And Emmy loves her, you can tell. It's really the only thing she cares about. She keeps wanting us to get back to searching for her, and other stuff keeps getting in the way. Even Nick doesn't seem to be too bothered. He shouldn't go off with that other woman, for a start. And the *dog*.' She sighed dramatically. 'What kind of a person keeps a dog like that anyway?'

'You might be right,' Thea acknowledged, feeling heartless and unobservant. 'But don't forget that stuff about the notebook. I think Emmy and Nick both care about that a lot – maybe more than worrying about Ginny being safe. But I agree they're much more interested in Ginny than they are in Alice. Which makes it awkward

159

for us. We ought to try and stay objective, if we're to be of any use – not cast judgement on anybody.'

'That's impossible,' said Stephanie. 'Even the police wouldn't manage that. I mean – you have to remember that people tell lies. Jessica told me that.'

Thea considered this as they walked up a gentle hill through long grass. 'Do you think there's a chance that Emmy might tell a few fibs if she thinks there's any risk that the police will suspect Ginny?'

'Do you mean to us, or the police?'

'Both, I suppose. She knows we're in cahoots with Gladwin, so she probably doesn't really trust us.'

'She's right not to, isn't she? But that makes it extra hard for us. How can we know what to believe?'

'Good question,' said Thea.

They went through a gate into a higher field that was suddenly much steeper. 'This must be the top field they keep talking about,' said Thea. 'You wouldn't think there'd be all that wildlife, so close to the house.' She looked back. 'Although it doesn't feel so close, actually.'

'It's a mess,' said Stephanie critically. There were dense patches of black thistle stalks, drying in the cool of autumn. Brambles rampaged all along one side of the field, leapfrogging onto the grassland and forming substantial mounds that would be impenetrable by all but the smallest rodents. Middle-sized trees straggled unimpeded and untrimmed, where once a sturdy hedge had been. Everywhere the grass was so long that it had bent over to form a spongy layer that was difficult to walk on. The ground under it was bumpy. 'Surely it can't have got like this in only two years?'

'Good point. I guess they'd been letting it go for a while before that. I'm still not clear about the family history.'

'No,' said Stephanie absently.

Thea was looking round, noting the way the low sun was casting creative shadows over the landscape, highlighting folds in the much-cultivated ground, making Thea think of Romans and Ancient Britons and Charles I, all scampering about on this very land laid out before her. Combined with the Weavers' valiant crusade to remove as much human trace as they could, it all made her go quiet and thoughtful. 'It makes nonsense of any talk about the planet needing to be saved,' she remarked, aware of stepping on sensitive ground. 'Look at how it recovers after just a few years. Not just *recover*, either. It goes mad. Abundance overflowing. Just by stepping back and doing nothing . . .'

'Mm,' said Stephanie uncertainly. 'You sound like Nick.'

'You can see what he means, though, can't you? It's probably paradise for a dozen different sorts of mice and voles and shrews. Stoats, weasels, rabbits, birds, hares, badgers, foxes . . .'

'Ants, bees, wasps, spiders, beetles,' Stephanie cheerfully joined in. 'I suppose that is rather wonderful in a way. Scary, too.'

'How come?'

'Those things bite and sting and kill each other. There might even be snakes.'

'We forgot frogs and toads and newts. Butterflies.'

'Dragonflies. Water boatmen. There's bound to be some water around.'

'Can't see any. The River Churn's not far away, though.'

'It's terribly un-Cotswolds,' said Stephanie. 'People must absolutely hate it.'

'I wonder. The Weavers have been clever enough to demonstrate that it has a commercial value, with the courses they run. And it's terribly fashionable, remember. I don't think many people would dare to protest too loudly. Apart from the thistle seeds – they must be annoying. But I guess the neighbours have no compunction about using weedkiller if they need to.'

'Like the man we saw just now in the village.'

'Indeed. Didn't he say he had adjacent fields? We'd need to look at a map and work out what land belongs to who. Or we could just ask Nick.'

'We still don't really know much about Ginny, do we?' Stephanie was clearly obsessing, even while enjoying the sudden wildness all around her. 'What did she think of all this ecological business? Do you think she fancied Joe, even if he's got a partner and kids? What if she's lying in a ditch somewhere with a broken leg? What if nobody ever finds her? Is she still *alive*?' The girl's face was flushed and crumpled as she worked herself up. 'I mean – it's so easy to get lost, isn't it? Right here in this messy field, a person could get stung or caught in the brambles, or be out in the dark and go the wrong way.'

'Hey, Steph!' Thea stopped and faced her stepdaughter. 'We can't carry on with this if you're going to get all emotional about it. You're scaring yourself for no reason.

You have to treat the whole thing as a puzzle, that's all. I grant you that Emmy's very sweet, and all that. And she does seem needy. But she's got Nick and friends, and we're not at all responsible for her or Ginny. We'll do our best – if we ever get a minute's peace to get on with it – and that's all. Whatever happens, we can only stay one more night after this. Your father isn't going to stand for more than that, and he's right. I'm not even sure we're doing any good at all – we might be making things worse, whatever Emmy says. She must think she ought to be feeding us, for a start.'

Stephanie shook her head impatiently. 'It just feels so *awful*. Hopeless. I thought we might find Ginny if we asked the right questions, but that hasn't worked. I just think us being here is silly. I don't understand what we're *for*.'

'Nor do I, not exactly. But it's nice here, and we don't have to be anywhere else, and Gladwin thinks we're useful. She explicitly asked me to stick around when she phoned. She and I both know that extra pairs of eyes and ears are fantastically useful, and if that's us, it can't be a bad thing. Besides – I did find Alice, and Gladwin seems to think that's important.'

'It's much more about Alice than Ginny, now, isn't it? And that's making Emmy sad.'

'So let's do our best to cheer her up,' said Thea as bracingly as she could.

They stayed another fifteen minutes, admiring the sweeping view over fields and patches of woodland, and awed by the colourful sky that lasted for a few brief minutes as the sun disappeared. They had views both to the east and the west, and kept turning to compare the contrasting panoramas. 'It's pretty fabulous, you have to admit,' said Thea. 'A world without people – you can't see anything human from here.'

'You can hear the road. And there's a plane, look. And a lot of telegraph poles. And I think that must be the village down behind those trees. I can see a roof. It's much closer than I thought.'

'Don't spoil it.'

Stephanie didn't speak for a moment, then she tried to voice her thoughts. 'The thing is, humans aren't very good at stepping back, are they? They never see themselves as a part of all this. You either march in and control everything, or you go away completely. And that isn't going to work, is it?'

'I'm sure there's a solution somewhere,' said Thea feebly.

Back in the farmhouse well after five o'clock, the Abby person was still there. Thea, Stephanie and the spaniel took themselves into the annex where they were to spend the night, and unpacked their minimal luggage. 'Time for Hepzie's supper,' said Thea. 'I suppose I can give it to her here.'

The spaniel was a messy eater. The family begged Thea to limit her diet to dry dog food that could easily be cleared up, but Thea insisted on using tinned meat, with jelly and gravy and small soggy lumps that could not be allowed to land on carpet. 'The dry stuff is unnatural,' she maintained, ignoring the scornful replies.

'Unless you give her a raw rabbit, it's always going to

be unnatural,' said Drew. 'Or a lamb.'

'Bathroom,' said Stephanie now with authority.

There were still several hours to go before bedtime, and the question of an evening meal was raising its head. 'Are you hungry?' Thea asked.

'Not very. But I've got to have *something*.'

'There's probably a supermarket still open somewhere.'

'We could get something delivered!' Stephanie's eyes sparkled. It was something they did barely twice a year, as celebration or in an emergency.

'What? Chinese, you mean?'

'No – we need stuff for breakfast and tomorrow night as well. A proper box of groceries. Don't the ads say they come any time, day or night?'

'Do they?' Thea seldom registered advertisements. 'Must be expensive. This exercise is going to leave us seriously out of pocket at this rate.'

'Emmy must be paying you, surely?'

Thea grimaced. 'We never quite got around to talking about that.'

Stephanie was already on Thea's phone. 'Yes! Waitrose look as if they'll do it. Quick – what do we want? You have to spend £40 or more. Plus a delivery charge. They do the Deliveroo thing. You'll have to fill in the form.'

'Blimey, Steph! Isn't that all a terrible hassle? We can just go there now and do it like normal. We can get what we want for half that money.'

'This is more fun. Let's have lasagne, soup, fruit . . .' She rattled off a shopping list faster than Thea could keep pace. There was a microwave oven in the annex, a small fridge, kettle and toaster. She supposed they could survive very

165

adequately for a day or so, and the sense of camping in a strange place where any adventure might happen would be spoilt by a mundane visit to Waitrose.

She obeyed Stephanie's instructions, completing a lengthy form on the mobile's tiny screen. 'What's the postcode here?' she asked.

'How would I know?'

'You know everything,' said Thea unfairly.

'There's a sheet of paper stuck to the fridge with useful information on it. Try that.'

Sure enough, amongst phone numbers, rules and instructions for working the microwave, Thea found the postcode. 'How very efficient,' she murmured.

'That'll be Nick. He's more businesslike than he seems.'

'Is he?'

'I think so. He just has his own way of doing things.'

The food was successfully ordered, expected to arrive by seven, and the evening free for whatever they chose to do with it.

It was shortly before six when Emmy came to the door with the woman Thea recognised from the previous day. 'This is Abby,' was the brief introduction. 'She wanted to have a little word with you.'

Youngish was the only word Thea had applied to Abby on her first very brief encounter. Now she looked more closely, observing light brown hair inexpertly cut, green eyes and snub nose. *I live right here*, she had said, and nothing else that Thea could recall. Emmy had mentioned that the woman came regularly to the farm for eggs – and perhaps to have a few moments talking to Nick about her predations on his land in the name of foraging.

'Hello again,' said Thea.

'I know who you are now, but yesterday I had no idea. You seemed a bit sinister, turning up out of the blue and finding that poor woman so soon after she was killed. To be honest, some of us thought *you* must have killed her. It all seemed so neat, you see. But then you obviously knew that detective and everything, so we thought you'd been deliberately looking for her, and it wasn't so odd after all. Now Emmy and Nick say you were actually trying to find Ginny. Which does sort of explain things, I suppose.'

It was a long speech, uttered falteringly, with apologetic smiles and glances at Emmy.

'Um . . .' said Thea. It didn't feel as if she was expected to say much.

'The police came to my house this morning and asked a lot of questions. I could tell they didn't believe me when I said I had *no idea* there was anybody living in that shed. I mean – you wouldn't, would you. I didn't even know it belonged to Mr Robinson-Finch until Dickie pointed it out. At least, I wasn't sure. Everyone else seems to have known. It's just a tumbledown old shed on a bit of land that can't be more than a quarter of an acre.'

'Robinson-Finch? Is that his name? We saw him again this afternoon.'

'Did you? His family's been here for ever. He owns property all over the place. Woodland as well, and at least one house in Cirencester.'

'I'm not a bit surprised,' said Thea. 'Who's Dickie?'

'He works for Robbers. That's what we call Mr Robinson-Finch. It's quicker.'

'Abby's a bit scared, you see,' put in Emmy. 'She lives there by herself and she's worried the killer might come back. I told her you could probably reassure her.' The look she gave Thea was one of mild derision at such needless timidity. 'She wants Nick to go back with her and check locks and things.'

Thea felt a surge of resistance to the role Emmy was allotting to her. She was expected to say something bracing and supportive of Emmy. It was irritating and she was tired. 'He could do that, I suppose. But it's a silly idea. You've imagined some monstrous murderer randomly stabbing women in quiet villages, which is pure fantasy. Whoever did it must have known Alice was there, and had a specific reason for wanting her dead. Nothing at all to do with you – unless you saw him, of course.'

The woman reared back as if a snake was attacking her. 'Silly? You think I'm being silly?'

'I do, actually. Or hysterical. Trying to get us to see you as some kind of victim. Did you tell the police you were scared?'

'I tried to. They weren't very interested,' Abby muttered.

'Good for them. Now look – if you want my reassurances, you can have them by the bucketful. Nobody's going to murder you. Make sure the door's locked and you've got a phone by the bed. Have a stiff whisky and read yourself to sleep with a nice romance. In the morning you'll realise there's nothing to be frightened of, and you can just get back to normal. Don't you have a job to go to? Family? Commitments of some sort?'

'I work from home. I'm divorced and my husband has custody of our daughter. She's twelve. I've had a few mental health issues – and I really don't like the way you're talking to me.'

Thea looked at Emmy through narrowed eyes. Emmy knew what Thea was capable of when it came to straight talking. *She set me up*, she realised. The whole thing was planned. Emmy knew just what Thea was likely to say to this shrinking violet and exulted in it. This was *bloody Abby* after all, who so conspicuously clung to Nick for comfort. 'Well, there it is,' she said unrepentantly.

'It's almost dark,' said Emmy briskly. 'You'd better get going.'

Abby looked startled, as if darkness had come as a complete surprise. 'Is it?' she said. 'But I walked here. How'm I going to get back?'

'You'll see well enough. Go down the road way, instead of over the fields, and there'll be some lights from the 417 to help. Once you're over the Whiteway Bridge you're practically home.'

'I can't. Nick's got to come with me.'

Even Thea was feeling sorry for the wretched woman by this time. 'It must be nearly a mile,' she said. 'Why did you leave it so late?'

'I don't know. We just got talking. I only meant to come for a bit, and that was *hours* ago.'

'Oh hell!' Emmy exploded. 'This is such a nuisance.

Come on, then. I'll drive you. Nick's got things to do. Hurry up.'

Stephanie had not spoken for some time. Once alone again, she said to Thea, 'You were very nasty to her, weren't you?'

'A bit. I can't stand women like that. So sorry for herself and waiting for other people to solve all her troubles. Emmy thinks the same as me, by the look of it.'

'Well, now she's got to get the car out and drive the woman home, so she didn't come out of it so well, did she?'

'At least she hasn't sent her off into the dark with Nick. If you ask me, Abby's inappropriately fond of him and doesn't care who knows it.'

Stephanie waved a hand, as if dispersing smoke. 'Too much information,' she said.

Outside there were engine noises – more than would be made by a single car. 'That'll be our delivery,' said Thea. 'Thank goodness for that.'

They sorted their purchases on the assumption that they would need an evening meal the next day too. 'Though whether we really are going to stay another night remains to be seen,' said Thea. 'Anything might happen.'

'And frequently does,' quoted Stephanie. It was something Drew said.

As if to reinforce the uncertainty, Thea's phone jingled. 'Just some sort of spam,' she announced, before noticing that there was an unread text. 'Uh-oh! Gladwin's been in touch. Listen to this: "Talk with Vanessa F arranged for early tomorrow. Be helpful if you could come and see her with me. Minus kid and dog. Stn 8.30 a.m.?" Now isn't that exciting.'

'Minus kid and dog? That's a bit rude. And eight-thirty's awfully early. What am I supposed to do when you've gone?'

'Emmy's going to have to keep an eye on you. I'm more worried about Hepzie than you. We really should have left her at home.'

'I won't let Joshua eat her,' Stephanie promised bravely.

'Thanks.'

Chapter Twelve

Thea was at the Cirencester police station two minutes early, to find Gladwin waiting for her in the reception area. The detective bustled her out to her car without a word until they were in motion.

'Where exactly are we going?' Thea asked.

'Duntisbourne Abbots. It's no distance.'

'I know where it is,' said Thea with a disturbing pang. 'That's where I did my very first house-sit. Must be five years ago now, or very nearly. I haven't been there since.'

'Let's hope nobody there remembers you,' said Gladwin. 'That might be unhelpful.'

'I don't remember anybody called Vanessa.' She thought of a man called Harry, who had fallen for her and remained a friend until he'd died a few months ago. A sad man, as old as Thea's father, with a neurotic sister. 'There weren't many people around, anyway. Not really.'

'Typical Cotswolds, then.'

'You could say that.' Her memories of the events in Duntisbourne Abbots had grown hazy. A nice young man had been killed, and Thea had been saved from depression and despair by another detective, named Phil. 'It all seems very long ago now.'

'Hollis,' said Gladwin with a nod. 'I heard all about that.'

'I expect you did,' sighed Thea.

'This is it,' came the announcement moments later. They drew up at a medium-sized house, with a modest garden, standing close to the road. Sudden questions filled Thea's head – ones she wished she had asked Gladwin before they arrived. Why was Alice living rough when her sister had a perfectly good house? And hadn't Gladwin said that Alice also had a house? What did Vanessa know about the reason for this interview? Who *were* these sisters, anyway?

'Is there anything I should know first?' she asked in a panic. 'Am I being set up in some way?' It seemed all too likely, after Emmy's little game of the night before. 'Why did you let me prattle on, instead of briefing me?'

'Best if you come to it with no preconceived ideas,' said the detective. 'Don't worry. At worst you'll just irritate her. But I'm hoping you can elicit a few bits and pieces that she'd never disclose to the police.'

'Huh!' said Thea. 'Here we go again.'

The door was opened by the tall woman Thea remembered so vividly from Monday. Capable, impatient, perhaps even slightly arrogant – she stood back to let the visitors in. There was no overt sign of grief for her sister, unless the shabby cardigan with buttons done up odd was a clue.

Gladwin stayed a step behind Thea as they moved into a sitting room that appeared to double as an extensive library. There were shelves of books lining three of the walls. There was something unreal, almost theatrical in the atmosphere of the room. The curtains were a deep red velvet, the sofa covered with a rich maroon leather.

Nobody said anything until they were arranging themselves on chairs and sofa. More questions poured into Thea's head. What were the chances that this woman was the one who had stabbed Alice? How responsible had she been for the welfare of the dead woman? How would the death of her sister change her? And many many more.

'Sorry to trouble you again,' said Gladwin formally. 'You probably don't remember Mrs Slocombe . . .' she waved at Thea, who was uncomfortably perched on a chair with a hard embroidered seat.

'Oh, yes, I do. She was enjoying the spectacle of my sister's humiliation in the middle of Cirencester on Monday. I'm sure she remembers me just as clearly.' The voice was strong and low. The woman looked closely at Thea. 'And they tell me you're the person who found my sister. Such a big coincidence! And I understand that the police generally regard coincidences as suspicious.'

'In this instance, that does not happen to be the case,' said Gladwin, still unnaturally formal. 'I was hoping that we might clarify just what did happen on Monday. It occurred to me that Mrs Slocombe might have a useful contribution to make – if you have no objection?'

'Rather late for that, I should have thought. Any objections I might have would look somewhat pointless now.'

'Be that as it may, we're here now and Thea is indeed the one who found Ms Ferguson.'

Before Thea could properly note the 'Ms', Vanessa was snatching up a book from a small table. 'Thea!' she exclaimed. 'Fancy that! The main character in this book is called Thea.' She waved the grey-covered volume. 'It's a Dorothy Whipple – do you know her? She's a favourite author of mine. Along with rather a lot of others, as you might have noticed.' The bookshelves seemed to loom in agreement.

The mere fact of holding a book seemed to bring the woman to life. She gazed on it as if at an adored child. 'It's a brilliant story. I never thought I'd meet another Thea.'

Gladwin and Thea looked at her in bewilderment. How could anyone get their values so skewed? What did a name matter at a time like this? Was she mad? As mad as her sister had appeared to be?

'Displacement,' said Vanessa with a sigh, as she observed their expressions. 'Anything rather than face up to what's happened. Only works for a bit, unfortunately.'

'So, what about Monday?' said Thea, slightly too loudly. Gladwin had given her no instructions, no warnings as to what not to say, so she opted to dive right in. 'With Alice.'

'Where to start? You were with a young girl. You stared.'

'Did we? Sorry.'

'I imagine we presented a somewhat unusual diversion.' She put the book back on the table and sat with her hands clenched between her knees. 'She wasn't drunk, you know, although on another day she might well have been. It was one of her "episodes", as we've always called them. Poor old Ally.' Her face turned pink and she sniffed. 'I know I should have watched over her better than I did. And you know the really awful thing? I'm actually not terribly surprised that somebody's murdered her. It was either that or drink or starving herself or some extreme manic moment sending her over the edge. We both knew it was going to end badly. I only hope it didn't *hurt*. I suppose it must have done, for a minute.'

'Was she bipolar?' asked Thea, feeling a flash of anger at Gladwin for not supplying more information.

'Right,' nodded Vanessa. 'Quite a severe case, in fact. It's remarkably common, you know, and the medication was of very limited help.'

'So on Monday – that was an episode, was it?'

Vanessa took a long breath, and stared at the floor. 'She was coming down from one of her manic phases, and wasn't making a lot of sense. And I have to admit I didn't have the patience to listen properly. All I wanted was to get her off the street, as you might understand.'

'How did you know she was there? You came across the road right to her, as if you knew already what you'd find.'

'Yes, I did. People know us. A woman living above one of the shops opposite the church saw her and phoned me. She'd been there for quite a while, talking to herself and drawing weird patterns on the pavement with her finger. Caroline said the police would be along any minute, and I should try and get her somewhere safe.'

'Which you did.'

Again, Vanessa heaved a deep sigh. 'I took her for a coffee and tried to calm her down. She had some of her pills with her, and I got two down her, which worked, luckily. She wanted to go, then, so I let her. There didn't seem to be any sense in trying to stop her.'

'Did you know she was living in that shed?'

'She wasn't *living* in it. I've said all that to the police already.' The woman looked up at Gladwin, whose silence was suddenly very loud. 'Why don't *you* say something?'

'I will when I need to. Go on – I'm listening.'

'It was funny the way nobody really seemed too bothered about her, in Cirencester,' said Thea thoughtfully. 'I mean – she really was being very odd.'

'They all thought she was drunk, I imagine. English people have a habit of averting their gaze, don't you find? What were *you* planning to do about it, if I hadn't shown up?'

Thea gave an embarrassed laugh. 'Nothing, probably.'

'There you are, then. It wasn't raining. She wasn't hurting anyone. I doubt that Caroline was right in thinking the police would take an interest. Just a poor crazy drunk making a bit of a nuisance of herself.'

'But she *did* drink? Most people think she did.'

'*Most people*? The fact is she very much liked beer and was a bit tipsy at times. It didn't agree with the medication very well. She was not an alcoholic, if that's what you're implying. Poor old girl,' she groaned again. 'Fancy getting herself killed like that. It's like something out of a book.' She looked up again. 'You might have guessed that I live my real life through books, most of the time. I write reviews, and do what I can to rehabilitate forgotten authors. When something like this happens, I have great difficulty in processing it. I suppose I'm a bit mentally ill myself, in that respect.'

'Oh dear,' said Thea, suitably chastened, and lost for words. Then she glanced at Gladwin and squared her shoulders. If she had been brought here to serve a useful purpose, then she'd do her best to comply. 'So, why would anybody murder her?'

Vanessa shook her head slowly. 'She practically asked for it, I suppose. Living like that, making herself so stupidly vulnerable, acting so crazy. She was almost a stereotype of a murder victim. I told her so, in fact. And that was before I knew the half of it.'

'But *why?*' Thea cried. 'Gladwin says she had a house – why didn't she live in it?'

'Ah – there's a question. Partly – well, *mostly*, I suppose – it was financial. She really didn't have any money – just the house, which she couldn't bear to sell. So she rented it out and lived off the proceeds. Which weren't much, because she had a lot of debts to pay off, and she insisted on giving far too much to obscure charities. It was working out quite nicely until she fell out with the tenant.'

Gladwin perked up. 'Oh?'

'It was a while ago now. I never heard the details. Listen – my sister was a grown woman, even if she did have pretty severe problems. She had a right to control her own life, and I for one respected that. She only accepted help from me when things got impossibly bad. She went her own way.'

'What about this tenant?' Gladwin persisted. 'Is it the same one that's there now?'

'As far as I know. But he won't have killed her. It wouldn't be in his interest.'

'You've thought about it, though,' said Gladwin astutely.

'I've thought about everything in the past twenty-four hours,' nodded Vanessa. 'Or not even that, yet. It must have been late morning when you finally caught up with me yesterday and told me the news.' She sighed. 'Time does very funny things. I expect it seems the same to you.'

She looked at Thea, who nodded wordlessly, as she mentally tallied the days – Monday in Cirencester, Tuesday finding the body and Wednesday all over the place trying to understand what had happened. 'Thursday today,' she murmured, slightly to her own surprise.

'You know why we're here, don't you?' said Gladwin, leaning forward. 'A follow-up from yesterday. There are a lot of details you can probably give us that we haven't established yet.'

The woman shrugged. 'The ways of the police are a complete mystery to me. Since nothing that has happened this week makes any rational sense, this is simply one more chapter in the fantasy. I feel rather as if I've been dropped into the pages of *Alice in Wonderland*. I suppose a lot of the people you talk to say that sort of thing.'

'Actually, no,' said Gladwin. 'But we do want you to tell us as much as you can about your sister. Thea is here quite unofficially. She's involved because she found Ms Ferguson—'

'Miss. She was Miss not Ms,' said Vanessa crossly. 'I told them that yesterday.'

'Sorry,' said Gladwin calmly. 'Well, as I was saying, Thea is here partly because she saw you on Monday, but strictly speaking she ought not to be party to any formal interview. So, can we take this as informal? We've already established that you were in London on Tuesday, so you're in no way under suspicion. Your role is purely as supplier of information and background.'

'I *was* in London,' Vanessa asserted firmly. 'And about twenty people can verify it.'

Gladwin nodded impatiently. 'I know. That's not in question, as I just said. But please – can you fill us in on Alice's situation? How long had she been in Baunton? Who knew she was there? How did she spend her time?'

'And how crazy was she really?' interrupted Thea, haunted by the memory of Alice tapping the pavement and weaving her head from side to side.

'Fairly crazy,' said Vanessa readily. 'I told you already. They applied various labels to her over the years, and the correct wording keeps changing as well. What used to be manic-depression is now bipolar something-or-other, heaven knows why. Some of the treatments she's been subjected to have been verging on the Victorian – although she always dodged the dreaded electric shock therapy. Pity, really – it might have worked. Somebody even mentioned lobotomy, thirty or forty years back. It

180

was an appalling idea, even then.'

'Surely not?' Thea was horrified.

'Well, I might have got it wrong. There are other things they do, with impossible names that nobody can remember. Alice had all the classic symptoms that made her a candidate for some sort of surgical intervention. In her forties she was absolutely bombarded with all kinds of ghastly efforts to make her normal. I have to admit she really was pretty bad at the time.'

'But she managed to maintain a house. Did she have a job?' It was Gladwin speaking.

'Oh yes – she worked on and off, all her life. But the house was thanks to Robert. Her devoted partner, Robert Williams.'

'Where is he now?'

'Dead, poor chap. Pancreatic cancer. But he made sure he left Alice somewhere to live. God knows where she'd have been without him.'

Again Thea and Gladwin both fell silent, filtering and organising the facts in an effort to construct a coherent picture. 'You've got other sisters? Is that right?' asked Thea eventually.

'Done your homework, I see,' said Vanessa tartly. 'Yes, there's Poppy and Jemima as well as me. Both rather a lot younger. One's an air steward, or whatever they call it now, and the other lives in Bermuda. She married a West Indian and has four children. They haven't seen me or Alice for ten years.'

'Let's go back to why she was living in—sorry, *using* a shed in Baunton,' said Gladwin. 'Because that's where she was killed.'

'I really have no idea.' The woman got up from her chair and started walking round the room. 'If I had thought about it at all, I would have assumed she'd got a bed with those farm people. I don't think I was in any state yesterday to take in what they told me about *where* she died. That seems to me one of the less crucial details.'

'Farm people?' asked Gladwin with a swift warning glance at Thea.

'Yes. The ones who run the courses. That's all she ever talked about. A man called Nick. Free-range eggs. Releasing long-gone species back into the English countryside. Beavers. *Wolves.*' She laughed. 'I must say I quite like the idea of wolves on the streets of Cirencester.'

'You didn't know she was sleeping rough?' Gladwin was bemused. 'Surely someone told you yesterday?'

'If they did, I missed it. What sort of a shed? Can I go and see it?' She faced Thea. 'And what were you doing snooping around, anyway? That's what I've been wanting to ask all along. Just who *are* you, Thea Whatever-it-is?'

Gladwin also got to her feet and flicked a hand at Thea to do the same. 'No need for that now,' she said sternly. 'I think we'd better go. You've been very helpful, but there's no need for anything further at this stage.'

Thea was more forgiving. 'I don't think it could have hurt too much,' she said gently. 'There was no sign that she . . . well . . .' How much was it safe to say, she asked herself belatedly.

'Thrashed about? Crawled across the floor searching for help? None of that?' Vanessa stared into Thea's eyes with no intervening barrier. Stark truth was what she wanted.

'No. Nothing at all like that. She was just lying there.'

'Did she look surprised? Angry? Scared?'

Thea shook her head. 'It's a myth, actually, that dead faces show any expression. All the muscles relax. You can't read anything into them.' She smiled. 'And I should know. I'm married to an undertaker.'

'Why does that not surprise me? Well, dear Thea, I really hope we'll meet again very soon.'

Chapter Thirteen

Thea was back at the Weavers' just before ten. She and Gladwin had spent fifteen minutes at the police station discussing their impressions of Vanessa. 'We didn't glean all that much about Alice, did we?' said Thea.

'We got as much as was reasonable. She was starting to get tetchy, which is understandable. I want to keep her onside. Normally there'd be a FLO to stay with her. She is the next of kin, after all. She needs a bit of TLC. But we never even dared to suggest it, given what she's like.'

'So Alice never had children?'

'Apparently not.'

'Can I go and see Vanessa again? By myself? I liked her.'

'Leave it a few days, maybe. If she didn't even know Alice was in that shed, then she's unlikely to have much useful information. I got the impression she's never even been to Baunton.'

'Who has? Unless they're keen on church paintings, there's nothing there to see.'

'I won't even ask about the church painting. Now get back to your girl and dog, why don't you?'

'I wasn't thinking of asking Vanessa for help with the murder. I just thought it might be nice to see her again.' Thea was wistful. Too many of her attempts at making friends in recent years had been sabotaged by murder investigations. People tended to be suspicious of her, and once a crime had been solved there were often embarrassing secrets laid bare, or incurably hurt feelings caused along the way. Perhaps it would be different with Vanessa Ferguson, who was reading about a person called Thea in a book by Dorothy Whipple.

Stephanie and Hepzie greeted her with mild relief on her return. They were both in the annex, the girl using Nick's laptop. 'Any news?' Thea asked.

Stephanie shook her head. 'Not really. Emmy's a bit more cheerful. I found somebody who knows Ginny, up in Liverpool. There's a muddle about her mother, though. What did Nick say about her?'

'Let me think. Her mother's mother, who is also Nick's mother, is in hospital, critically ill – right? So I think we assume Ginny's mum is close by, visiting or whatever. He seemed rather cross about it, for some reason. She's called Anita, and she's his sister and they don't really get on.'

Stephanie worked her shoulders like a tired manual

labourer. 'So why isn't he there with her? It's his mother as well. Why isn't he desperately worried? Are there any more brothers or sisters?'

'I don't know, Steph. You're the researcher here. But I agree it isn't at all clear. Although Nick says he did go up to Liverpool a couple of weeks ago. I suppose it's difficult for him to leave the farm, even if there aren't any animals. There's a whole lot of family business to do with the farm that they never properly explained.'

'It's too hard for me,' the girl admitted. 'I can do Facebook and Instagram, but I'd need to sign up for ancestry.com or something to get all the background. But there *is* this person I've found in Liverpool who says she knows a Ginny Chambers aged twenty-one, who'd been working on a farm. Says she had a WhatsApp from her about ten days ago.'

'That's something,' said Thea warmly. 'More than I could have managed. But ten days . . . wasn't she still here then? She went off last Wednesday, which is only eight days. Are there any more clues? What did the WhatsApp thing say?'

'Only something boring about the weather and how she was sharing a house with a dog as big as a bear. That's how I knew it really was her.'

'Did you tell this Liverpool person she was missing?'

'Sort of. But I kept it vague and low-key. I mean, I didn't say it was desperate or anything.'

'Good girl. Now let me tell you about my morning . . .' and she recounted as much as she could remember about the visit to Vanessa Ferguson.

'That doesn't sound very useful,' Stephanie summarised

at the end. 'She didn't know any of the people that Alice knew.'

'So she says. But she remembered us from Monday – and she's reading a book with a character called Thea in it. Which is completely irrelevant, but she seemed to find it interesting.'

Stephanie smiled faintly, and then asked, 'What happened next? On Monday, I mean?'

'Vanessa took her for coffee and made her swallow some pills and then left her to get on with it.'

The girl's shoulders slumped. 'It's too much for me,' she admitted. 'I don't really understand sisters. Shouldn't she have been more worried than that and really *done* something? Isn't that what a proper sister would do?'

Thea laughed. 'I'm not sure it's possible to understand sisters, probably because they're all different. Take me and mine. I never see Emily, for a start. And Jocelyn is a law unto herself. We get along perfectly well, but I wouldn't say we really know each other, since we grew up. She was very sweet when she was little.'

'Seems a bit of a waste,' said Stephanie.

'Yes, it does.' Thea remembered how she had just been hankering for a friend, ignoring completely the fact of two sisters. 'I suppose it just doesn't work out sometimes. Vanessa and Alice Ferguson haven't seen their other two sisters for ten years.'

'Have they got friends instead?'

'She didn't say. Alice had a partner called Robert, who died.'

'He must have been a nice man, to put up with her being so crazy. Mentally ill, I mean. It's rude to say "crazy".'

'There was quite a lot that wasn't very logical, now I think about it. Gladwin got a bit excited about the lodger, or tenant, or whatever he is. It sounded as if he and Alice couldn't live in the same house, so she moved out. But we didn't get anywhere with that. The subject got changed somehow. Vanessa vows she had no idea about the shed, though.'

'So where did she think Alice was living?'

'Here, apparently. At least, she knew Alice came here sometimes to help when the courses were on. But there's an awful lot that still hasn't been explained.'

'People tell lies,' said Stephanie, as if this was a recent discovery. 'We thought yesterday that even Emmy might be lying. I don't properly understand what she *wants*. I can tell she's worried. She can't sit still and keeps looking out of the window. Then when Joe turned up, she was peculiar. Wasn't she?' The girl stared helplessly at Thea. 'We don't know what Caz thinks of her, do we? She's always clever when it comes to people.'

'That's true. But I think the really big question is how Ginny and Alice are connected. I think they must be, somehow. Lots of people knew both of them, because of coming here on the courses. Oh – and we mustn't forget about the diary they say Ginny stole. That seems important.'

Stephanie gave her a patronising look. 'Yes, it does. *I* hadn't forgotten about it. But I don't see how it helps anything.'

'What if Ginny was a compulsive thief, taking things from other people, not just the Weavers? And what if Alice was as well? Maybe they worked together, and somebody caught them and were so furious they killed both of them?'

Stephanie laughed. 'That's the sort of theory I usually come up with. Alice doesn't sound like a thief to me. When we saw her, she didn't look as if she cared about *things* at all.'

'You're right. There was hardly anything in the shed. I'm still not sure I believe Vanessa when she says she didn't know Alice was living there.'

'Do we believe her story about how she knew Alice was in Cirencester? I suppose we have to, because nothing else makes sense. I don't suppose she was just shopping and happened to see her by the church?'

'It sounded quite convincing, and it doesn't show Vanessa in a very good light, so I guess it was all true.'

'Or maybe Vanessa was *tracking* her,' said Stephanie, wide-eyed. 'I bet that was it. People do that with their kids, you know. There's a boy in my class—'

Thea interrupted, 'I don't think so, love. She'd know about the shed, then – wouldn't she? How does it work?'

'There's a map. So, yes – Vanessa would probably figure out that Alice was somewhere that wasn't a house.'

'Hm. I don't think that's it, then. I don't think Vanessa *cared* enough to do something like that. I think it's right that the Caroline person saw Alice being odd in the street, and phoned Vanessa about it.'

'Except that would still be a coincidence, wouldn't it?'

'How?'

'Caroline would have to know both of them.'

'True. But Vanessa said they're well known in the town, which isn't very surprising.'

'What did Mrs Gladwin think about it?'

'Don't call her that. It sounds funny.'

'I can't just say *Gladwin*, can I? It's disrespectful. Maybe I'll try *DS Gladwin*. It's annoying, being so young. Things like this happen all the time. What's her first name?'

'Sonia. You can't call her that, either. Stick with *Mrs*, then. You're fine with Caz, at least.'

'Caz is different. She's like Jessica. Friendly.'

'Anyway, to answer your question – I don't know what she thought. She left almost all of it up to me. I assume she was watching and listening to everything we said and did.'

'Did she take notes?'

'Not at the time, no. I wonder what Caz made of the Weavers?' mused Thea, sidetracking. 'I wonder how they're getting on this morning? Gladwin seemed to have a plan of some sort, although she didn't tell me what it was. We were going to walk round the village together, but that seems to have been abandoned now. I did see more people than Abby and that double-barrelled man on Tuesday. Maybe we could go and see who's around today.'

Stephanie shook her head. 'Not again. We keep doing the same thing, and just hoping something's going to turn up. How many people are you talking about, anyway?'

'Three. An elderly couple and a man of short stature. At least, I *think* it was a man. The voice was quite deep.'

'They don't sound very interesting. What did they say?'

'If I remember rightly, the short person and the man in boots both said they didn't live nearby, and the couple said they lived round the corner. They all knew Mr Robinson-Fortescue, or whatever he's called.'

'Robinson-Finch,' said Stephanie. 'I wrote it down this morning.'

'You're amazing,' said Thea, again put in mind of the boy called Ben in Barnsley village, who made dossiers and flowcharts and solved murders by means of a computer.

'It's just good sense,' said Stephanie modestly.

'Well, he's on my list of suspects,' said Thea, half joking. 'If he knew Alice was living in his shed, he'd surely want to get rid of her.'

Stephanie looked doubtful. 'I'm wondering about that Abby. She didn't seem very real to me.'

'We shouldn't throw names about like this. It's the sort of thing Gladwin tells me off about.'

A noise outside diverted them, and Thea went to the door of the annex for a look. She came face to face with Detective Sergeant Caz Barkley, and almost threw her arms around her. 'Hey! It's you! How lovely!' The pleasure and relief took her by surprise. 'Just the person we need.'

Caz took a step back and smiled tightly. 'Steady on!' she cautioned. She looked down at the exuberant spaniel pawing at her knees. 'You and your dog need to curb your enthusiasm. Is Stephanie here?'

The girl appeared in the doorway, grinning broadly. 'Hi Caz,' she said. All three of them glanced around the yard, checking for Emmy or Nick appearing from the house or barn. Caz's car stood boldly in front of the annex. Nobody put it into words, but the implication was clear that Caz wanted her presence to be observed.

'You're both staying here, then?' she said to Stephanie.

'I wasn't sure whether it was true. It seems very odd to me.'

'It *is* odd,' said Thea. 'We can hardly understand it ourselves. But Emmy insisted and it's half-term, and . . . well . . .'

'You couldn't resist. I know. I can see it's nice here.'

'You were here yesterday – you passed us in the road. We stayed away on purpose, to let you get on with it. We're not being very useful, really. Everything's too muddled up. We were supposed to help with finding Ginny Chambers, as I expect you know by now. Stephanie's making a bit of progress, I think . . .'

Caz put up a warning hand. 'Not here,' she said, looking round at the outbuildings and farmhouse. 'Let me come in and tell me then. I've got some time. I've left Erik and a couple of uniforms tracing paths through the village and over the fields, trying to figure out how everything connects. There's loads more to it than we first thought.'

In some confusion, Thea led the way back into the main room of the annex. 'We were just wondering what to do next,' she said.

'I need to get some things straight. Like why *exactly* are you here? What *exactly* did you find on Tuesday? And what's your connection with Virginia Chambers? I've seen vague bits of answers from the interviews, but it's a long way from a clear picture.'

'I've already told Gladwin all of that.'

'Except you haven't, or not in the right order. That interview yesterday was all over the place.' There was an implied criticism of Caz's superior, which Thea found worrying. 'There's been no serious attempt to connect the

Chambers girl with the attack on Ms Ferguson – which seems to me a mistake.'

'She's Miss, not Ms,' said Thea, automatically. 'She's never been married, and neither has her sister. At least . . .' She stopped, wondering what had made her assume Vanessa was unmarried.

'You think Ginny killed Alice?' It was Stephanie, cutting through the implications and careful language. 'Is that what you mean?'

'No,' said Caz forcefully. 'I did not say that. But it's a line of enquiry that's fallen to me, and I'm here to follow it up.'

'What did the Weavers tell you yesterday?' asked Thea.

'Not as much as I'd have liked. Lots of stuff about the courses, and the way people come and go and form friendships and get into arguments. Ginny was only here for a month or so, but she got friendly with a man called Joe. Her grandmother's in hospital, but nobody seems to go and visit her . . .'

'We noticed that,' said Thea. 'The family background's all over the place. I don't think either of them really care about their relations.'

Caz nodded, with a complacent smile. 'Well, we've checked all the facts, and the old lady is definitely in hospital in Liverpool. We've also spoken to Virginia's mother, as it happens. She's not entirely well herself and hasn't seen her daughter since last July. She said a lot about goings-on in Bristol and how she washed her hands of a girl who could behave like that. Words to that effect. She gave the impression that everything was too much for her and she didn't need the worry.'

Thea remembered her first encounter with Emmy. The girl had been unable to face the unhappiness of her grandmother's move into a home and the dismantling of the family house. She might have some sympathy with Ginny's mother, trying to dodge the harsher realities of family life. She said some of this to Caz.

'So you think Ginny's like that as well and has gone off to avoid bother?' Caz pursed her lips sceptically. 'Surely, she'd do the exact opposite – I mean, she's got family here in the shape of Uncle Nick and Auntie Em, who were nice to her and gave her food and shelter, and interesting things to do. Besides, there hasn't been any bother here, has there? Not until this week, anyway.'

'You're saying you think somebody abducted her, are you?' Thea asked. 'Because nothing else really fits. Can she really be hiding away somewhere? What does she do for money?'

'How does she clean her teeth or go to the loo?' Stephanie added, with a mischievous smile. 'What does she eat?'

Caz shook her head. 'It's not very likely, is it? Nobody her age knows how to just disappear – they can't resist putting it all on Facebook or something.'

'TikTok,' said Stephanie.

'And the rest,' sighed Caz.

'But they can't *all* be like that,' Thea objected. 'Emmy says Ginny was quite outdoorsy and not glued to the phone like most of them. If Ginny met someone on Emmy's course, that person might well be off the grid, or whatever they say. I mean – that's the sort of person who'd come here. Joe's like that, for a start. Did you get a list of all the people Ginny might have met?' She looked at Stephanie, wondering whether she had asked for such a list already.

'I did,' said Caz, tightening her lips. 'It wasn't easy. They blustered about confidentiality and data protection.'

'So you really are making a proper effort to find her, then?' Thea found herself quite surprised at this development. 'After ignoring it last week when Emmy and Nick reported it.'

'Because you think she might be dead,' said Stephanie. 'Don't you?'

'It has to be a possibility,' said Caz, with a direct look. 'Everything changed when the Ferguson woman was killed.'

'Because if she's not dead, she might be the murderer.' Again it was Stephanie stating things in the plainest terms. 'And Emmy might know that's what you're thinking. And she might be asking me to find Ginny because she thinks I'm just a kid and can't possibly find anything out that would matter.'

Caz's head went up. 'You don't trust Emmy?'

Stephanie looked to Thea for rescue. They both grimaced and wriggled, before Thea tried to explain. 'That's going too far. But she does seem a bit *tense*. On edge. As if she has to watch what she says. It might just be the pregnancy, I suppose.'

'What about the husband? Nick.' Caz glanced at the notebook she had put on the table in front of her.

'He drifts away mostly, with his ridiculous dog, and doesn't say much. Ginny's his niece, and he does seem to be worried about her, but he leaves most of the talking to Emmy.'

'The thing is,' said Caz slowly, 'they asked you here specially, just a day before Alice Ferguson was killed. They made a real effort to convince you to come. They wanted you for something, which they must have discussed between themselves first. That's what Gladwin says. But *what*? Have you been set up? Does this all include Alice Ferguson somehow? And what other people are there in the picture?'

'Wait.' Thea flapped a hand. 'They couldn't have thought of me before Monday. That was when Emmy saw my car by the church and left a note on it. There's no way that could have been planned. It was just a massive coincidence that Stephanie and I came here when we did, and Emmy was on the spot to see the car.' She paused. 'A *massive* coincidence,' she repeated unhappily.

'Explain,' said Barkley.

'Nobody walks along that little street looking at the cars. Not unless they're delivering leaflets or something. Visiting a neighbour, maybe. It's absolutely quiet and deserted, like all these villages. But Emmy was doing what pregnant women do, taking herself on a long walk every few days, around the footpaths. It was only natural that she'd go past the church, and she says she recognised my car the moment she saw it. She remembered it from Chedworth.'

'And you believed all that, did you?' said Caz. 'Because I'm thinking that maybe she saw you in Cirencester earlier in the day and followed you here. That maybe she saw all that carry-on with Alice and her sister by the big church and fitted you into something that was already going on. Or somebody helping her did it. You're pretty well known, Thea Slocombe, let's face it. If you showed up in Cirencester, there's a few people who'd recognise you right away. They could call Emmy and suss out what you were doing, and make it all look like a coincidence. Although I have to say, if it'd been me, I would have been sceptical, right from the start.'

'I was just so excited to be seeing her again,' Thea admitted. 'I didn't think of any of the other stuff. I never thought to question it. And her explanation made quite good sense. I did believe her, yes.'

'So did I,' said Stephanie supportively.

'Your theory doesn't feel right,' said Thea. 'Emmy's not that devious. Nor is Nick, from what I can see of him.' She looked at Stephanie. 'We've got a bit carried away with conspiracy ideas. Stephanie was just speculating that Vanessa might have been tracking Alice, before you showed up. We thought the way she suddenly appeared out of nowhere on Monday was a bit neat, although she gave a perfectly credible explanation to me and Gladwin this morning.'

'It's all much too neat,' snapped Caz. 'The way these explanations strike you as so *credible*. I can't see it like that at all. You finding the body five minutes after she was killed, for another thing. That feels to me like Emmy Weaver again, as well. Sending you out on a vague mission to explore the village. I mean – what is there to explore? What did they think you would find?'

'I got the impression they thought I might find Ginny under a hedge somewhere. And they really couldn't have known where I would go. I could just as easily have headed off along the Monarch's Way to the big road, where Stephanie and I went on Monday.' She blinked at a sudden memory. 'There was another ramshackle old shed that way, as well. The place is full of them.'

Caz heaved a sigh. 'These villages drive me crazy. At first glance they're nothing more than a pretty picture, with no people anywhere to be seen. And then you show up and there's a violent death and all kinds of horrible things start crawling out from under the lovely Cotswolds stones.'

'Don't blame me,' said Thea, well aware that this was a familiar observation. 'I'm just a catalyst.'

'People know Thea,' said Stephanie. 'They *recognise* her. Sometimes, anyway. It makes them think up clever plots where she can be useful to them.'

Both women stared at her. 'Careful, pet,' said Caz. 'You'll be agreeing with me in a minute, if you don't watch yourself. Isn't that what I just said?'

'Oh,' faltered Stephanie. 'Is it?'

'With a bit of teenage imagination thrown in, maybe. Like drones and fake birds and trackers stuck to your car – all that superhero stuff.'

Stephanie laughed. 'Drones are real, you know. So are trackers. There's a boy in my class—'

'Fake birds?' queried Thea. 'What are they, then?'

'Little models perched somewhere inconspicuous, filming and recording everything going on around them,' Caz elaborated.

'You're joking,' said Thea. 'There's no such thing.'

'Gladwin found one last week in Evesham. It was incredibly realistic. Technology can do anything these days,' she finished with a severe look. 'You need to be on your guard all the time.'

Thea was deeply intrigued. 'Gosh! That would make so many things possible. But where do superheroes come in?'

'They don't,' said Stephanie. 'This stuff doesn't need any special powers. She's trying to talk teenage,' she added with a cheeky grin at Caz.

'Foiled again!' laughed Caz. 'And actually, you could be right about people thinking they can use Thea for their own ends. That's very clever of you.'

'So where does that get us?' asked Thea, losing patience. 'And what happens next?'

Chapter Fourteen

It was half past eleven when Drew called Thea in a state of some agitation. 'I can't leave Timmy alone all afternoon,' he insisted. 'Fiona can't come and keep him company and none of his friends seem to be available.'

'Why? Where are you going?'

'An old lady in the Hollies wants to prearrange, for one thing. And they think there might be one or two others, if I want to go and chat to them. It could be a lifesaver if it works out.'

'Hm. You can't take him with you, then?'

'Hardly.'

'I suppose I can come back. I'm not doing anything in particular here. I've seen Gladwin and Caz today already, and Emmy seems to be ignoring us. We're just brainstorming, basically.'

'Is Stephanie all right?'

'She's fine. In her element. The Hollies is the one down this way, isn't it?' She had a thought. 'Why don't you bring Tim here? I could meet you somewhere and you could hand him over.'

'It's almost in Burford. I turn off at Hampnett.'

'There's a lay-by near the crossroads, I think. I could meet you there. Then you can come here afterwards and collect him. There isn't anywhere for him to stay overnight.'

Drew uttered a sound of exasperation, which was rare for him. 'Why do you have to stay there if you're not doing anything? Isn't it a colossal waste of time?'

'No, Drew. Being at home would be a waste of time. I do feel useful here, in a vague sort of way. Just being on the spot seems important. Stephanie's actually making some very sensible suggestions as well. Emmy's happy that we're here. You can take Hepzie back with you, though, if you like. She's not having much fun.'

'Tim will be happy about that. Okay, then, we'll do it your way. I haven't got time to argue about it. Can you meet me at one o'clock in that lay-by?'

'If you're sure.' She was having second thoughts, as the implications dawned on her. 'I can't remember exactly where it is. Maybe it's a daft idea.'

Drew's feelings were apparently going in the opposite direction to hers. 'We'll find it. If all else fails, I'll turn into that little road that leads to Hampnett the back way and just park at the side of the road.' He spoke with confidence, all annoyance evaporated.

'All right.' Thea's head was still swirling with images of fake birds and surveillance drones. Would somebody be watching as she and Drew transferred a small boy from one car to another? 'And I'll get the postcode of this place. You won't find it otherwise.'

She explained the arrangement to Stephanie, who took it calmly. 'Tim's going to love Joshua,' she said. 'He's been much better with big dogs since Grandma came with hers. Although it might not work the other way round.' Drew's mother had paid a memorable visit six months earlier, accompanied by a most alarming mastiff. Unaccountably, the dog had taken a great liking to Timmy and a bond had been instantly formed.

Thea pushed the subject of large dogs to one side. 'We should go and talk to Emmy. I haven't seen her at all today. Make a note of the postcode, will you, and we can give it to your father so he can find his way here.'

'It's already in my head,' said the girl. 'Isn't it in yours? How did you find your way here on Tuesday if you didn't know it?'

'Emmy gave very good directions. Like in the olden days.' Thea could still just remember a time when she was in her early twenties and people miraculously found their way around without technological assistance.

'What're we going to do with Timmy? How long will he be here?'

'For a start we make him feel he's wanted and not just a nuisance. If Nick's around, he might let him play with Joshua. If you really think that's a good idea.'

Stephanie chewed her lip. 'It might not be. I know Tim would like him, but he might take against Timmy and try to kill him. Anyway, Nick isn't around. I haven't seen him all day.'

'So let's go and see Emmy.'

Yet again, it was almost time for lunch, as Thea only realised when she caught a whiff of frying onions coming from Emmy's kitchen. 'Oh damn – she's cooking,' she muttered. 'She'll think we've come begging food off her.'

'It's not twelve o'clock yet. We'll tell her we're not staying long.'

'We can't, anyway. We're meeting Drew at one.'

Emmy greeted them with a warm smile despite looking pale and droopy. 'Hey!' she said. 'Sorry I've neglected you. I see you had a visitor just now.'

'DS Barkley,' nodded Thea.

'The one who came yesterday? She seems quite nice.'

'She is. And very good at her job.' Thea knew there was a subtext to her words, and felt mildly sorry about it. Caz's words – *You don't trust Emmy?* echoed in her head along with all the wild speculations about plots and conspiracies. 'At least they're finally taking Ginny's disappearance seriously.'

'Only because they think she's done a murder,' said Emmy bitterly.

'Well, that's not very likely, is it? Why on earth would she kill a woman she barely knew?'

'She *did* know her, though. And there were some pretty strong feelings flying around on that course. The one they were both here for.'

'Oh?'

'Didn't we tell you?' Emmy swept a distracted hand across her forehead, pushing back a strand of hair. 'I can't remember who said what now. It's all got so *horrible*.' Tears filled her eyes. 'And here I am bringing a baby into the middle of it all. Every time I try to calm down and think straight, the baby kicks me and I just want to crawl into a dark hole and stay away from everybody.'

'Even Nick?' asked Stephanie.

'Even Nick.' Emmy gave a shaky laugh. 'Only don't tell him, will you?'

'The course,' Thea prompted. 'Tell us what happened on the course.' She glanced at her watch. 'Although we've only got twenty minutes or so.' She explained about Drew and Timmy and her domestic complications. 'Are you busy?'

'I'm doing a big lot of bolognese for the freezer. People keep telling me that's what you're supposed to do before you have a baby. Of course, in my case there's a little matter of Christmas getting in the way as well.'

Thea waited hopefully for some relevant information, which did finally come. 'Oh – the course. Yes. It was the middle of September. The focus was on birds – nightingales and curlews and bullfinches and things like that. We had somebody come from the RSPB to give a slide show. Some people went out at first light with cameras and sketchbooks. Ginny did breakfasts for them. Alice came two or three times as a general dogsbody. There were two or three people who had no idea how to behave. They dropped litter and made a noise and talked about hunting down hares and deer and red kites. Plus slaughtering every sheep in the country for good measure. And I did tell you about the day the kite snatched the leveret. That was all part of it. Ginny and Alice both had a go at them and tried to get them to see how wrong they were. They did change a bit, to be fair. But it sparked off a huge argument about whether humans had any right to interfere at all. Silly, of course. Nick and I know perfectly well that there'll never be a time when people genuinely stand back and leave it all to nature. But you get a few idealists who think that's got to happen. I tried not to get involved and it died down by the end of the week, but people did say some awful things. And Ginny was badly upset about it.'

'Which side was she on?' asked Stephanie.

'What? Oh – well, she was anti-hunting of course. For sport, anyway. But she did point out that sometimes human intervention did good. Like reintroducing the kites. Then one of the oiks started on about cane toads . . .' She noticed her listeners' expressions. 'Never mind that. The point is, I suppose, that Ginny took things to heart and brooded on them. Joe was good with her, and I think she got a bit of a crush on him. She was already an emotional mess when she got here, and I have to admit we didn't help. If anything, she got worse.'

'Was she upset about her grandmother being ill?' Again it was Stephanie directing the conversation.

'Well, a bit, I suppose, when it first happened. But she'd already made a decision to forge her own way in life and stop trying to please her relations up there. She was sorry about her gran, of course. They'd been quite close when she was little. But the woman's in her eighties, and I think deep down Ginny thought they should just let her go, and stop all the medical stuff. But Nick thinks she suddenly realised she might have some sort of claim on the property, when her gran dies. After all, we have got three hundred acres of prime agricultural land. That's quite an estate. Of course, our child – or children – will probably take it on eventually. But Nick was prepared to give Ginny a role here if she wanted it. Now she's gone off with that diary, he's pretty much changed his mind about that.'

Stephanie was clearly finding this all very difficult to digest, so Thea took up the reins. 'There's a subtext here, isn't there? Or perhaps it's the main concern? The business and the family complications. I think the police have come to that conclusion, as well.'

Emmy looked close to tears. 'Don't be nasty. I honestly have tried to tell you everything, but there are so many different strands to it, so many people, and everything's so *confusing*. I don't know what I should feel – worry about Ginny, shock about Alice, fear for our future and the baby. It all just goes round and round my head, and I know it's bad for me. Nick tries to calm me down, and I put on a show for him, but inside I'm in meltdown.'

Thea dropped a soothing hand on Emmy's shoulder. 'I'm sorry,' she murmured. 'I was pushing you much too hard. We're just as confused as you are, if it's any consolation. But I really don't think you need worry too much. Your job is to take good care of yourself and let everything else wash over you. Let Nick take the strain. After all, it's his niece that's caused all this trouble, isn't it?'

'Poor you,' said Stephanie, with the disabling sympathy that only a child can provide. 'We were being horrid, weren't we?'

Emmy's tears overflowed, and she leant her face on Thea's front.

'Do you want us to go?' Stephanie went on. 'We will if you think that's best. Won't we?' she asked Thea. 'Although, we *are* in the middle of it all now, and Timmy's coming here soon.'

Emmy shook her head. 'No, you need to stay. We have to see it through. I should pull myself together until we've got some answers. I have to accept that the most likely thing is that Ginny either killed Alice or has been killed herself. Those are the only things that make any sense.'

'Yes,' said Stephanie, almost triumphantly.

Thea groaned softly. 'Steph! Don't be so . . .'

'What? Honest? Why?'

'It's all right,' said Emmy, fishing for a tissue and blowing her nose. 'We've all been thinking it, haven't we? Except Nick. He won't even let me say it out loud. He's always been ever so fond of her, since she was little.'

'I got that impression,' Thea nodded. 'I assumed it was his idea to notify the police that she was missing, last week.'

Emmy pulled a doubtful face. 'Sort of,' she said. 'He panicked when he realised she'd gone without saying a word.'

'But she took all her stuff, didn't she?' said Stephanie.

'Not all of it, no,' Emmy said in a muffled voice. 'Not that she had very much anyway.'

'So perhaps that means she hasn't been killed. Although . . .'

'Stop it, Stephanie,' said Thea. 'We're going round in circles. As Gladwin would remind us, what we need above all is *evidence*. Just making wild guesses never gets anybody anywhere.'

Stephanie sat back and folded her arms. 'So what are we supposed to do, then?'

Thea looked at her watch. 'In five minutes we're going to meet your father and collect your brother. Then we'll go and have lunch somewhere. Then we'll have a walk round the village again. We can show Timmy how Monarch's Way goes under the big road. After that, who knows?'

Emmy heaved a great sigh. 'You two,' she said. 'You make me feel pathetic. I'm a real mess today. Sorry to dump it all on you.'

'Where *is* Nick?' said Thea, thinking this was becoming a somewhat repetitive question.

'Oh, I don't know. I have a suspicion he keeps going off over fields and into bits of woodland, still hoping he might fine Ginny. Totally irrational, of course. More likely he's planning what to do with the rest of the fields, and keeping busy that way. He's talking about taking fences down and seeing if there are springs he didn't know about. We've got another ninety acres that's still ordinary pasture. People put cattle and sheep on it, since we got rid of all our own livestock. He likes to croon over new baby trees. He disappears for hours at a time. This rewilding stuff has really got under his skin – there's always something new to be excited about. It'll be mushrooms next. He still can't believe there's so much money to be made out of it, at the same time. He's got such a rosy vision of the future, it's almost scary.'

'It *is* exciting,' said Thea. 'Even the little look we had yesterday was a revelation. And the courses you run are genius.'

'We thought so at first. They certainly are lucrative. And they mean we don't have to waste years applying for grants and all that. It's the bureaucracy that's stopping far more people doing the same sort of thing. But it hasn't all been smooth sailing – and when there's a baby as well . . .' She looked down at herself and rolled her eyes. 'I can't think how it's all going to work, to be honest.'

'It'll be fine,' Thea assured her. 'Babies are very portable. It'll just fit in with whatever you need to be doing.'

'Is it a boy or a girl?' Stephanie asked.

'Don't know. We don't approve of knowing in advance. Spoils the surprise.'

'Oh,' said Stephanie, with a blink. 'I thought everybody knew the sex before it was born.'

'Well, you thought wrong.'

'Emmy – you do know we're only staying one more night, don't you?' Thea put in. 'So, whatever you think we might be doing to help, say now, because it'll be too late otherwise.'

Emmy wiped a hand across her brow again and closed her eyes. 'I know. The whole idea was probably bonkers. But when I saw your car by the church, everything just seemed to fall into place. I phoned Nick before I left that note, and he said to go for it. I'd told him about you, of course. I told him that if anybody could find Ginny and work out what was going on, it was you.'

'I can't imagine why, quite honestly. I've never actually found a missing person in my life.'

'Just dead bodies,' said Stephanie.

'But not Ginny's,' said Emmy. 'Which is something to be thankful for.'

'Okay – we'll see you later this afternoon, then – probably. Everything seems to have gone quiet, which is not usually a good sign. But let's stay hopeful.' Thea gave a vague smile to go with these words and led Stephanie out to the car in the yard.

It was not entirely straightforward, getting from Baunton to Hampnett, but Thea had the route firmly memorised – turn right at North Cerney, then left when that little road emerged onto the Fosse Way, or A429. It was only six or seven miles. 'I thought I remembered a lay-by just before the turning into the village, but now I'm not sure,' she worried.

'We'll find him,' Stephanie assured her, waggling her stepmother's phone. 'It's right near Northleach, isn't it? Where we were a while ago. There was a girl called Millie then, as well, which was what you called Emmy when you knew her before – remember?'

'It's a common name these days. The Northleach Millie was rather a nice little thing.'

'Emmy's nice as well,' Stephanie said. 'Don't you think?' There was anxiety in the girl's voice.

'I'm not sure. I want to like her, but she isn't easy to really get to know. I think she's very self-absorbed, which I suppose is natural in the circumstances. I'm still amazed that she recognised my car the way she did. She never struck me as very observant when I knew her before.'

'And I discovered that her name really is Emily, as I

guessed. Like your sister. Did you ever call her Millie?'

'No,' said Thea. 'Just Em.' She did not often think about that particular sister.

'Names are funny, aren't they?'

'Very,' said Thea, finding the conversation oddly disconcerting.

It turned out that Drew had parked outside the defunct Lion Café, which had been part of the Prison Museum. It was on the main road, and he was standing with Timmy beside the car. Thea swerved into the space at the last moment, with Stephanie yelping beside her. 'Sorry!' Thea said. 'It came sooner than I thought.'

Timmy was grinning broadly, and threw himself into the back of the car without a word. The spaniel greeted him with lavish affection. 'Monarch's Way!' he announced without preamble. 'I want to go there.'

Thea opened her window and spoke to Drew, handing him the slip of paper that Stephanie had provided. 'Here's the postcode. It's just outside the village. I won't try to explain. Use the satnav.'

The Slocombe satnav was a family friend, given the name of Ernie and heavily relied on. Drew claimed to find the Google maps on the phone impossible to use and the voice unbearably jarring. Ernie had a soothing Australian accent. 'Okay,' he said. 'It'll be a while. I want to do some shopping as well.'

'No problem,' said Thea.

As she drove off, she could see Timmy behind her, unfolding a large map. 'We can start with the Monarch's Way, then White Way, then Welsh Way,' he explained. 'They run together in some places. This is amazing!'

Thea felt pangs of guilt, admiration and affection towards her stepson. Instead of reproaching her for leaving him behind, he had thrown himself into the unexpected thrill of walking his favourite footpath at first hand, on a stretch he hadn't seen before.

Stephanie seemed to be feeling much the same. 'Hey, Tim!' she said. 'It's lucky Dad's busy, right? We haven't done any of the footpaths yet. You can show us the way.'

'Can we start at the church?' The boy was positively bouncing with excitement. What an odd child, Thea thought, to get so elated about lines on a map. The three-dimensional reality on the ground was secondary to the history and associations – especially when it came to the Monarch's Way. 'Why is it called White Way?' she asked.

'Don't know. I can't find much about it. A lot of it just goes along big roads now.'

Thea duly parked close to the church and stood for a minute thinking about Monday, and the careless inspection she and Stephanie had made of the building and its environs. 'Those are ancient water meadows,' Timmy told her, pointing to the fields below the church wall.

'I thought they looked as if they flooded sometimes,' said Thea. 'Lucky nobody's been daft enough to build on them.'

'We saw people over the other side,' Stephanie remembered.

'So we did. Walking along the edge of the woods.'

'Did somebody get murdered?' Timmy asked. 'Dad wouldn't tell me properly, but I worked it out. Are you being detectives?' He didn't sound envious or annoyed at being excluded. Stephanie's young brother had no interest in solving crimes or grasping malicious motives. The convoluted Pokemon games he played with his friends was the closest he got to tackling puzzles.

'Yes,' Stephanie answered him. 'An old mad woman called Alice was killed. And a young one went missing at the same time. So we've got two things to think about, and we can't understand how they're connected.'

'They're probably not,' said Timmy casually. 'Why would they be?'

'Because they happened in the same place at the same time. And they knew each other, and the people we're staying with knew both of them, and they're *obviously* part of the same business, somehow.'

'It wasn't really the same time, though,' Thea corrected her. 'There was nearly a week in between.'

'There you are,' said Timmy. 'You're jumping to conclusions.'

'We're not,' said Stephanie in a big-sister voice. 'Just you wait and see.'

They rapidly repeated the earlier walk from the church to the big road surging noisily overhead, Timmy leading the way at a brisk pace. 'I just want to mark it off as seen,' he explained. Having achieved this purpose, he briskly ordained that they retrace their steps down to the middle of the village. Eight minutes later they were at the little patch of grass where Thea and Stephanie had met the Robinson-Finch man. Timmy masterfully directed them around a bend to a point which he said was part of two footpaths for a short way before they diverged. 'This is great!' he enthused. 'There must have been monks and merchants and drovers and all sorts of people all coming and going along here.'

'On their way to Cirencester,' said Thea, trying to keep up. 'It's only two miles from here.' She paused to look round. 'I never did get to this bit of the village. Gladwin said she'd walk round it with me, but she seems to have abandoned that plan, probably for good reason. The fact is, there's hardly anything to it.' She eyed a little cluster of houses in what could only be a cul-de-sac. None of them had gates, she was pleased to note.

'Have you been searching for the missing person?' asked Timmy. 'What if she's here all the time?'

'Someone else would have found her by now. They've had police people working out all the pathways and how it all fits together. I expect they're still at it somewhere around here. Where would she hide?'

Stephanie gave a wordless sound that contained scornful disbelief. 'What about Alice, then? She seems to have managed to hide well enough. Wasn't that just here somewhere?'

'Over there.' Thea waved to her left. 'Where the houses stop. It's different here – it's much more open.'

'We need to go down here,' said Timmy, clutching his map. 'Through that gate.' There was a short stretch of road that suddenly ended with a metal gate leading into a field. They opened it by means of undoing a hook-and-chain contraption and went through. The field they were in had little to entice them, and Timmy jogged across to an open gateway directly ahead. The others followed, and then all three stopped dead in surprise.

214

'What *are* they?' wondered Stephanie. Spread across a large expanse of grassland was an array of assorted wooden structures. Some looked like chicken runs, some like little houses. Two were giant wooden seats and a few could be recognised as the sort of jumps you saw at horse shows.

'It must be for training horses,' said Thea doubtfully. 'But there aren't any hoofprints or horse muck.'

'There are two horses over there,' Timmy pointed over to the right. 'The other side of the river.'

'River?' Thea peered. 'Oh yes.' The little Churn was dawdling inconspicuously around the side of the field.

'What were we just saying about there being nowhere to hide?' said Stephanie. 'What about all these things? Some of them are big enough for a person to sit in – and nobody would ever see them.'

'And you could hide behind them if somebody was coming,' said Timmy. The two children suddenly rushed off to demonstrate, leaving Thea holding Tim's map. Hepzibah followed, yapping in delight.

'Which way is the footpath?' she asked, when they finally came back to her, having enacted a brief game of hide-and-seek. It was indeed true that the erections offered cover for somebody intent on remaining unseen.

'Straight ahead and into those trees,' said Timmy with total confidence.

'Rather like the place by the church,' said Stephanie. 'But steeper.'

There were people emerging from the woods, too far away to see faces. Timmy resumed his jogging pace and the others followed. A stile took them into the trees, where a path zigzagged upwards. Looking back, Thea was struck by just how small Baunton was. A forgotten little settlement, once on a junction of important pathways, now barely relevant. Insignificant enough for road builders to fly over their heads and never bother about the disturbance caused. Only a handful of people would be affected, they must have told themselves.

From the top of the patch of woodland, the traffic noise was once again very evident. 'Does the big road run over there, then?' Thea asked. 'I've lost my bearings.'

'It must curve all round the village,' said Stephanie, looking over her brother's shoulder at the map. 'Yes – it goes under the White Way over there somewhere.'

'And that's Cirencester, that way,' Timmy told them, looking to the right. 'It would be easy to walk there.'

Thea was trying to construct a hypothesis involving Alice and unseen comings and goings, which might involve any of the people she had met in the area. 'Anyone walking across that big field would be very conspicuous from here,' she murmured thoughtfully. 'The wooden things are too far apart to really hide anybody who wanted to get over here without being seen. They'd only be useful if you stayed inside or behind one of them. There must be less visible ways to get up here.'

Timmy gave her a pitying look. 'Plenty,' he said. 'Follow me.' He veered off to his left, along a narrow track that seemed to lead into the middle of the woods. After a few minutes they came to another stile, and another left turn saw them into a classic 'green lane': grassy underfoot, but wide and level enough for vehicles to use. On their right were open fields containing sheep, and very soon they were overlooking the field of strange obstacles, on a much lower level to the left. 'We keep going along here,' said the boy.

A few minutes later they were emerging onto a lane which Thea did not instantly recognise. Then she saw the big yew tree towering over the wooden shed where she had found Alice. 'Blimey!' she said. 'Look at that!'

The children were baffled. 'What?' said Stephanie.

'That's where Alice was. That cabin or shed or whatever you call it. It looks bigger from this angle, weirdly. I climbed over that fence at the back, when I could have got in up here more easily – though it's still a scramble.' There was a steep slope up to the overgrown tangle of brambles and ivy that almost concealed the building. 'The police have cleared a way up to it now. It was much more covered up before.'

'Here?' Stephanie cocked her head, and walked a few paces down the lane. 'It's so close to the houses! How could Alice have stayed out of sight?'

'It wouldn't be hard if she kept quiet and didn't have a fire,' said Timmy. 'And look – she could use that green lane to get up to the White Way and then to Cirencester. If anybody saw her, she'd just look like another walker. But there must be times when nobody's around.'

'This is all very useful – thanks, Tim,' said Thea. 'It's connected up a whole lot of stray bits and pieces. I can work it out much more clearly now.'

'So what's up that way?' the boy wondered, pointing up the track. 'A farm, I suppose.' His map was not helpful, it seemed. 'I don't think it's part of one of the footpaths.'

'It doesn't look very inviting,' said Thea. 'It's time we got back, anyway. We've been out for nearly an hour.'

Timmy allowed himself to be persuaded and they started back towards the car, which was just around a bend where the various arms of the village all met. 'Where are we going now?' he asked.

'Nowhere,' said Thea. 'I mean – back to the farm. Your father will be here for you before long.'

'No he won't. He said it would be nearly four o'clock at the earliest.'

'And I just bet you it'll be sooner than that,' said Thea, knowing that Drew did not like leaving the Broad Campden house empty for long.

'I'm glad we saw the place where you found the dead body,' Timmy said.

'Why?'

The boy shrugged. 'You'll be talking about it at home for ages, won't you? I want to be able to imagine it.'

That was sweet, Thea admitted to herself. Timmy *was* sweet, and somehow never got due credit for it. As the son of an undertaker, he was in no way morbid or nervous around the dead, taking bodies for granted just as his sister did. It was an effort to be included, to share the experience, that motivated him. Stephanie enjoyed the story and the puzzle of what had taken place, assuming she was an integral part of it all – but Timmy had to work harder, and Thea could not deny that this was unfair. 'Well, now you can,' said Thea, looking back one more time and thinking of poor dead Alice.

'That's Abby,' said Stephanie, a few seconds later, ducking her chin at a woman walking ahead of them with a basket on her arm. 'Doesn't she look old-fashioned.'

'This must be her house,' said Thea, indicating a typical Cotswold building on the left. 'Or possibly the next one.' She frowned. 'Actually, it could be any of these.' There were four or five separate dwellings within a few yards, but all of them struck her as rather large for the modest woman they were observing.

Abby had stopped to peer at something on the ground, and the little group caught up with her at the foot of a short flight of steps. Nearly all the houses had steps up to their front doors, Thea noticed. Perhaps it was a safeguard against flooding, if the River Churn chose to misbehave. 'Hello,' said Thea. 'It's me again.'

Abby's attention was all on her discovery. 'There's a puffball, look. Just starting to grow. They like grass verges.'

Timmy was the first to share her excitement. 'It's very small,' he criticised.

'Give it a week and it'll be bigger than your head. Literally. Haven't you ever seen one?'

'I don't think so. Can you eat them?'

'Oh yes. Sliced up and fried in butter. Full of good minerals and so forth. But not very flavourful, I must admit.'

'What would eat it if you left it here?'

Abby blinked at him. 'Slugs, I suppose. I don't really know. Some insect might lay eggs in it.' She pulled a face.

'Are you a forager, then?' Timmy asked, suddenly much bolder than usual.

'I am,' she said proudly and showed him her basket. There were red berries, acorns, hazelnuts and one small mushroom in it. 'Those are rosehips,' she said, fingering the berries.

'What do the Weavers think about that?' Thea wondered. 'Wouldn't they rather it was all left for wildlife?' Her thoughts were stumbling over a number of vague arguments all going on at once. 'Surely human beings already take far too much? Isn't it a bit greedy to go pillaging around the hedges and taking what must rightly be theirs?'

'I think so,' said Stephanie, rather loudly. 'I definitely do.'

Abby went pink. 'But it's free food. Nature's bounty. Nick doesn't mind – although . . .' she faltered. 'He's not really *keen*, I admit. He won't put on a foraging course, even though I keep nagging him to. He never properly explains why.'

'You'd have people digging up burdock roots, and wood sorrel and goodness knows what,' said Stephanie. 'It'd end up spoiling his rewilding.'

'How do you know all that?' Thea asked.

'I was at the farm most of yesterday, remember. They were talking about it then.' The girl looked at Abby. 'But they didn't say it was you who wanted to run the course about it.'

Abby looked mulish. 'Emmy doesn't think there's anything wrong with it. She likes the things I make for her. She thinks they're good for the baby.'

'You need to be careful,' Stephanie informed her. 'Some things are poisonous.'

Abby gave a scornful laugh. 'I know that,' she said. 'Obviously.'

Thea was giving Abby a close scrutiny. 'You stopped feeling scared, then? That was quick.'

'What? Oh – yesterday, you mean. I was having a wobble, wasn't I? Emmy gave me a lecture in the car, and told me Nick was certain nothing could possibly happen to me. He's always so logical. Yesterday he made me see that Alice had a troubled life, and must have upset a lot of people along the way. Even her sister wanted to be rid of her, or so he says. I felt really bad when I heard she'd been living just a few yards from me and I never knew. I did see her in the fields now and then, and just thought she was blackberrying like me, and just . . . you know . . . pottering about. She was on the farm every now and then, but I never spoke to her. I assumed she went back to Cirencester to sleep. It's not far to walk, after all.'

'You know Vanessa, do you?'

'Who?'

'Alice's sister.'

'Oh – no, not personally. Nick told me about her.'

'Did the police interview you?' It was Stephanie asking. 'They'd want to know what you saw, living right where the murder happened. And you probably know Ginny, as well.'

Abby's head jerked back and the basket swung on her arm. Timmy gave a little laugh. 'I don't think that's any of your business,' the woman said. She looked around at the three people, including the spaniel in her sweeping gaze. 'I don't know who you think you are, but I know I don't have to answer your questions. Certainly not from *children*.' She said the word witheringly.

'It's okay, Steph,' murmured Thea. 'We can ask

Gladwin.' She looked directly at Abby. 'That's Detective Superintendent Gladwin. She's a friend of ours.'

The effect was not as expected. 'Oh yes – we all know about you and the sneaky work you do for the police. Why do you think Emmy dragged you over here in the first place? If I were you, I'd keep my mind on Virginia Chambers and forget all about old women being stabbed in a shed.'

Chapter Fifteen

Thea and the children arrived back at the farm shortly before three o'clock and made themselves drinks. The sky was brighter than it had been all day and they chose to sit outside, carrying kitchen chairs out and setting up camp in a corner of the farmyard. Timmy wanted a table to spread his map on, but Thea told him that was going too far. He ended up squatting on the cobbled ground with the map in front of him. The spaniel flopped down with her front half obscuring one corner of the paper. Timmy made no attempt to push her off.

'Baunton's a lot more complicated than I thought,' said Stephanie, looking over his shoulder. 'I've been trying to imagine where I'd go if I'd just stabbed somebody. Obviously they didn't go back into the middle of the village, because you would probably have seen them,' she told Thea.

'Not necessarily. I don't think I was as close as that to it. I mean – it could have been half an hour or so after it happened before I found Alice. I was parked near that memorial thing, so I couldn't see the cow gate or any of the little road up to it. I just sat in the car for a bit and had a packet of crisps. And the killer probably didn't run madly down the street covered in blood. He probably had a car nearby and just calmly drove away.'

'But look at all the possibilities,' insisted the girl. 'Fields in all directions, pretty much. You could be in Cirencester in twenty minutes, or off up the White Way – or back past the church. No need for a car at all.'

'Is it somebody you've met, do you think?' asked Timmy. 'That woman said Alice had lots of enemies, didn't she?'

'She implied that, anyway. And it could well be a total stranger, I suppose. But somehow I don't get that impression.'

'So who are the suspects?' asked Tim.

Thea laughed. 'Just about everybody. The Weavers. The sister. The owner of the shed. The people in the village. Joe. Ginny. Except not one of them has the slightest hint of a motive.'

'It can't be the Weavers,' protested Stephanie, with a cautious glance at the farmhouse twenty-five yards away. 'Can they hear us, do you think?'

'Of course not. We're much too far away,' Thea assured her. 'And the windows aren't open, look.'

Stephanie was not convinced. She eyed the barn, which was closer, and a wall beyond the house. 'There's a garden behind that wall,' she whispered. 'Emmy might be out there.'

'I think it must have been a man,' said Timmy. 'You have to be quite strong to stab someone.'

Thea bit back a temptation to argue. 'You're probably right,' she said. 'But let's not think too much about that.'

'I think DS Gladwin thinks it's Ginny who did it,' said Stephanie.

Thea whipped round on her stepdaughter. 'What are you talking about? You haven't even *seen* Gladwin. You can't possibly know what she thinks.'

'I've seen Caz,' said Stephanie stubbornly. 'They're sure there's a connection.'

'Caz never said anything of the kind. They don't work like that. There's absolutely no evidence whatsoever concerning Ginny, so they can't *possibly* have that idea.'

'Why are you so cross about it?' asked Timmy. His hand was on Hepzibah's neck, gently fondling the soft hair.

'I'm not,' Thea began, before noticing her dog's worried eyes on her face. 'Am I?'

'Yes,' said the children in unison.

'I didn't mean to be. It might be because it makes me feel as if the whole thing is some sort of trick. A conspiracy. We talked about that before, and I just thought it was silly then. I still do, mostly – but what if it isn't? That would be so horrible.'

'You put the Weavers first on the list of suspects,' Stephanie pointed out. 'Just now.'

'I was *joking*. I was putting the most unlikely people first. You jumped on me right away and said it couldn't be them. You're right. Of course it can't.'

'Good,' said Stephanie, obviously unconvinced.

'Here's Dad,' said Timmy, as a car drove into the yard. 'Can I take Heps back with me?'

'If you want. It's not much fun for her here.'

'You haven't seen Joshua,' Stephanie realised. 'I wonder if he's in the house.'

Thea was musing about the protocol of having her husband and his children dropping in and out of the Weavers' yard without consultation. Drew had met Emmy when she was known as Millie, in Chedworth, but only fleetingly. He had not expressed any desire to reacquaint himself with her. Given the way they opened the place up for residential courses, it did not seem likely that they would care about privacy – although everybody who showed up had presumably been properly invited. 'Just jump in the car quickly,' she ordered Timmy.

'I can't. I need a wee first.'

'Hurry up, then.' She went to meet her husband as the boy ran into the annex.

'He doesn't know where the loo is,' Stephanie observed.

'So go and show him,' Thea called back over her shoulder. Drew had stopped the car beside her, and she bent down to talk to him through his window.

'They haven't seen us since we got back with Timmy,' she said. 'I don't suppose they'd mind, but—'

'Best not to put it to the test,' he finished for her. 'So, where's the boy? And am I taking the dog?'

'He's gone to the loo and yes please.'

'When will you be home?' He was looking after his daughter, who was not hurrying after her brother. 'What's the matter with her?'

'Nothing. She's showing Tim where the loo is – or

supposed to be. We've only been back here about twenty minutes.'

'That's his map, is it?'

Thea went to collect the Ordnance Survey, which was marked in various colours by Tim, along with added notes. She folded it up and handed it to her husband. He was slow to take it, gazing blankly into the middle distance. 'What's the matter?' She echoed his question about Stephanie and Drew echoed her reply.

'Nothing. Just thinking about Miss Porter. The old lady whose burial I've just prearranged. She's a real character.'

'You always say that.'

'Do I? No, but she really is. Her body's disintegrating, but her mind is as good as anybody's. Better than most. She *rants*. It was exhilarating.' He grinned. 'I keep hearing her voice in my head.'

Thea felt torn. On the one hand she wanted Drew and Tim and the dog to go quickly before the Weavers appeared, and on the other she was intrigued by Drew's obvious preoccupation. 'What did she rant about?'

'Climate. Not very original, I know. She even thinks the same as most old people who insist they've seen it all before and talk about their grandparents being snowed in for a month in the 1880s – but she linked it all up with politics. It really made me think.'

'Oh.' She was disappointed. Strong feelings about the climate were too similar to zealotry about religion, as far as she could see. The same language was used, and the same excommunication of heretics went on. It was fundamentally boring when it wasn't being irritating. Even Timmy could see through the blatantly biased indoctrination that he was exposed to at school.

'Here he is! Come on, Tim. Where's Hepzie?' The appearance of the boy came as a relief. Miss Porter's observations could definitely wait until a more propitious time.

Stephanie came out of the house with a bag, the dog at her heels. Drew sat tight, frowning slightly. 'Nature versus capitalism,' he said softly. 'That's the crux of it.' Then he lifted his head and looked around the yard. 'You said these people run courses about rewilding and all that? Maybe they've put their finger on the solution.' He smiled. 'Same as I have, according to my old lady. She positively *bathed* me in approval.'

'How nice,' said Thea, taking the bag from Stephanie and putting it on the back seat with Hepzibah. Timmy went round to the front passenger seat. 'I'll see you tomorrow,' she said, kissing Drew through the window.

'What time? And what's in that bag?'

'Just some food we won't get round to eating,' said Stephanie. 'We did a Deliveroo thing last night and got a bit carried away.'

'Good God,' said Drew. 'Did you tell me what time tomorrow?'

'I don't know,' said Thea. 'But definitely before supper, I promise.'

'I'll hold you to that,' he replied with a serious look. 'Bye then, Stephanie.'

'Bye, Dad. Wish us luck.'

He blinked, obviously not sure what she meant.

'Go!' ordered Thea. And they went.

* * *

'Now what?' asked Stephanie five minutes later.

Thea shook her head, noticing a strong feeling of anticipation. Something was going to happen. Gladwin would sweep into the yard in a frenzied rush and order them to jump into her car. Or Nick and his dog would appear and shout for their assistance. Even Vanessa Ferguson might show up, keen for further conversation. This last was the most appealing, and probably the least likely. 'I suppose we should make something happen. Isn't that what we usually say?'

'I don't know.' The girl was looking oddly bereft. 'Like what?'

'Are you all right? You've gone very quiet.'

Stephanie took a deep breath and averted her gaze. 'Not really,' she admitted. 'The thing is . . .' she swallowed. 'The thing is, I'm a bit scared.'

Thea was astonished. 'What? Why? What of? What do you mean?'

'It feels . . . this sounds weird, but it feels as if we're being watched all the time. Those windows . . .' she nodded at the farmhouse. 'And every time a plane goes over us, I think it's a drone filming us. I had a dream . . .'

'Have you felt like this all day?'

'More or less, I suppose. It was better when Tim was here. And Hepzie. Now it's just us. And Caz said we shouldn't trust Emmy or Nick . . .'

'She didn't say that, Steph. She asked if *you* trusted them, but she never said whether you should or not.'

'But she usually says *trust no one*, doesn't she? That's scary. The thing is – I don't understand why we're even here. Not really. It seemed like a bit of a game to start with, but it's not like that at all now. For a start, Emmy's ignoring us. And where's *Nick*? Everything's got in a horrible muddle. And that man, Joe. Where did he go? Nobody *tells* us anything.'

'You should have gone home with Dad,' Thea realised.

'I wanted to, but nobody seemed to have even thought of it. And I can't leave you all alone, can I?'

'Of course you can. I've been alone countless times when there's been a murder, and nothing bad's ever happened to me.'

'But it could have done,' said the girl stubbornly.

'No, I'm not having that. You know how I feel about *What ifs*. That's a mug's game and you know it.'

'Like *better safe than sorry*,' nodded Stephanie. 'Yes, I know. But most people can't keep on like that all the time. It's not even rational. Maybe poor Alice thought the same, and see what happened to her.'

'Stop it,' begged Thea, feeling her foundations wobble. 'What are you trying to do to me?'

'It's *me* we're talking about,' Stephanie reminded her. 'You asked and I told you. Okay?'

'Oh, God – you are so grown up it's frightening. Thirteen going on thirty, as they say.'

Stephanie smiled then. 'I'm really not, though,' she insisted. 'So, what do we do now?'

The answer came via a call to Thea's mobile.

Chapter Sixteen

'Robinson-Finch here,' came a voice that sounded oddly shaky. 'Can we talk?'

'How did you get my number?' Thea often found herself asking this; the answers were generally either obvious or vague.

'From Emmy Weaver, of course.'

'Oh.' Not vague, but nothing like as obvious as he seemed to think. 'What do you want?'

'I saw you today, on the footpath with two children and a dog.'

'Did you? I didn't see you.'

'My land is nearby. I was in a gateway . . . well, that doesn't matter. I need to understand what your role is in all this. Who *are* you? You drop in on us out of nowhere and start asking questions and ferreting about. I just don't understand.'

At least he didn't say 'snooping' thought Thea, wondering what she should tell him. 'Well – most people know about me, actually. I used to be a house-sitter. Now I live in Broad Campden. My husband's an undertaker. We've got a natural burial ground—'

He cut her off. 'Most people know you? Really? Well, I'm obviously not most people, because I still don't get it.'

'Why does it matter? What is it that's bothering you? You sound worried.'

'*Of course* I'm worried. A woman was murdered on my property. Dickie swears he never knew anything about it, and I believe him. But it looks very bad, anyone can see that.'

'Dickie?'

'My manager. I'm not here all the time. I've got a place in Argyllshire . . . well, that doesn't matter either. Dickie does all the estate management, runs the farm and so forth. You must have seen him on Tuesday.'

'Must I? What does he look like?'

'He's small. Shy. Knows his stuff, though. Excellent with horses *and* cattle. Very rare, that.'

'Ah!' said Thea, recalling the person of limited stature and indeterminate gender who had drifted quietly away on Tuesday. 'I remember him now.' Was this another name to add to the not-very-serious list of suspects?

'Anyway, you asked what's bothering me and it's not something I want to discuss over the phone. As they say.' He huffed a quick laugh that made him sound suddenly very human. Did the man actually have a sense of humour? 'I know it's an awkward time, but do you think we could meet? Where are you?'

He really doesn't get what's going on, Thea realised. 'I'm at the Weavers' farm, in their annex. How could you possibly not know that if you've spoken to Emmy and got my phone number from her?'

'I thought you would have gone by now,' he said meekly.

'Well, you can come over, if you like. We're not going anywhere.'

'Thank you. Fifteen minutes, then.'

Stephanie was listening impatiently. 'Who *was* that? Not the double-barrelled man, surely?'

'The very chap. He sounded completely different. Much less arrogant and bossy. He says he saw us with Timmy just now. He wants to talk. He doesn't seem to know anything about what's going on.'

'The police will have interviewed him,' said Stephanie with certainty. 'And he knew you were working with them because he saw you in Gladwin's car. And he doesn't like the Weavers. What will they think if they see him coming here?'

Thea groaned. 'Not again! It was bad enough having Drew turning up. But it can't be helped now. I suppose it'll be all right.'

'It might not. He sounded as if they were *enemies*.'

'Well, he sounds different now. Something must have happened to change his mind. And it wasn't enemies – he was making fun of them, wasn't he? Scornful and disapproving, but not more than that.'

'Did you say he was spying on us today? We didn't see him, did we?'

'He says he was in a gateway. Try to ease up on the conspiracy stuff, okay? It's not very realistic.'

'Sorry,' said the girl with disarming meekness. 'So who's Dickie?'

'His farm manager. I saw him by Alice's shed on Tuesday, as well. He's very short. Robinson-Whatnot says he's shy but good with horses and cattle. I almost forgot about him.'

'Another suspect,' said Stephanie, with a cautious look at Thea. 'Possibly.'

'I thought that as well. I doubt if we'll ever see him again, though. You heard me promise your father we'd go home tomorrow. We're not likely to solve anything by then, are we? Emmy will just have to get along without us.'

'Do you think we should go and tell Emmy the man's coming? Just to be polite?'

'Probably, but I don't think there's enough time. He'll be here in a minute.'

Which he was, and before another few minutes had elapsed a good deal of trouble had ensued.

Thea and Stephanie had left the annex door standing open, and heard the car engine approaching down the farm's driveway. At the same time, Emmy emerged from her own front door, making quite a noise over it. Thea remembered being sent round to the side on her initial visit because the front door scraped on the ground and didn't open easily. 'There's Nick,' said Stephanie, pointing to the nearest field. 'And Joshua.'

Emmy heard the words, and the car engine. She walked down to the gate in the wall between the house and the yard, which was permanently open, and watched for the oncoming vehicle. 'Who is it?' she called to Thea. 'Is it somebody else for you?'

Thea walked a few steps towards her. 'I'm afraid so. I hope it's all right? He was quite insistent.'

'It depends who it is,' said Emmy, before focusing on the Range Rover that had entered the yard. 'Oh God!' She looked towards her approaching husband with something like terror. 'If Nick sees him . . .'

'Too late,' muttered Stephanie, from behind her stepmother.

'Calm down,' said Thea. 'It can't be that bad. Surely, he wouldn't have come if—'

'Go!' shouted Nick Weaver, from a distance of fifty yards. 'Get off my farm, you damned swine.'

Afterwards Thea deduced that Joshua had wrongly interpreted these words as an order to him personally. After a moment of lumbering indecision, the giant dog found an untapped reserve of energy and flew at the visitor just as he was opening the door of his car. Robinson-Finch was hurled back into the vehicle with the animal on top of him. Sounds of snarling and muffled shrieks filled the farmyard.

'Call him off!' Thea screamed at Nick, who did nothing of the sort.

'He doesn't bite,' said Emmy, looking extremely pale.

'He doesn't need to,' yelled Thea. 'He'll *crush* the man to death.' She had already run to the car and was trying to find purchase on the shaggy coat to pull the animal off the man. She got her hands round one back leg, but found it impossible to move it. 'Help me!' she ordered Nick, who began to move slowly towards her. Stephanie was quicker and was already grabbing for the other leg.

'Get away,' said Emmy. 'He'll hurt you.'

'No he won't,' argued Stephanie. 'Not unless he bites

us.' She pulled again, but was obviously more worried about causing damage to the dog than risking injury to herself. 'I don't think this is going to work,' she gasped.

'He's got huge teeth,' Thea remembered, still speaking too loudly. The more static and silent the others became, the more she wanted to throw herself about and scream. 'And all dogs bite if they're provoked.'

'Aarghh!' came the voice of the trapped man. 'Get it off me.'

'Oh, for God's sake. Get out of the way.' Nick Weaver had finally reached them. He stretched past Thea and Stephanie, leaning into the car. 'Joshua! Leave!' he ordered. There was a sudden slackening of tension as the dog's master got his arms around the furry torso and hauled it backwards. One hand managed to grasp the collar, and there was a tangled expulsion of man and dog, like a ghastly birth, with Robinson-Finch as a crumpled retained placenta still lying across the front seats.

Joshua was not happy. He rounded on his master and seized his lower leg in the very large teeth. 'No!' roared Nick as the jaws clamped down.

Inside the car there was silence, causing Thea to completely forget its owner. Nick Weaver sprawled at her feet with his dog still holding tight to his leg.

'Call an ambulance,' she told Stephanie, already aware of prolific blood loss. 'My phone's on the table in there.' She nodded at the annex and then turned to Emmy. 'Get this dog away, somehow.'

'He won't let go,' groaned Nick.

'Shoot him if you have to,' came a voice from the Land Rover. 'I've got a gun in the back.'

'Shut up,' snapped Nick.

Emmy marched into the fray, smacked Joshua hard on the side of his face, and said 'Drop it!' Which he did. She then led him, rather as if he were a small pony, into the house and slammed the recalcitrant door on him. Heading back to Thea and her husband, her steps slowed and she made a slurring sound. Stephanie came back with the phone, and said, 'She's fainted. Gosh! I never saw anybody faint before.'

Thea was struggling to tear away Nick's trousers, so as to examine his wound. The thick denim was sodden with blood. 'Take them off,' she ordered him.

'Is that an artery?' he asked wonderingly. 'It doesn't hurt.' He showed no concern for his wife. Robinson-Finch was very slowly unfolding himself from the front seats of the vehicle, his dignity in shreds.

Thea was in full nurse mode, which was rare, but not unknown. The basics had been drilled into her and her siblings by a conscientious father. 'I hope not. But you're losing a lot of blood. We have to press down on it as hard as we can. Have you got a hanky or something?'

'Of course I haven't. Have you?'

'No. Take the trousers off and we can use them.'

'What about a tourniquet?'

'Bad idea,' said Stephanie, who was hovering between him and Emmy. 'They can do more harm than good.'

'They did a first-aid course at school, and I remember that's right, as well,' Thea explained. She was suddenly feeling unnaturally calm after the brief frenzy. 'Is the ambulance coming?' she asked Stephanie.

'I think so. They're still on the line. Do you want to talk

to them? You can ask about a tourniquet.'

'All right. In a minute. Let's see the wound first.'

Nick was co-operatively fumbling at his belt and zip and lifting his bottom to pull down the jeans. 'Now it hurts,' he reported. 'Dog bites are meant to be painful, aren't they?'

'Very,' said Thea briskly. 'I'm taking your shoes off now. Pity you weren't wearing wellies.' Instead, he had sturdy trainers fastened with double-knotted laces that were difficult to unpick.

'It's still fairly dry in the fields. I only wear boots when I have to.'

The calm conversational tone was starting to feel bizarre – which Stephanie seemed to have noticed. 'Emmy *fainted*,' she repeated. 'She hasn't come round yet.'

'Has she?' Nick raised his head for a look. 'Where's the dog?'

'She took it into the house. I hope she hasn't hurt herself.' The girl had left the phone for Thea and was kneeling beside the prostrated woman. Thea had one shoe off and was tugging the leg of the jeans clear. 'These won't work as pressure pads,' she complained, and picked up the phone.

'Are you still there? Good. Listen – it's a deep dog bite. Two holes that I can see. It's bleeding, but I think it's slower than before. I'm wondering about a tourniquet . . . All right . . . How long will the ambulance be? . . . Bloody hell. There's an unconscious pregnant woman as well, if that incentivises you to get a move on.'

Stephanie was gazing at her in horror as she ended the call. 'You were rude,' she said.

'I know. I couldn't help it. They agree with us about the tourniquet, especially as the bleeding's slowed down. They are trying to be quick. I've got to put pressure on the site of the bleeding.' She tugged again at the jeans and tried to fold the material over the wound, before pressing down on it. Nick yelped and tried to push her off.

Emmy stirred and Stephanie leant over her. 'Are you okay?' asked the girl. There was no coherent answer, but Emmy's eyes were open.

Robinson-Finch was hovering beside his car, eyeing Nick with almost comical apprehension. 'I hit my head,' he said. 'Your dog will have to be destroyed.'

'Not by you,' Thea told him. 'Have you really got a gun?'

'Just an air rifle. Enough to kill a dog, probably. Better on crows and squirrels.'

There was the sound of a car coming closer. 'Is that the ambulance?' asked Nick, more faintly than before.

'I think not,' said Thea. 'It might be the police.'

Which it was. DS Gladwin was at the wheel and a familiar young man sat beside her. They both jumped out of the car, eyes wide. Five people were scattered across the yard, two of them horizontal. Gladwin went first to Emmy. 'What happened to her?' she asked Stephanie.

'She fainted after she shut Joshua in the house. I think we're all in shock, actually. Everyone's being weird.'

Detective Constable Erik Something approached Thea and her patient. 'Lost a lot of blood,' he observed.

'The dog bit him.'

'Nasty. And who's this?' He looked at the other man, who was leaning on the bonnet of the car, looking dazed. 'Is he bitten as well?'

'No. He says he banged his head. He's been rather quiet.'

'Good grief. Did the dog do all this?'

'Well – yes. I suppose he did. These two don't like each other, which is really the cause of it all.'

Gladwin was keying her phone, with a worried frown. 'It's more than just a faint. She's completely out of it. Erik – come here, will you? Prop her up a bit and talk to her. Good girl, Stephanie. Looks to me as if you're about the only sensible person here.'

'I've been *very* sensible,' protested Thea. 'I've saved a man from bleeding to death.'

'Hm. I have a hunch it's nothing like as bad as it looks. The worst risk is infection with a dog bite. I assume the animal doesn't have rabies.' She laughed fleetingly. Then she had a thought. 'Was it the giant that Caz told me about? A Saint Bernard or something?'

'Newfoundland,' said Nick. 'Never bitten anything before, man or beast.'

'He'll have to be destroyed,' repeated Robinson-Finch.

'And you are?' asked Gladwin.

'William Robinson-Finch of this parish,' he told her with a sickly smile. 'You'll have notes on me, thanks to the accident of ownership of the building in which this lady found the body of a woman, two days ago.' He tried to stand up straight, swaying much as Emmy had done. 'And I feel very peculiar.'

'Concussion,' diagnosed DC Erik.

The arrival of the ambulance did not initially do much to reassure anybody. The paramedics hesitated, looking around and asking irrelevant questions. Finally, they opted for Emmy as the most urgent case. She was carried into the vehicle and wrapped in a red blanket. Torches were shone into her eyes and her 'vitals' taken. There seemed to be anxiety as to whether or not she was going into premature labour. In sheer irritation she soon recovered enough to insist she was perfectly all right and they would do far better to tend to her husband. 'He's bleeding,' she said in a shrill voice.

'Oh!' said Nick, hearing her. 'That's it. She can't stand the sight of blood. It's a physical thing. It always makes her keel over. I forgot,' he admitted.

With no sign of urgency, medical attention was transferred to his leg. 'Hardly bleeding at all now,' one of the men remarked.

'I stopped it,' said Thea, not really expecting praise, but annoyed that it was not forthcoming. It had happened before – paramedics seldom thanked members of the public for any assistance they might offer, in her experience. Mostly they just pushed you out of the way. They would have done it this time, if she hadn't already got to her feet and gone to join Gladwin and Stephanie.

'You got the 999 call, did you?' she asked the senior detective. 'I'm impressed.'

'Come on, Thea. It's routine to cross-reference addresses and people of interest, especially if they're involved in an ongoing investigation. The computer flagged the address and a message was put through to me.'

'I'm still impressed. These things don't usually work, as far as I'm aware.'

'What about Mr Double-Barrelled?' asked Stephanie. 'I still can't remember which way round the names go.'

Constable Erik and William Robinson-Finch both heard her and both smiled. The latter pushed himself away from

241

his car and walked the few yards to join the all-female group. 'It's all your fault,' he said to Thea, his tone far more pleasant than his words. 'When you think about it.'

'I disagree,' said Thea. 'There were several things I couldn't possibly have known. And it was your idea, not mine, to come here.'

'We knew he and Nick didn't like each other,' Stephanie pointed out.

'But none of this has anything to do with the murder, has it?' asked young Erik, which had a miraculous effect on them all.

Chapter Seventeen

A decision was made to take Robinson-Finch to Gloucester Royal Hospital for observation, but leave both Weavers at home to watch over each other and talk to the police. Everyone – including a watchful Detective Superintendent and an eager-looking Constable – drifted into the Weavers' kitchen in silent accord and sat around the big table. Joshua was ordered outside, into the back garden.

'Robbers,' said Emmy suddenly. 'Ginny always called him Robbers.'

'We've been calling him Mr Double-Barrelled,' said Stephanie. 'Did Ginny like him?'

Gladwin rapped on the table and Thea half expected her to call for order. Nick's leg had been professionally cleaned and bandaged and an antibiotic injection administered. He sat sideways to the table with his leg propped on a stool, wearing baggy pyjama bottoms. Emmy was still pale, but had recovered completely in animation. She showed every sign of wanting to talk.

'None of this has *anything* to do with Alice Ferguson,' she burst out, looking at Constable Erik. 'I don't know why they think we need you here. It has nothing to do with the police,' she added, with an annoyed look at Thea. 'I'm starting to feel sorry I asked you here now. You've brought nothing but trouble and haven't been the slightest use in finding Ginny.'

'Steady on,' said Nick in a low voice. Then he addressed Stephanie. 'And no, Ginny didn't like that man, any more than I did, or anybody else you care to mention. He's the worst kind of capitalist vandal, thinking of nothing but killing anything that gets in his way.'

'He wanted to shoot Joshua,' said Stephanie with a nod.

Thea watched Gladwin's knuckles hover over the table, preparing for another authoritative rap. 'He certainly doesn't approve of you,' she told Nick, in a perverse desire to defend the absent Robbers. 'I can see you two are at opposite poles when it comes to the use of land and so forth.'

'Is this relevant?' asked Erik. There was something painfully perky about him that gave force to Gladwin's complaints on Tuesday and explained why Caz Barkley found him a trial. As far as he could see, the only matter of any significance was the murder of Alice Ferguson – and Thea was inclined to agree with him.

'Do you want us to go, then?' she asked Emmy. 'Right away?'

'You can't,' said Gladwin. 'You told those paramedics

you'd be on hand in case these two had relapses or something. We're not staying long, so it's up to you.'

'He wanted to tell me something,' Thea remembered. 'That's why he came. And I would really like to meet Vanessa Ferguson again. I liked her.'

'You think he was going to confess to killing Alice?' Nick grated. 'Him and that Dickie who does all his dirty work for him. That wouldn't surprise me.'

'Shut up, Nick,' said Emmy. 'You don't know what you're talking about. Nobody could possibly think Dickie would stab someone. It's unimaginable.'

'Who's Dickie?' asked Erik, flipping through his digital notebook.

'Nobody,' said Emmy. 'Nick's just being stupid.'

The rap finally came. 'This is hopeless,' Gladwin complained. 'None of you are talking any sense. Thea – come with me. Erik – stay here and watch Mr and Mrs Weaver for a minute. Mrs especially. I don't want her fainting again.'

'I won't unless Nick's leg starts pouring blood again.' Emmy shuddered. 'I can still see that horrible pool of it.'

Thea sighed and followed the detective outside. 'It wasn't anything like a *pool*,' she muttered. 'His trousers soaked most of it up.'

'I think she was milking it a bit,' Gladwin agreed. 'She soon recovered when those paramedics started fussing round her.'

'So what do you want to say to me?'

'Vanessa Ferguson was very taken with you and has asked if you'd go and talk to her again. I'm assuming it isn't about her sister – more likely to be books or politics or something. Caz went back there this afternoon for a bit, trying to get more background on Alice.'

'Did it work?'

'Up to a point. It's like a blizzard of information, but none of it feels very useful. We've got about a dozen pictures of that shed pinned up, trying to imagine what she thought she was doing there. She can't possibly have intended to stay much longer. No water, no loo, no electricity. It's beyond primitive.'

'And all in an affluent little Cotswold village,' teased Thea. 'Although I don't think she was exactly living there – just using it as a hideout. She probably went to Cirencester for food and a wash every day – maybe just slept in the shed. That wouldn't be so bad. Even so, it really isn't the sort of image you get from the Cotswolds.'

'Exactly. And not a single person admits to knowing she was there. Never any noise or smoke or unusual smells. What would anybody *do* in a place like that?'

'Watch birds. Read. Think. Don't forget she was quite seriously ill, mentally. And I think I'm right about the way she used it. The kids and I walked right round the land to the east of the village today, where those bizarre little buildings and things are, and we worked out how she could easily have come and gone to Cirencester without being noticed. If she only went there to sleep, that would explain why nobody realised she was there. I bet that's right. After all, Stephanie and I saw her in town on Monday. It's easy to believe she just roamed around the pathways all day, keeping out of sight as much as she could.'

'But *why*? What was behind it all? Was she hiding from someone? Waiting for something? Or just stark-staring bonkers?' Gladwin spread her hands in a gesture of helplessness. 'How did she fit with all these other people? Where did she stand in this feud that's going on?'

'Feud?' Thea frowned.

'Come on! The Robinson-Finch man and his minions enraged by all this eco business, letting the weeds rampage and having the nerve to make *money* out of it. It flies in the face of everything country landowners have stood for for a thousand years. I must admit to a certain sympathy for them.'

'Times are changing,' said Thea fatuously. 'And have you seen that top meadow? It is rather wonderful. I had a little argument with the Abby woman today about it – sort of. She goes foraging, and apparently Nick doesn't mind. But it seems like *pillaging* to me. Taking even more for human beings. She didn't even seem to have thought about it.'

'Abigail Seldon,' Gladwin nodded to herself. 'If anybody knew about Alice's shed, it would be her. She's about sixty yards away from it, and is one of the few people in the village who's at home all day. If you ask me, she's got to have known.'

'Why would she lie about it?'

Gladwin cocked her head. 'Think about it. It's pretty obvious, surely?'

'You can't be thinking she's the murderer? She hasn't got enough sense.'

Gladwin laughed. 'Since when does killing anybody take sense? Rather the opposite, in my experience.'

'No, but,' Thea persisted, 'are you really thinking it could have been her?'

'She had means and opportunity in spades. Motive remains unclear – for just about everybody in the picture. If you trusted algorithms, you'd have to say the sister came out pretty high on the list. She's likely to get the house, for a start.'

'And Alice was a serious nuisance in her life,' added Thea. 'But we don't think it was her, do we?'

Gladwin gave herself a shake. 'This is not the place to talk about it. I just wanted to pass on the message from the sister, and suggest you follow it up quickly. She might say something useful – the way people do.'

'How quickly?' Thea looked back at the farmhouse. 'Will Joshua have to be destroyed?'

'What?'

'The dog. It bit its master really badly.'

'I think it's up to him, in the short run. But there's a baby coming. There'll be health visitors and so forth, who are highly likely to raise a concern – especially if they get to know that it bites.'

'Oh dear. I thought that's what you'd say. Well – I suppose I could go this evening to see Vanessa. Stephanie and I are back in Broad Campden tomorrow, and quite honestly, I think we'll be glad to see the back of all this.'

'What time tomorrow?'

'Afternoon, probably. There won't be any rush if Drew's going to be in to mind Timmy. Things aren't too busy just now.'

'It was wrong to bring Stephanie, you know.' The detective spoke these words with some difficulty, as if they'd been sitting on her tongue for a long time and had to be spat out somehow.

'She's perfectly all right. Learning about life, seeing other people, using her brains. What's wrong with that?'

'It's not *predictable*. Anything can happen and you wouldn't be able to keep her out of harm. Things around here are unstable. There's obviously a lot of strong feelings flying around. She's at a very impressionable age. You can't be sure of the effect it's all having. And this place is so *open*. Strange bods coming and going. Caz says there was some weird long-haired character here yesterday, just lurking about doing nothing.'

'Joe,' said Thea. 'He's meant to be helping to find Ginny.'

'Well, I'm sure you see what I mean where Stephanie is concerned. You've been leaving her here on her own, haven't you?'

'You know I have. You *told* me not to bring her to yesterday's interview. She had the dog,' she finished weakly.

Gladwin looked round. 'Where is it now?'

'Drew took her home, with Timmy. She wasn't having much fun here. Nobody could guarantee that Joshua wouldn't kill her.'

'What a stupid name for a dog,' Gladwin sighed. 'I keep wondering who you mean. Pity we can't finger him as Alice's killer.'

Thea gave a weak laugh, remembering one of Drew's stories from his earlier days. 'It can happen,' she said.

'So – I'll have to get back. I need to boost some morale, with so little progress to keep them all on track. They lose heart, poor things.'

'Young Erik seems to be pretty focused. What's his surname, by the way?'

'Sampson. It's his mother who's Swedish.'

'Yes, you said – only it was Norwegian before.'

'It doesn't matter,' snapped Gladwin. 'He's as English as any of us, when it comes down to it. But I have to keep reminding people about the "k" at the end of Erik, for some reason. And yes, he's keen and clever and when I get tired of him, I give him to Caz for a bit.'

'Right,' said Thea, trying to summarise to herself the scraps of advice and information she had just been subjected to. Most of it was criticism disguised as advice, she concluded crossly. She found herself wishing very passionately that she had never stumbled upon Alice Ferguson's body. 'You don't sound very hopeful of solving the murder this time. That's bound to be depressing.'

'Oh, we'll solve it,' said Gladwin fiercely. 'Just you wait and see.'

Only after the detective had gone did Thea realise that she would have to leave Stephanie alone again if she were to go and see Vanessa Ferguson as intended. She would also have to abandon Nick and Emmy, who had both been told they should have somebody to keep an eye on them for the rest of the day. Common sense suggested that this could be achieved by letting them watch over each other. Nick at least was unlikely to collapse or become incapable as a result of a bitten leg. As for what happened to the dog, Thea placed that question firmly outside her sphere of interest.

The mystery of what had happened to Ginny felt as if it was fading into far less significance. Nobody had found her lying dead in a basement, and no computer had logged her as flying off to California, so she was to be presumed alive.

The implications of fecklessness led to the suspicion that she had simply decided to move on, finding it easier to just go, avoiding arguments or any inclination Nick might have to try to impose his authority as an uncle. His subsequent anxiety about her might have been a delayed attempt to acknowledge that he had a degree of responsibility for what happened to her. Thea suspected that Stephanie was coming to much the same conclusions.

Back in the Weavers' kitchen, Stephanie was sitting quietly by herself. 'Emmy's gone to lie down.' she reported. 'Nick thinks he'll join her. They can take it in turns to make sure each other's all right. Or something.'

'What about Joshua?' Thea asked, in spite of her determination to leave the dog out of her worries. 'Is he still outside? Is somebody going to feed him?'

'Probably,' shrugged the girl. 'I feel all peculiar. It's been a horrible afternoon and my head aches.'

'Don't tell me that! You never have headaches.'

'It's only a bit. But can we go for a walk or something? It's nice and bright out there and there'll be another pretty sunset in another hour or so. The Internet says it's going to rain tomorrow and go on for days.'

'Yes, I heard that as well, yesterday. We knew the dry spell couldn't last much longer.'

'So can we?'

'Yes, of course we can. It's just what we need. Where's Nick? I'll tell him.'

'In the sitting room, I think.'

Thea found him and informed him that she and Stephanie would be out for half an hour, if he thought he and Emmy could survive without them. His agreement

251

was tetchy and unsmiling. *He thinks it's all my fault* Thea realised. Some people might think he had a point, she admitted to herself.

At Stephanie's suggestion, they walked down towards the village and then turned northwards where the church still seemed to beckon. 'This is where it all started, only three days ago,' said the girl solemnly. 'A lot's happened since then.'

Thea smiled uncertainly. 'Has it been too much for you? Gladwin thinks I was wrong to bring you into all this. It's all very messy, let's face it.'

'I don't mind really. I did ask if I could come, after all. Nobody's going to hurt me, are they? They hardly even notice me most of the time.'

'I'm trying to persuade myself that it's good for you. Seeing the real world, and all that. I suppose I think it's a healthy alternative to looking at a screen all day.'

'I've still been looking at a screen quite a lot.'

'Granted. But at least it's been with a purpose. More productive than playing games or calling your friends rude names.'

'We don't do that. But it does get silly sometimes. And I charged my phone, look.' She produced the device with an air of triumph. 'You never know when you might need it.'

'I'd like to disagree, but I suppose after what's been happening this week, that would be misguided.'

'It would,' said the girl firmly.

'This road noise is worse than ever,' Thea noticed. 'It can't be good for people to live with it all the time.'

'Rush hour,' said Stephanie. 'It's twenty past five.'

'Is it? Gosh. Where do you want to go from here?'

'Let's go all the way to the road, and stand under it again. I liked that. Pity we haven't got Hepzie – she could run free along here.'

'Dad'll take her out, I expect.' Thea was trying not to enjoy the sense of irresponsibility that came with the absence of the dog. There was no need to keep a perpetual eye out for her, monitoring and anticipating any deviations that might lead into danger or disapproval. The spaniel had a tendency to run into people's houses if the door was open, or to start digging in private gardens if she got the scent of a mouse. 'Besides – she might go and sniff out another dead person, and that's the last thing we need.'

Stephanie laughed and did a little skip. She too was evidently experiencing a sudden onset of liberation. Something about the constant traffic noise gave everything a heightened reality. The need to slightly raise your voice, the sense of rush and forward momentum going on above you, and the unseen mysteries at ground level that totally escaped the notice of the drivers – it all created a strange atmosphere.

They reached the road itself and Stephanie ran all the way from the path to the far bank at the end of the flyover and then back again. Looking up, they again admired the fresh clean materials on the underside of the highway that had yet to be weathered and colonised by wildlife. The white supports had a few streaks on them, but still stood out against the browns and greens of the natural surroundings. Directly overhead was the road's invisible underbelly, an incongruous golden colour. The low sun sent deep shadows across the little field beyond.

'It's even better this time,' said Stephanie. 'I love it. Imagine making something like this! It's got to be so *strong*.'

'And the noise gets much quieter when you're right under it.'

They stayed for ten minutes, walking around the huge supports, speculating on building methods and the usefulness of bridges of every sort. 'Maybe I'll be an engineer when I grow up and not an undertaker, after all,' said Stephanie.

'My great-grandfather was an engineer. He made a lot of money inventing things.'

'What sort of things?'

'Um – some sort of furnace, I think. I've never taken much interest, to be honest. He was very rich when he died.'

'Who got the money?'

'His three sons had to share it between them, and my granddad was very careless with his, and lost nearly all of it. My mother never forgave him.'

But Stephanie had stopped listening and was turning back the way they'd come. 'I'm hungry,' she said.

'And I'm supposed to be phoning Vanessa, in case she wants to see me this evening.'

'We could meet her in a pub, then, and have some supper.'

'There's still some food in the annex to be eaten up, even after you sent the surplus back with Dad. I hate to say it, but I don't think she's going to want you there.'

'Oh.' Stephanie stopped walking and tapped her foot on the ground for a moment.

'What? Is that a problem?'

'A bit. It'll be dark. What about Emmy and Nick? I'm sure

you're supposed to be there in case one of them gets worse.'

'I might be able to leave it until tomorrow morning, maybe – unless you don't want to be left then either. Or she might agree to come to us this evening. You can go to bed while we talk.'

Stephanie started walking again, her gaze on the ground ahead. Thea waited for a reply, but instead, in a brief lull in the traffic noise, they both heard a cough. It was a single sharp note, quite loud. Thea and Stephanie looked at each other, eyebrows raised. There was nobody anywhere in sight, nor any buildings close by. 'Hello?' called Thea.

Stephanie waved a hand to silence her, whether to facilitate better listening or to stop being embarrassing was uncertain. But Thea saw no reason to comply. 'Somebody's hiding up there,' she concluded. 'Behind these trees.'

Stephanie began to scramble up the slope, which had a flimsy wire fence at the top. Thea experienced a powerful stab of déjà vu. 'Stop!' she hissed. 'Come back! There's that old summer house or whatever it is up there, look. We saw it before when we came down here. It's just like Alice's shed.'

'So what? We're not going to find another body, are we? Bodies don't cough.'

'No, but . . .' Seeing that the girl had no intention of coming down, Thea had little choice but to join her. Hauling herself up with the aid of sturdy bushes, she drew level with Stephanie and together they crested the slope. Ten yards to their right was the wooden summer house she remembered from their walk on Monday. 'Hello!' she called again. 'Is anybody there?'

It was probably the owner of the big garden they could

now see more clearly, in the corner of which stood the small building that was little more than a shed. It had windows and a pitched roof but seemed quite neglected. It was likely that the person who coughed would take exception to being accosted on his or her own property. But Thea was not persuaded by her own arguments. From the first she had been in the grip of a wild idea.

'I'll go over and look,' said Stephanie.

'No need,' came a female voice from the other side of the building. 'I've had enough of this game, anyway. It's terribly lonely, for a start.'

'I'm guessing you must be Ginny Chambers,' said Thea.

'And you'd be guessing right,' said the girl, coming into view.

Chapter Eighteen

'We've been looking for you,' said Stephanie in her usual direct manner. 'Were you here all along?'

Thea was desperately trying to think. 'No, you can't have been,' she answered for Ginny. 'You'd never have survived that long.' She examined the girl's appearance for signs of injury or sickness. The face was grubby, the hair lank, but nothing shouted for urgent attention.

'Who *are* you?' Ginny demanded. 'How do you know who I am?'

'Come down here and we can talk properly.'

'Let me get my stuff, then. Have you got a car? Can you take me somewhere I can lie down?'

'No, actually. We walked from the Weavers' place.'

Ginny froze. 'I'm not going back *there*, whatever you say.'

'We never said anything like that. Calm down.'

'We can go and sit in the church,' said Stephanie as if

this was the most obvious thing in the world.

So they did. It was chilly, but empty. Ginny unself-consciously stretched out on one of the pews using a kneeler as a pillow. 'Not as good as a bed, but better than that summer house floor. There were *things* running all over me. I had to stay sitting up all the time, in case they got on my face.'

Stephanie leant towards her. 'What things? Spiders? Ants? Centipedes?'

'All of them, as far as I know. It was horrible, and I didn't dare put the torch on in case somebody saw.'

'How many nights were you there?' asked Thea.

'Three. Monday, Tuesday, Wednesday. Today *is* Thursday, isn't it?'

'Where were you before that?'

'In Alice's house.'

Thea and Stephanie looked at each other. 'What? The shed, you mean?'

'No! Her proper house. She took me there last week, when I left Emmy and Nick's. But we couldn't stay because she promised the guest – or whatever she calls them – he could have it all to himself. She's got it on Airbnb, you see. Most people don't like it if the owner's there, so she has to go away. It's only a small house, with one bathroom, you see. *Do* you see?'

Thea shrugged. 'Sort of.'

'You still haven't told me who you are.'

'I knew Emmy a few years ago in Chedworth. She was called Millie then. It's not the only thing that's different now. But we were thrown together then, and she thought I could help—'

Ginny interrupted. 'What's your *name*?'

Thea introduced herself and Stephanie and made no further attempt to give an account of her presence in Baunton. 'We live in Broad Campden,' she said.

'Never heard of it,' said Ginny. She was not looking at them as she spoke, but gazed straight up into the church roof. 'I can see a spider,' she said with a sigh. 'They're everywhere. I never noticed that before.'

'Tell us more about Alice,' said Thea, with a warning glance at Stephanie. There was a definite implication that Ginny did not know the woman was dead.

'She has let me down very badly. The deal was for only two nights living rough, and then we'd meet up and compare notes. But she didn't show yesterday, and I was worried somebody would tell Emmy if they saw me, so I stayed here another whole day and night – and all of today. It was horrible. There's nothing to do without my phone. Most of the time it was even too dark to read a book.'

'You brought a book?' queried Stephanie in disbelief.

'Why not? They don't need batteries, and it's a very good story. But you have to have enough light.'

'Mm,' said Stephanie, lost for words.

Thea spent the next thirty seconds scrutinising their discovery. Ginny Chambers was of medium height and slightly chubby. Her hair and face were familiar from the photos Emmy had shown her, but she seemed older. Her clothes were crumpled, and she carried a well-stuffed rucksack. 'What did you eat and drink?' she asked.

'I took that with me. It's all gone now. Sandwiches, biscuits, apples, bottles of water. Cheese, crisps. That wasn't a problem, except I ate it too quickly because I was so bored. I am quite hungry now, actually.'

'So am I,' agreed Stephanie. 'We were going back to eat when we heard you.'

'But what did you think you were doing?' Thea burst out. 'It's crazy. Why cause such worry to poor Emmy? It's an awful thing to do.'

Ginny gave a sound like an amused groan. 'Oh, yes – poor old Emmy! Everybody always puts her first, don't they? Just because she's having a baby. Any fool can do that, let's face it.' Stephanie giggled and Ginny went on, 'It's not crazy, though. It's all part of the same thing as we've been doing at the farm. Using the land as it was intended. Ask Joe – do you know Joe? He's got all the right ideas. Nick's not bad, but he doesn't stick to it properly and he gets all obsessed about things. That *dog*, for a start.'

'It bit him today. Just a little while ago,' Stephanie informed her. 'Quite badly, actually.'

'I knew that would happen. The thing's a brainless monster. It caught a hare a few weeks ago – tore it to bits.'

'Really? I thought hares could outrun anything but a greyhound,' said Thea.

'He caught it unawares, I suppose. Hares are having a tough time, with the kites taking their babies. I hate kites now!'

'So you're on Mr Double-Barrelled's side, then?' said Stephanie.

'Who?'

'Robinson-Finch. You call him "Robbers" apparently.

There's a feud going on, mostly about the kites, as far as we can work out. Or thistles. And somebody said something about bracken as well.' Thea shook her head impatiently. 'The police think it might be relevant, the way they're such antagonists.'

'Police? Relevant to what? What are you talking about?'

'Ah.' Thea grimaced. 'I wasn't sure we ought to tell you that part. There's been a lot going on down in the village this week. You must have missed it. Haven't you got a phone that keeps you up with news and stuff?'

'I left it in Alice's house. She said people could track me if I had it with me.'

'So they tracked her instead?' asked Thea sharply.

'No,' said Ginny with the exaggerated patience of a young person speaking to an elder. 'Because she kept it switched off and she didn't carry it round with her anyway.'

'You've been less than half a mile away,' Stephanie pointed out. 'Surely you must have known something was going on? The police have been crawling all over the village. Why didn't they find you?' She gave Ginny a similar searching look to the ones Thea had been throwing.

'Were they looking for me especially? Or what?'

Again, Thea gave Stephanie a warning look, which was received with an unspoken *Yes, yes, I know.* 'But you have been deliberately hiding, haven't you?' the girl accused.

'Not the way you think. It was part of the game, not to be spotted. Alice was doing it the same, in her shed.

She was even nearer houses than me. And my summer house is bigger than hers, with better windows. It was just a *game*, don't you see? You'd need to know Alice to understand. She had times when she did that sort of thing. We weren't doing any harm. Just seeing what it would be like not to have electric or water or anything. It was a great idea. But she spoilt it by not showing up when she said.'

'She couldn't,' said Stephanie.

'Why not?'

'Er – let's take this slowly, okay?' Thea felt herself entering deep water and could see no way of avoiding it. 'The police were told you were missing, more than a week ago now. Emmy and Nick reported it almost as soon as you disappeared. But seeing you were an adult and there was no sign of foul play, there was little or no action taken. So then Emmy asked me to come and help find you.'

'And me,' said Stephanie.

'Yes. But it was never going to work. It still feels as if they wanted me for some other purpose that I don't understand. We've not been here very long – only since yesterday. But I've met Robinson-Finch, and Abigail and Joe. And Vanessa.'

Ginny was following this with scant patience. 'Get to the point,' she urged. 'What did you think of Abby?'

'That isn't the point you want me to get to,' said Thea with a sigh. 'The thing is, I went out on Tuesday to look round the village, and found Alice in that shed. Right next to Abby's house. Somebody had just killed your friend Alice with a knife,' she finished flatly.

'Oh my God!' said Ginny, her hand to her mouth while she still lay flat on the pew. 'That can't be true. Not *dead*?'

'Sorry,' said Thea. 'There's no painless way of telling you. That's why there's been police everywhere.'

Ginny said nothing for a whole long minute. Her face was white, her jaw clenched. 'Somebody killed her? But why?'

Thea merely spread her hands helplessly. Ginny sat up slowly and looked at Stephanie. 'That's why she couldn't come yesterday, then. Sorry – that sounds stupid, doesn't it? I'm not thinking straight.'

'That's okay,' said the younger girl kindly. 'And yes, you're right. Now do you see what we've been talking about?'

Ginny was still trying to order her shocked brain into some kind of rational thought. 'It must have been someone in the village, I suppose. Robbers, most likely. Has he been arrested?'

Thea shook her head. 'Nobody has. Some people think you must have done it, actually.'

'Oh,' said Ginny, with a bitter smile. 'Well, it wasn't me. Poor old Alice. What a ghastly thing. She was rather mad, you know.' She looked down at the floor, her eyes flickering rapidly. 'Why would anybody kill her, though? We all liked her, even if she was peculiar. She was fun as well. Full of ideas and jokes and stories about her life. I took to her the first time I saw her, when she came to help with the first course I was here for. Although Emmy and Nick tried to keep her out of sight of the punters.' She laughed sarcastically. 'Those courses! They're bedlam, you know. There's never enough food, and somebody always gets stung or bitten and they *argue* all the time. Nick always tries to keep off climate change – he says it's of "peripheral significance" compared to biodiversity and cultivation of trees and letting wild things live their natural lives. Endless debates about red kites. That sort of thing, all muddled up together. There's always somebody who connects oil with plastic and that leads to carbon dioxide and the greenhouse effect and whoever it is tries to persuade him he's got it all wrong.'

Thea knew enough to understand that the prattle was a vital part of the process of absorbing the shocking news. Drew had described numerous instances arising from his funeral work.

'But what did Alice think about all that?' asked Stephanie.

'She laughed. Basically, she thought it was all far too complicated for any proper conclusion, and that whatever humans did to try and put it all right was doomed to fail. Reintroducing the kites was just one daft thing among many.' She frowned. 'Nobody would kill her for saying that, would they?'

'What other reasons could there be?'

'Let's not get into it now. I really am starving, which probably seems heartless, but I can't help it. If I stay here, do you think you could get me some food?'

'I might, but where are you going to sleep tonight?'

'Here, I suppose. I can't possibly go to the farm – it'd be too embarrassing. Nick can get very overbearing sometimes. And he talks too much about my mother. I don't care about her in the slightest. She's never been much use, quite honestly. But the really boring thing about Nick is that he tries to plan my whole life for me. That poor baby – it's never going to escape from his control. And they'll go on about Alice now, as well. I don't think I could cope with that.'

'That doesn't sound like enough reason to sleep in a cold church – if you're only worried that he'll talk about things you find boring or difficult.'

'You don't understand,' Ginny sighed. 'Anyway, this isn't bad. A lot better than a cold summer house, believe me. It's really rather comfortable, actually.' She wriggled herself down onto the pew again and folded her arms across her chest. 'Do I look like somebody on a tomb?'

The resilience of the young, thought Thea, with a pang that mixed disapproval with envy.

'It sounds to me as if you're scared of the Weavers,' blurted Stephanie. 'And I don't see why you should be. They've been so worried about you. They're desperate to know you're alive. Some people think whoever killed Alice killed you as well.'

'I'm not *scared* of them, exactly. But they've got no idea what it's like being there with them. It was bad of me, I know, just sloping off, but they'd have locked me in my room if I'd said anything.'

'We've got to stop all this talking and find some food,' said Stephanie, urgently. 'I'm starving as well. Shall I stay here with Ginny while you go and get something?' *To keep an eye on her*, she added silently. Thea understood perfectly.

'If you like. The quickest thing would be if I sneak back to the annex and load up everything that's there.

It won't be much. What about water?'

'Yes please,' said Ginny. 'I ran out ages ago.'

'You can die of dehydration, you know,' said Thea sternly. 'It's important to keep drinking.'

'Yes, Mum,' sighed Ginny sarcastically. 'Everybody seems to be wanting me dead. Have you noticed that?'

'Nobody wants you dead,' said Thea. 'That's the whole point.'

'Poor Alice. It's still only just dawning on me. How did you say they did it? Was it quick?'

'I'm going.' Thea was at the door of the church. 'I'll be fifteen minutes – or more if I walk back. If I start the car, Emmy or Nick might hear me. More like half an hour, I suppose. Stay here and keep quiet.'

'Good luck!' said Stephanie, as if her stepmother was going on a trek across the Sahara.

Thea laughed. 'I just hope Joshua's not on the loose.'

Walking back to the farm took just over ten minutes and felt very strange. The sun had almost set and there was an eerie silence for the last few minutes, the traffic noise muffled by a row of trees. She was torn between a sense of urgency and a reluctance to betray Emmy by colluding with Ginny. The responsible adult thing to do would be to go straight to the farmhouse and report her discovery. She could not properly identify just what was stopping her. Nothing terrible would befall the girl if her aunt and uncle were told she was alive and well, but wanted to stay away from the farm. But that too would be a betrayal, of course. Ginny trusted her not to tell. And the Weavers would hardly settle for such minimal news, despite the distractions of their afternoon experiences.

All of which slowed her progress. More and more questions forced themselves on her attention. What was she actually *doing* here, anyway? Drew and Timmy – not to mention Hepzie – were being shamefully neglected. Drew had made his feelings perfectly clear: the time for amateur detecting, house-sitting, interfering, was over, as he saw it. In the early years of her widowhood, it had made sense and been a useful diversion. She had the wits, time and personality to be of genuine help to the police. But now was different. Now she should turn her talents to something closer to home. She knew he was right.

There had been a time, indeed, when Drew himself had been closely involved in murder investigations. He had wanted to put things right, to expose the truth. His first wife had been fatally injured after witnessing a murder. His natural sense of justice had motivated him in a number of adventures. All of which meant he understood Thea's own commitment to helping the forces of the law – and which also meant that his arguments carried considerable heft when he urged her to give it all up.

This case, with its jumbled implications and odd cast of characters, was proving to be deeply unsatisfying. Whoever killed Alice, it was from motives that Thea suspected she would condemn wholeheartedly. The link with Ginny had now been made, and could be passed to Gladwin. Emmy and Nick would have to be told about the latest development before long, even if Thea could bring herself to leave the girl in the church all night – which she rather doubted.

In the annex, her phone was on the table where it had been left after the ambulance and police had departed. Thea picked it up with a vague sense that she ought to keep it with her. Idly she turned it on and saw that there was a text message waiting for her. Its first words were displayed, and she quickly accessed the rest of it.

'The detective woman gave me your number. Are you free this evening for a chat? I really would appreciate it. Vanessa Ferguson.'

'*Oh!*' muttered Thea impatiently. 'Now what am I supposed to do?' The sudden solution to the mystery of what had happened to Ginny Chambers was only half the story, after all. Nothing the girl had said led to any greater understanding of who had murdered Alice, and Gladwin for one would expect Thea to see the business through to the end. There would be time to do it all before bed, if she got herself organised. She texted back, 'I think so, but give me an hour before arranging anything. I'll phone you.' She remembered that she had fully intended to go and see Vanessa that evening anyway. Now that began to feel more like a mildly irritating duty than anything essential. Ginny's situation very much took priority.

She filled a bag with everything edible she could find and threw it into the car. Something told her she might be glad of a vehicle before the evening was finished. If the Weavers heard the engine, they could wait a while for an explanation.

'That was quick,' said Stephanie, when she got back to the church. 'Eighteen minutes. We timed you.'

'I came in the car. I thought it might be useful.'

Ginny grabbed the bottle of water and drained it. 'That's better,' she sighed. 'I can feel my veins taking it up.'

Stephanie giggled. 'You can't,' she accused.

'Honestly – my head was hurting and now it already feels better. Brains need lots of water, you know.'

'Brains or veins?'

'Both. Arteries, to be precise,' Thea informed them. 'Now, listen. We can't stay here much longer. I don't think I can let Ginny stay, either. It's irresponsible. Everything's coming to a head – I can feel it. We really should all stick together.'

'You sound like the Famous Five,' said Ginny.

'I'm serious. But first I have questions.'

'Fire away,' Ginny invited.

'Why did you take that notebook? Emmy and Nick are distraught about it. They say it's crucial to the business, and also very confidential. Can I have it and take it back to them – or leave it in the annex, at least? I don't really want to talk to them again until tomorrow if I can help it – which I probably won't be able to, when it comes to it.'

Ginny's blank stare was disconcerting. 'What notebook? I didn't take anything. Who says I did?'

'You must have done. They both said it. It sounded as if that was about the most worrying part of you going missing.'

'It's a trick. They're lying to you. I *promise* you I didn't take it – whatever it is.'

'They said it belonged to your grandmother, and had all sorts of details in it that mattered enormously. Nick seemed to think you were intent on sabotaging the farm and the courses and all that.'

'Bloody Uncle Nick,' Ginny snapped. 'He's put it somewhere safe and then forgotten where, and decided it must all be my fault. He can get really paranoid sometimes, you know.'

'The way you talk about him makes him seem very different from how he's been with us,' said Stephanie through a mouthful of bread and ham.

'Emmy saved him, you know,' said Ginny, also with food in her mouth. 'The whole place was out of control for years before she married him. Weeds everywhere, straggly hedges, complaints from all sides. My gran lived with him, and they struggled with it after Grandpa died, but there was hardly any money and they argued all the time. My mother and I went there when I was about ten, and it was all scruffy and muddy then, although things were still more or less working. They had a lot of cows and milked twice a day. I loved drinking it from the tank – all creamy and delicious. Grandpa had died about a year before that. Uncle Nick liked me and told me the place would be my inheritance if he never had children – I'm an only child and there weren't any cousins, so I suppose he was right about that. It didn't mean much to me – just felt stupidly old-fashioned to talk about inheriting anything. Still does, really.'

'So then Emmy turned up and put it all right, overnight?' Thea was sceptical.

'It wasn't so difficult, once the whole rewilding thing hit them. All they had to do was sell all the cows, organise the courses, paint the house, fix up the annex, and bingo!'

'What happened about your gran? Where did she go?'

'Oh, that was sad. She was meant to live in the annex permanently. She and Emmy got on quite well most of the time. But then she went to stay with an old friend in Liverpool while the building work was done and she got sick when she was there so she stayed. She was actually getting better until she ran her car into a stone wall and nearly killed herself. Now she's in a coma, poor thing. The friend is absolutely devoted to her, luckily.'

'They hardly ever mention her,' mused Thea. 'You'd think they'd be more upset.'

'The baby changed everything, I think. And they're much too busy to go up to see her – though Nick went up for a day or two when she had to go into hospital. The friend does Zoom every little while, and updates them. They know she's never going to get better, so they've moved on already.'

'They'll be sorry when she dies,' said Stephanie, with the voice of experience. 'I know about these things, because my dad's an undertaker.'

'Yuk!' said Ginny, which did nothing to endear her to either of her listeners.

The food was soon consumed and outside the light was fading. Thea had exhausted all the questions she could think of to ask Ginny and Stephanie was restless. 'What now?' she asked – twice.

Thea was very much aware of her promise to Vanessa and her sense of obligation to Gladwin. She also needed to process the events of the past few hours without interruption. Amongst all that were her uncomfortable thoughts about Drew and their future.

And she had two girls in her care whose safety might well depend on what she chose to do.

'I don't know,' she said. 'I seem to need to go in about three directions at once.'

'Leave me. I'll be fine,' insisted Ginny. 'I'll make a little camp for myself, and I bet I'll sleep for about ten hours. It's lovely and quiet in here. I can go for a wee behind one of the graves when it gets dark. Nobody's going to see me.'

'There are houses just across the road,' worried Thea. Then she remembered the reports of strange happenings in this very churchyard and her anxiety increased. 'No,' she concluded with a heavy heart. 'I just can't do it. I know you're an adult of sound mind and all that. But if anything happened and it came out that I knew you were here, I'd never hear the end of it.'

'That sounds like a "What if . . ." to me,' said Stephanie. 'How about if I stay here as well and you go and talk to Vanessa, if it's that important?'

Thea shook her head. 'That's almost worse. You'll get talking and shining lights and somebody's sure to find you. And on top of everything else, I'm meant to be keeping an eye on Emmy and Nick.'

'We found Ginny,' said Stephanie, slowly and loudly. 'They owe us for that. There's a limit to what else we can be expected to do. You want to solve the murder – I can see that. I do too, sort of. But how's Vanessa going to help with that? Hasn't she told you all the important stuff already?'

'How do I know? If she wants to talk to me, that

implies that she has more to say. Besides,' she added wretchedly, 'I liked her. I don't want to let her down.'

They were sitting on a pew near the front of the church, in semi-darkness. Suddenly there was the sound of the church door opening and the lights suddenly went on. 'What's going on here, then?' came a male voice.

Chapter Nineteen

The three women turned as one, expecting to see a vicar or church caretaker. Ginny was the first to realise her mistake. 'Joe!' she cried. 'It's Joe. Of all people.' She got up from her pew and ran to him. 'How on earth did you find us?'

'Saw the car,' he said, looking at Thea.

Her mind was working fast. 'That doesn't explain anything,' she protested. 'What were you doing down here? It doesn't go anywhere, and it's dark.'

'Not important,' he said, with an arm around Ginny's shoulders. 'Am I glad to see you looking so bonny,' he told her. She grinned up at him. 'I actually did think you might be dead – you know that?'

'They found me just now. They've been very kind – got me some food and everything. But I'm not going back to the farm.' She gave him a fierce look.

'Come back with me, then. Sunny's going to be thrilled to see you. It's only forty minutes away. I'd have gone back sooner but I haven't got enough diesel and I'm out of cash.'

Ginny grinned at Thea and Stephanie. 'He doesn't use cards, you see. Strictly cash. Except that half the time he hasn't got any.'

'So you have to pay?' said Thea.

'Right. Seems fair, don't you think?'

Joe laughed. 'Looks like a win-win to me. We can give you a bed and settle all the loose ends in the morning.'

Thea found herself still in 'What if . . . ?' mode. What if this man was in fact a killer, and had his own sinister reasons for disposing of Ginny? What if he seduced her in the back of his camper van, or whatever he was driving? What if they *both* disappeared, never to be seen again? 'Er – are you sure that's a good idea?' was all she could think to say.

He gave her an appraising look. 'Don't you trust me?'

'Well . . . most people wouldn't . . .' she faltered.

'Thea!' Stephanie was staring at her. 'He's fine. What's wrong with you?'

'Ginny?' Thea appealed to the girl. 'What do you want to do?'

'I'll go with him,' came the ready answer. 'He's been a good mate to me. Stuck up for me a few times when Uncle Nick was being a pain. It's a miracle he's shown up just at the right moment.'

'Maybe a bit *too* miraculous,' Thea muttered.

All three looked at her with exasperation. 'If you must know, I was having one last search for Ginny before going home,' said Joe.

'Thinking you might find my dead body,' Ginny put in.

'Something like that. I remembered that day when Nick was having a go at you, and you stormed off – down in this direction, wasn't it? I ran after you, and we walked up and down this path for about an hour while you cooled down. You went on about him controlling your life and it being stupid to come here, and what the hell were you going to do with your life. Remember? All that angst just because he said you had a lot to learn and if it hadn't been for you, he'd have sold up five years ago.'

'He was vile that day. Even Emmy thought so.'

'He was. But the trouble is, I think he genuinely had your best interests at heart. He was really upset later on. But that's not the point. I remember how much you liked it down here, by the ghastly road. You got all philosophical and whimsical about two worlds clashing. I can't remember much of it now. It made me think maybe you'd come here again – and I was right! Have you been here all along?'

'Only since Monday. I'll tell you in the car. Can we go?'

'It's the camper, not the car, and yes, we can go. I've left it half a mile away, in a gateway. I take it you can walk all right? No physical damage?'

Ginny laughed and waggled all her limbs. 'Fit as a flea,' she said. 'Which reminds me – I think I might have a few fleas from that shed. I'll need a very hot bath, if that's allowed.'

And then they were gone, leaving Thea and Stephanie sitting in the car wondering what to do next. 'We have to tell Emmy we've found Ginny,' said Stephanie. 'We just *have* to.'

276

'I know. Just give me a minute. I'm still scared that Joe isn't what he seems. I mean, what if—'

'Don't start that again. Ginny *wanted* to go with him. He was the answer to the problem of what she was going to do. It was providential. As if he was sent by God.'

'An unlikely angel,' Thea chuckled. 'But he does seem a bit other-worldly, I admit. He seems to understand Ginny pretty well, anyway. I just don't trust my own judgement when it comes to people's characters.'

'Your judgement's fine,' said Stephanie loyally. 'So . . . ?'

'Don't hassle me. I'm thinking. I want to go and talk to Vanessa. I suppose you'll have to come with me. But I'm not happy about doing that.'

'Just get on with it!' Stephanie almost shouted. 'It's stupid just sitting here. I want to go back to the farm and tell Emmy about Ginny. I can stay there while you go, if that's what you want to do. I can't see why it can't wait until morning. It'll be midnight at this rate.'

Thea gave a low moan. 'You're right. I'm letting the woman bully me. She probably does that a lot. I don't know why I give in to women so much more than men. Must be something to do with my mother, I suppose.'

'Women are much more difficult to resist. It's the same at school. The women teachers are much tougher than the men.'

'Gladwin. Emmy. And now Vanessa.'

'Not to mention Caz, and even Ginny,' Stephanie finished for her. 'And maybe Alice was a strong character as well. Poor old Robbers, and Joe and Nick probably never got much of a say in anything, even if they look as if they're in charge.'

'We can only guess,' said Thea, feeling tired and rather hopeless. 'I take the point. Let me phone Vanessa and tell her we've had enough for one day. Thanks, Steph. You've put me straight yet again. Without you, I'd have gone dashing off to Duntisbourne Abbots without even thinking about whether it was a good idea.'

'Good,' smiled the girl. 'Just so long as nobody murders her in the night.'

Thea shuddered. 'If that happens, it'll be all your fault.'

'Pooh,' shrugged Stephanie, but there was a worried look in her eye.

There was one light on in the Weavers' house when they got back. Thea went to the side door and knocked, Stephanie at her shoulder. Nick came to open it within seconds. 'Where on earth have you been?' he demanded. 'We've been worried sick.'

'We've been doing what you asked us to do,' said Thea. 'Can we come in? How's your leg? I thought you were going to bed.'

'It's throbbing, but I can walk all right. Emmy's gone to bed. She's got a headache. I wanted to sit down here with a coffee and have a think.'

'Oh.' Thea realised that it was Emmy she wanted to talk to. Nick on his own was much less satisfactory. 'That's a shame. She's going to want to hear our news.'

'What news?' He stood tall, the bandaged leg thrust forward, the pyjama bottoms incongruously mismatched with the shirt and jacket on his top half. 'I don't think I can take very much more today, if it's all the same to you. I've got to decide what to do about Joshua.' Pain flicked across his face, and Thea understood that the dog was actually of great sentimental value to his owner. 'Emmy says we'll never be able to trust him with the baby.'

'No,' said Thea sadly.

'We found Ginny!' Stephanie burst out, unable to keep it back another moment. 'She's perfectly all right. We *found* her, just like you asked us to.'

'What? Where?' He peered behind her, as if assuming his niece was hovering somewhere near the door. 'Is she here?'

Thea put a hand on Stephanie's arm, silencing her. 'Let me,' she said softly. Then she addressed the man: 'She's somewhere safe for the night. There's no great mystery about it, really. She needed a bath and a good long sleep. It'll all be explained in the morning. We're both pretty tired as well. So, if you and Emmy are all right, I think we should all have a very early night, and leave it till tomorrow.'

'No! I have to know now – where has she been? What did she tell you? Why did she go off like that?'

'Sorry, Nick. If we start on all that now, we'll be here for hours. There's nothing that won't wait. Nobody's going anywhere. We'll all lock our doors and go to sleep.' She looked round. 'Where's Joshua? He can guard you for the night, if you're worried something might happen.'

'Sleep!' he muttered angrily. 'You're joking. I've shut the dog outside. He's been barking, though, so I'll have to let him in. He sleeps in here usually.' He rubbed his head. 'It's all gone mad. I still can't believe he bit me like that.'

Thea took a step backwards, drawing Stephanie with her. All three of them had quite obviously had enough. 'Didn't those ambulance people tell you to take aspirin or something? That should knock you out. You've had a shock – a trauma, even – I bet you'll crash out for ten hours once you lie down.'

'Ginny's okay? Really? Well, that's a relief. Bloody girl, causing all that worry.' He looked into Thea's face. 'What did she say to you?'

'Tomorrow,' said Thea again, and pushed Stephanie ahead of her out of the door.

Chapter Twenty

Friday was wet, as predicted, but Thea and Stephanie in their small, shared bedroom were awake before seven. 'Well, we survived the night,' said Thea, finding her increasingly dark mood had not evaporated in the least. 'And today we go home, whatever happens. That's a promise.'

'I don't mind if we stay,' said Stephanie.

'Do you *want* to?'

'I don't know. I suppose not. I feel bad about Joshua, mostly. But I can't do anything about that, can I? We're not going to adopt him, are we?'

'Don't even entertain that as the most wild fantasy that ever happened,' said Thea, grabbing for words strong enough to express her reaction. 'Not in your craziest dreams.'

'I wasn't. I don't really like him much. But it isn't his fault, is it?'

'No. It was completely down to Nick. The bite served him right. But Joshua's going to take all the flak.'

Stephanie sighed. 'It's not fair.'

'It really isn't,' Thea agreed. 'And we really are not staying. We'll go and talk to the Weavers as soon as we think they're up, and then I'll phone Vanessa and see if she still wants me, and then I'll phone Gladwin and tell her about Ginny, and then . . .'

'Phone Dad. Why didn't you call Vanessa last night? You said you promised.'

'I forgot,' Thea admitted. 'I was too tired to think straight by about half past eight. Why do I have to phone Dad?'

'Because he'll want you to. He doesn't know what's happening. But it's not finished, is it?' Stephanie realised. 'I thought it was when we found Ginny, but nothing's been explained. If anything, it's more confusing than ever. What about that notebook? Was Nick telling lies? Why's Ginny so scared of seeing him again?'

'And who killed Alice?' Thea finished. 'Which of these people is a murderer? Because I'm pretty sure one of them is.'

'It might even be Vanessa,' said Stephanie in a hollow voice, only half serious.

'It wasn't her because she was in London. For which I am truly grateful.'

Stephanie acknowledged the reference with a little laugh. 'There's no breakfast, I suppose?'

'Milk. Three slices of bread and a pot of honey. We won't starve.'

'You always say that.'

282

'Well it's true.'

'What time can we start phoning people?'

'Eight? I don't really know.'

But the question proved academic, because at twenty-five past seven, Nick came banging on their door, followed ten minutes later by a call from Gladwin, and from there the morning was consumed in a whirlwind of activity.

'So – will you talk to us now?' Nick demanded. 'Emmy can't wait any longer. She's beside herself. Come over to the house, will you?'

Thea was holding a mug of coffee and for an instant was tempted to throw it at him. 'Let me get my phone, then,' she said. 'You're not the only person who wants to talk to me.'

Stephanie went with them without any discussion, although Thea wished she'd had the sense to warn the girl not to say too much. It might not be too difficult to resist Nick's loud demands, but it would be far harder to fob his wife off with half-truths and evasions.

They gathered in the kitchen, the huge dog in his customary place on the rug at the end of the room. Emmy saw the visitors' glances and reassured them. 'All is forgiven – or nearly,' she said. 'We couldn't leave him out all night, and he's forgotten all about it now. Poor boy – he's not very bright, you know.'

Thea scrutinised the pregnant woman for signs that she was 'beside herself' as Nick had claimed. Emmy was pale, with shadows under her eyes, but she was sitting up straight and seemed to be quite composed. 'Did you sleep?' Thea asked.

'Not much. Bizarrely, I was mostly thinking about Joshua. Now Nick tells me you've found Ginny and she's all right, and he's desperate to know where she's been and what she told you.'

'He said *you* were desperate,' said Stephanie.

'We both are,' said Emmy. 'Obviously.'

'It's all rather silly,' Thea began with an effort to convey to Stephanie that the talking should be left to her. 'She and Alice had this sort of game going on, where they both slept out all night in ramshackle sheds. It seems there's a ready supply of them around here. We were walking back from where the road goes overhead, and heard her coughing. She was quite pleased to be found, as it turned out. She'd been waiting for Alice to come, and felt she had to stay where she was until that happened.'

'So where is she now?' It was Emmy speaking, while Nick stood close to her, intently absorbing every word.

'Somewhere safe,' said Thea awkwardly. 'I don't really understand it, but I think she'd rather I didn't say exactly where. I'm sure she'll contact you today and tell you the whole thing herself.'

'She didn't know about Alice?' said Nick slowly.

'No. She was shocked when we told her. They were friends, by the sound of it. Unlikely as it might seem.'

'It's right,' said Emmy. 'I saw them fooling about a few times. Alice liked taking photos with Ginny's phone, and they joked about the clients and their weird beliefs.' She sighed. 'It was nice to watch them – Ginny seemed to make Alice happy.'

'Ginny's phone,' Nick repeated, with a half-dazed

expression. 'Didn't Alice have a phone of her own?'

Emmy gave him an impatient look. '*I* don't know. Why does it matter?'

He put his hands up. 'It doesn't. I'm just trying to keep up, that's all. I assume she's had it with her all along?'

'Did she show you the notebook?' Emmy asked suddenly. 'Have you got it off her?'

Thea looked again at Stephanie, and gave a tiny shake of her head. 'The subject didn't arise,' she lied. 'We were too busy getting her some food and somewhere to sleep.'

The question about Ginny's phone hung in the air, until Emmy said, 'Well, we can ask her today. If she doesn't phone by about nine, we can call her. It's great that she's safe, and a miracle that it was you that found her. I can't tell you how grateful we are.'

'That's right,' said Nick, much less convincingly. 'Although I don't get why she's still hiding away from us. We're her *family* after all.'

'I'm sure it was just for the night—' Thea was interrupted by her phone ringing. 'Oh, it's Gladwin already. I can tell her we've found Ginny. It'll be one less thing for her to worry about.'

Nick made an odd jerk forward, as if intending to snatch Thea's phone, but he controlled himself before doing anything of the sort. Thea ignored him and turned towards the door, more from politeness than with any intention of concealing the conversation, but then remembered that it was raining outside. Emmy picked up on this and whispered, 'Take it into the living room if you like.' Which Thea did, leaving Stephanie in the kitchen.

'Did you see Vanessa?' Gladwin started. 'Did she tell you anything helpful?'

'I never got there,' said Thea, and proceeded to give a report of the previous evening, which was less succinct than was ideal.

Gladwin interrupted after a few sentences. 'You let her go off with the Joe person? How could you?'

'It was her choice. She's an adult. He's not at all threatening. I've told the Weavers.'

'About Joe?'

'No, actually, because Ginny seems to be a bit scared of them. They'll phone her in a bit, to check she's okay.' Then she had a thought. 'Except they can't, because her phone must still be at Alice's house. That's awkward.'

'Meanwhile, what about the small matter of a murder?'

'No progress,' said Thea shortly. 'How about you?'

'A few fingerprints to follow up. Her bag turns out to be of more interest than we first thought.'

'What about the tenant who didn't like her?'

'Ah – now there we've been particularly thorough. It's a succession of people, using it as an Airbnb. Most only stay two or three nights. A lot of them complain. We spoke to the most recent ones. She was a very poor landlady, or whatever they call someone in that position. A tendency to turn up at odd times, getting the money mixed up, putting the keys in funny places. It's quite a saga.'

Thea laughed. 'I don't think that's very unusual.'

'Made her unpopular, though. Have to take it into account.'

'I assume she was desperate for the money, poor thing. Exploiting her only asset.'

'Right,' said Gladwin hesitantly. 'Yes, I imagine that must have been it.'

'Stephanie and I are going home today regardless of developments, if there are any. I'm sorry I ever came, to be honest. I like Baunton a lot, but I don't feel I'm doing any good here. Harm, if anything. Nick's leg would never have got bitten if I hadn't been here, for a start. Which reminds me – is there any news of Robbers, I mean Robinson-Finch?'

'Not that I've heard. I guess someone would have told me if he was dead.'

'You sound as jaded as me,' Thea observed.

'That Friday feeling. It's been a long week.'

'And you can't just drop it all and go home, like I can. I wouldn't change places for a bucketful of gold.'

'I don't blame you. But Thea . . .'

'What?'

'You *do* help, you know. More than you realise, probably. You're so amazingly good at making connections, for one thing.'

'More like coincidences that I'm the only person to notice.'

'You're a catalyst. I'm sure I've said that before.'

'I'm sure you have.'

They left it that Thea would phone Vanessa and see if she still wanted a visit. Stephanie could help Emmy somehow – cutting up apples or brushing out the sleeping quarters in the converted barn. Ginny remained a loose end, but to far less an extent than before. 'Although she

287

still could turn out to be the killer,' Gladwin said, before ending the call.

'Emmy's got about five hundred apples to deal with,' said Stephanie, when the conversation was relayed to her. 'Most of them get turned into juice, but she makes a lot of blackberry and apple stuff for pies and crumbles and all that.'

'We used to call it "splodge",' said Thea reminiscently. 'We lived on it for weeks in the autumn.'

'Sounds nice. Anyway, she'll be glad if I can help her. She said so yesterday and the day before. Did you notice all those boxes full of apples in that little room at the back?'

'No, but I could smell them, now I think about it. I wondered what it was.'

'And there are still lots left on the trees, but Nick says the wildlife should have most of them. He says nearly everything in nature likes an apple.'

'They do have a central place in a lot of old legends,' Thea said.

'Like Adam and Eve, for instance.'

'Precisely.'

'And yet you don't hear much about blackberries. Emmy says Nick lets Abby pick as many as she likes, because most birds don't bother with them.'

'Well, it sounds as if I can safely leave you here, being nice and constructive. There's another course starting this weekend, isn't there? Emmy must be feeling a bit of pressure about that.'

'She hasn't said. Do they use the annex for the students, or whatever they call them?'

'I think the visiting tutor gets it. There's always some sort of expert roped in to do talks or walks or whatever.'

'Like Joe?'

'I suppose so. I'm still a bit hazy as to how exactly it all works. I do know that people pay a lot for the experience, so they'll expect something substantial for their money.'

It was suddenly nine o'clock and Thea made the call to Vanessa Ferguson, preparing to grovel about her failure the previous evening.

'Ah – Mrs Undertaker, at last!' was the unexpected greeting. 'I thought I'd been abandoned.'

'I'm terribly sorry. It all got rather busy over here. We were exhausted by nine o'clock last night, so I wouldn't have been any use to you.'

'No harm done. Are you available today?'

'I can come this morning for a bit, if you like.'

'I would appreciate that enormously,' came the heartfelt reply. 'The sooner the better.'

Going back to Duntisbourne Abbots again brought another surge of memories from her very first house-sitting commission. She remembered the people she'd met there, and the shock of being involved in a vicious killing for the first time. Everything had been wrapped in a film of grief and unreality, in the first day or two, so that emotion was muted. She had talked to people, asking questions and jumping to conclusions because there had been nothing else to do. Hepzie had been a young mindless creature, supplying essential comfort and amusement and getting herself into pickles. Nothing had seemed to matter very much. With a stab of alarm, she found herself wondering if that attitude had persisted far longer than she realised.

Vanessa was waiting on the doorstep, having seen her car. 'Coffee?' she suggested.

'Thanks.'

The book-filled room felt smaller and warmer than before. There were cobwebs in the corners of the ceiling and fluff in the corners of the floor. The windowpanes were smudged. Thea settled onto the leather sofa that embraced her wholeheartedly. It was much more comfortable than the chair she'd used before.

Vanessa brought the coffee in, holding a mug in each hand, and put them on a small table that was already cluttered. 'Sorry about the mess,' she said carelessly. 'Although I'm really not, am I? It's just something people say.'

'And I'm supposed to say it's nice and homely, and it shows you have a life, and don't waste precious time on dusting.'

'Which would be true, but does not need saying.' They both laughed.

'Alice was messy as well,' said Vanessa. 'And her house is half the size of this one. She kept trying to keep everything under control, but everything conspired against her. Either she was too depressed to lift a finger, or so manic she adopted five new hobbies in a week. Mind you, that was a while ago now. The medication changed her a lot. She did start tidying up and throwing things away. She got the bedrooms almost respectable.'

'She'd have to for the Airbnb people.'

'Up to a point, yes. She just shoved it all into cupboards and locked the doors. It's amazing what people will tolerate when they realise they're occupying someone's home.'

'I was told there were complaints.'

'Oh, well . . . you can't please them all,' said Vanessa vaguely.

'The police wondered if that might be significant.'

'They think one of the tenants killed her? Far-fetched, don't you think?'

'Probably. It's all a sort of process of elimination. Crossing suspects off because they've got no motive or opportunity or whatever.'

'And who's left after they've done that?'

Thea mentally ran through the list she had only half-seriously voiced a short time ago to Stephanie and Timmy the day before. *The Weavers. The sister. The owner of the shed. The people in the village. Joe. Ginny.*

'I had a sort of list,' she said. 'You were on it, actually.'

Vanessa smiled ruefully. 'Tell me – who else is under the spotlight?'

'It started with the Weavers, as a sort of joke. My stepdaughter soon threw that out of the reckoning. Then there was the landowner man, Robinson-Finch. And the missing niece, Ginny. A chap called Joe – and the people in the village. I've only met three or four of them.'

'Let's take them one at a time, then. I've never met any of them, but I might make a useful sounding board.'

Thea was surprised. 'Really? Is that why you wanted to talk to me?'

'I want to know who killed my sister. Wouldn't you? I

have the same desire to see justice done as I assume most people have. Did you ever read *Crime and Punishment*?'

'Actually, yes. I can still feel that horrible atmosphere. I think about it quite often.'

'It's a kind of wish-fulfilment fairy tale, don't you think? The notion that even if a murderer is never caught, the guilt will cripple him for the rest of his life. We all want that to be true.'

'And is it?'

'Who knows? It is in books, which is better than nothing.' Vanessa looked round the room. 'I do live my real life through fiction, I suppose. It's been a lifelong habit since I was about seven. All those wonderful worlds . . .' She sighed. 'And then something like this happens and I'm forced to wake up and look at it all as others do. If I'm to exist at all, I have a responsibility to engage with what people call reality. Before it's too late,' she added softly.

Thea sat back and tried to think. 'I see,' she said. 'Maybe we need a pencil and paper, then.'

Vanessa produced a pad of lined paper and invited Thea to repeat her list. One by one names were written down, with comments beside them. 'It's means, motive and opportunity,' Thea remembered. 'I always like saying that. It feels like sticking to the rules of a game. And evidence, of course. The police never do anything important until they've got proper evidence.'

They started another page headed 'Evidence', listing the knife left beside Alice's body, the probable timings, the layout of the village and all people known to be within striking distance at the time of the killing. 'Which brings us back to page one,' said Vanessa.

'We don't know everything the police have discovered. Witness statements. Who saw who when and where.'

'Who can we eliminate, then?' asked Vanessa, turning back to the top page.

Thea hesitated, trying to concentrate. Her eyes scanned the shelves of books, without registering any of the titles or authors. They were just shapes and colours, in no discernible pattern. 'I'd like to say all of them,' she admitted. 'Even the Robinson-Finch man is nicer than I thought at first. He was very decent yesterday.' She told Vanessa about the drama with Joshua, making her laugh.

'Alice would have loved that,' she said. 'She could be very childlike at times.'

'Yes, so I gather. Emmy told us about her playing about with Ginny. And the whole thing with Ginny hiding out was meant to be a game, apparently.'

'You've lost me.'

'Oh, sorry. So much has happened. I don't think I'll ever be able to bring you up to date with it all. You knew Ginny was missing – right?'

Vanessa consulted the notes. 'Yes, you said so just now. Nick's niece. Friendly with Joe, as well as Alice. I don't recall Alice ever mentioning her. But games? Hiding out?'

'It probably isn't relevant. Except she would have to be an amazingly good liar if she is the murderer. She really seemed to have liked Alice – and I can't imagine any conceivable motive.' She remembered the inconsistent accounts of the Weaver notebook and frowned.

'What?' asked Vanessa.

'Emmy told us that Ginny stole a vitally important notebook – diary – belonging to Nick's mother. Full of important stuff about the family business. When I asked Ginny about it, she said she had no idea such a thing existed, and she certainly hadn't taken it. So somebody was lying.'

'And you don't think it was her?'

'No. But I don't think it was Emmy, either.'

'Which leaves Nick.'

'It could all be perfectly innocent. He might have misplaced it, and just assumed Ginny had it. After all, it's a very odd thing to tell lies about.'

'It would cast Ginny in an unfavourable light.'

'You mean – give me and Stephanie more reason to hunt her down? Put more effort into looking for her? I suppose it did, a bit.'

'Or simply be a red herring of some sort.'

Thea lapsed into further concentrated thought. 'I can't make that fit,' she concluded. 'It feels more like the opposite of a red herring. As if we were being pointed in a very relevant direction, if that makes sense.'

'I read too much detective fiction,' Vanessa sighed. 'I expect I'm making it all much more complicated than it need be.'

'I've had a lot of first-hand experience of this sort of thing, as you might have gathered. I don't remember anyone actually deliberately trying to divert my attention. Although . . . perhaps there have been one or two. They tend to merge together in my memory after a while.'

Vanessa gave her a close look. 'I do find you fascinating,' she said. 'You're a real live amateur detective.

And married to an undertaker for good measure. You couldn't make it up!'

'It's been quite a ride at times.'

'You sound as if it's coming to an end. What's that about?'

Thea sighed. 'Nothing lasts forever, as my father used to say. My husband is more and more unhappy about it. Now his daughter's getting involved, he's really worried. I can see it looks dangerous – and upsetting at times. Stephanie is very young, but she's also very sensible and wise. My own daughter's in the police, and I can see Stephanie going the same way – which would be perfectly fine, even though Drew quietly hopes she'll take a role in his business when she's older. I should be earning proper money in a proper job. I'll soon be too old to get started on anything new – and I can't think of anything I really learnt to do, anyway – I'm not trained for anything. It's all a bit of a dilemma just now.'

'So I see,' said Vanessa. 'But I have no advice to offer you, other than that life is short and you have an obligation not to waste it in doing stuff that makes you miserable or frustrated or guilty.'

'Thanks,' said Thea. 'Let's get back to looking for evidence, shall we?'

'I'm not convinced we're getting anywhere. Maybe a different approach is called for. Tell me about these Weavers. They seem to be at the crux of everything. And you did put them first on your list of suspects.'

'That's exactly what Stephanie said. And yet . . . they can't possibly have killed Alice. They were on the farm at the time.'

'Were they? Look at these timings. How long did you take to walk from them down to the village on Tuesday?'

'I didn't walk, I drove, and then sat for quite a while in the car. I don't know how long it would take someone on foot.'

'Well I know for a fact that you can get from the shed to the farmhouse over the fields in barely ten minutes.'

'Can you? How do you know that?' Thea's head began to thrum. Was it possible that Vanessa was, after all, to be suspected? Had she cleverly arranged a false alibi? Had she really hated her sister, or really wanted to inherit her house?

'Because Alice told me. I admit I didn't always pay attention, but she said it a number of times. It's only two or three fields away. I think there's even a footpath.'

'Which the forager woman – Abby – must use as well,' said Thea slowly. 'They might have seen each other, even walked along together. And Nick – he walks around with Abby, as well.' She frowned deeply. 'How is it nobody seems to have thought about that? Which way does it approach the farm from, though? I can't get my head round the geography.'

Vanessa shrugged. 'Don't ask me.'

'Gladwin and I were going to walk it all out, days ago. We never got round to it.'

'Pity. Look – I don't think we're doing this right. This evidence stuff is what the police are good at. I would think your input would be more about impressions and connections and flights of fancy.'

Thea laughed. 'That's just what Gladwin says. But I don't think it's working very well this time.'

296

'Well, *I'm* getting some impressions myself. Look – there are lots of interlocking triangles here. Nick/Abby/Ginny, Nick/Abby/Alice. Maybe Alice/Emmy/Nick. Always including Nick. He seems to be everywhere.'

'Yes,' said Thea, faintly, not quite sure what was being suggested. 'Because he owns the farm. He's at the heart of it all.'

'And everybody knows him. He's got the most to lose. He has passions and obsessions and young Ginny sounds as if she's scared of him.'

'None of which makes him a murderer,' said Thea with conviction. 'If we're talking about impressions, then I'd say he's completely in the clear. He's just stressed with everything and worried about his business.'

'Okay.' Vanessa tapped her pen on the notepad. 'Though I'm not sure I can see why you're so sure.'

'If we're going back to impressions, then the person who really looks most suspicious to me is Abby. She flits about with her basket like some kind of hedge witch, has a pretty ropey backstory, and turns on the defenceless female tap when it suits her. I bet she's lying when she says she didn't know Alice was using the shed, as well.'

'What does she do for a living?'

'Good question. She's always around, so I don't think she goes to an office or anything. She said something about working from home. I'd say "software", although she doesn't seem the type for that. Maybe she writes blogs about mushrooms.'

'Stranger things have earned a good income.'

'Of all the people on the list, I like her least,' Thea said, rather to her own surprise.

'Well, let's hope it was her, then,' said Vanessa darkly. 'It would be awful if somebody *nice* did it.'

Thea found herself unable to take that as a joke. 'Yes, it would,' she said with a sharp flash of foreboding.

Chapter Twenty-One

It was almost eleven o'clock when Thea got back to the farm and still raining. Her thoughts were as mangled as ever, with no clear indication of what might happen next. A lot of what Vanessa had said was circling around in her mind, like a picture trying to come into focus. Thea had liked her very much, recognising similarities with other women of a similar age and background encountered in the Cotswolds over the years. When they were all gone, the place would be far less interesting or enjoyable. The next generation were so much more conformist, materialistic and unimaginative. The fact that it was Thea's own generation only made her more depressed.

She was paying scant attention to her surroundings as she drove into the farmyard. Indeed, there was very little to attract attention, at least at first glance. No big dog or strange vehicle. No smoke or flood, although it was still raining. The door of the barn stood wide open, which made Thea wonder if Stephanie had been recruited as a cleaner or bed-maker, in preparation for the imminent arrival of people for the next course. The rain would be a damper on the proceedings, if it kept on, she supposed. Didn't most of the activity take place outdoors? She pulled up the hood of her jacket and opened the car door.

Instantly, she could hear loud voices coming from the barn. 'But where *is* it?' Emmy was demanding shrilly. 'It was in that top drawer. I know it was.'

'Stop asking me,' came Nick's calmer tones. 'I don't even remember what it looked like.'

'Don't give me that, you liar. Honestly, Nick, I never know when to believe you these days. Of course you know what it looks like. You've peeled about a thousand apples with it, for heaven's sake, since Alice gave it to us.'

Thea's blood slowly turned cold. She walked towards the barn, to be met by Stephanie in the doorway. 'Knife?' she said, in a whisper.

Stephanie looked dazed, as if events were going on above her head and she could not find any meaning in them. She shrugged helplessly. Thea acted quickly. Grabbing the girl, she dragged her back to the car, fumbled for her phone in the bag on the passenger seat and then pushed Stephanie into the vehicle. 'Sit there,' she ordered. 'I'm calling Gladwin.'

'Why?'

'Why do you think?' said Thea heartlessly.

'I don't know. I don't understand.' Tears were forming in Stephanie's eyes. 'I want to go home.'

Thea was beyond thankful when the detective answered on the third ring. 'Come to the farm right away,' she ordered. 'We need you.'

Anyone else would have asked endless questions, argued, made excuses. 'Okay,' said Gladwin. 'Six minutes tops.' Thea found a moment to worry for any loitering creatures in the lanes leading to Baunton.

She sat with her stepdaughter, marvelling at the workings of the human brain. How many microseconds had it taken for her to see the whole picture, crystal clear and inescapable? It could only be that the truth had been lying there, just below the surface, since some point the previous evening. It had nudged at her again that morning, when talking to Vanessa. Now it was sitting there, newborn and vivid, and Thea had no idea what to do with it.

'Thea? What's happening? Emmy can't find the knife she uses for cutting up apples. What's so odd about that? She's cross with Nick about it. He's been out in the barn all morning, and we've been putting covers on duvets. We were laughing about it, because it's a horrible job. We were going to make apple juice. Why've you called Gladwin?' Stephanie was trying to speak normally, to convince herself that all was well, and there was not about to be something cataclysmic taking place. 'It's just a knife,' she insisted pathetically.

'Knives kill people. It was Alice's knife – Emmy just said so. I'm sorry, Steph, but I think that's all the evidence we need.'

'We?' echoed the girl bitterly. 'What does it have to do with us? Why did we ever come? Without us, it would all have been all right.'

Looked at a certain way, Thea had to agree.

In the barn, the marital argument raged on, and Thea knew she ought to be listening to what was said. There was a strong risk that Emmy would draw the same conclusion as Thea had done, and find herself in danger as a result. 'I'll have to go and talk to them,' she said. 'You stay here.'

'Don't worry, I will,' muttered Stephanie.

Inside the barn, Emmy was sitting on a wooden bench in what was now a kind of hallway leading to the two dormitories. She was staring dully at her husband, tears on her cheeks. 'Is it anything to do with Abby?' she asked huskily. Then she noticed Thea and put a hand over her mouth. 'I didn't know you were back,' she said, with no sign of relief or gladness.

Nick was standing against a wooden partition, like a wild boar at bay. *Where's Joshua?* Thea wondered, by a rapid piece of association. The man's bandaged leg was thrust out in front of him at an unnatural angle.

'You're not making any sense,' he told his wife. 'I have no idea what you're thinking, or where all this is coming from. I don't concern myself with kitchen utensils and I certainly can't see what anything has to do with Abby.'

'You should have put it back,' Emmy said. 'That would have been the clever thing to do.'

Nick glared at Thea. 'Well?' he snarled. 'Heard enough? I thought you'd have gone by now.'

Thea went to Emmy and sat down beside her. She could hear a police siren not far away, and thought how foolish it was to use it in such a situation. Crass, dangerous and unnecessary. But the others showed no sign of noticing it.

Nick spoke again. 'Come on, love. We've got work to do. The apples can wait. If it keeps on raining, we'll have to change the programme. We might be able to find the film that people are talking about. The one that follows the life of a cow. That should get them thinking.'

'Shut up,' said Emmy wearily. 'You know as well as I do that there isn't going to be a course. There might never be one again.'

Panic filled the man's face. He limped a few paces along the wall and back. 'You don't know what you're saying. You're in some sort of fugue state, seeing visions or something. There's absolutely no need for anything to change. We *have* to keep it going, don't you see? It's all we have. It's our future.' He looked at her middle. 'It's our *baby's* future.'

Emmy shook her head, and leant against Thea. 'I can't live with a murderer, Nick. And I can't let my baby do that either.'

Gladwin was directed to the barn by Stephanie, who refused to go with her. Detective Constable Erik was in attendance, and Thea supposed further reinforcements might be on their way. The tableau in the barn was probably not what the police officers expected. The Weavers were in each other's arms, both sobbing. Thea was slumped on the bench, doing nothing.

'So?' asked Gladwin.

'It was Nick. Emmy can probably supply the evidence, along with Abby Seldon. I'll talk you through what I think happened, if you like – I might be wrong in some parts, of course.'

'Um,' said Gladwin, uncharacteristically floored. 'I can't just arrest him on your say-so. And a wife can't usually testify against a husband.'

Erik spoke up. 'She can, ma'am. If it's voluntary and her husband doesn't raise an objection.'

Gladwin glared at him. 'Thank you, Constable. I'm not sure that helps just at the moment.'

'He'll go with you,' said Emmy, pulling away from Nick. 'He knows he hasn't got a choice. He'll give you a full confession – won't you?' she appealed to her husband.

He nodded wordlessly, his face ravaged by horror and despair.

'He's lost everything, you see,' Emmy explained in an eerily calm voice. 'That's what he was trying to avoid by killing Alice. I suppose she saw him and Abby together.'

'Is Mrs Seldon an accomplice, then?'

'Probably,' said Emmy.

Nick raised his head. 'No!' he cried. 'She has no idea. It would never even occur to her. Leave her out of it.'

Thea winced at the sudden passion in his voice. Emmy had heard it too, and her face changed to one of fury. 'You really love her, do you? That pathetic mess of a woman? To hell with you, then. Go and confess your sins and leave me in peace.'

'I guess that's what we'll do, then,' said Gladwin. She faced Nick. 'Mr Weaver, I am taking you in for questioning, but you are not under arrest. I am proceeding on the assumption that you are willing to accompany me to the police station?'

The whole group moved out into the rainy yard. Gladwin paused to address Thea. 'Will you be all right?'

'Oh yes. I'm not so sure about Stephanie, though. Or Emmy.' *And what about the dog?* A crazy voice was asking somewhere.

'I've got work to do,' said Emmy, standing squarely in the rain like a defiant statue. 'I have to cancel the course, and get the dog destroyed.'

Gladwin turned away, helping Nick onto the back seat of the police car. She met Thea's gaze, and then glanced again at Emmy. Here was one hell of a strong woman, they silently agreed.

Fifteen minutes later Thea and Stephanie were driving back to Broad Campden. The girl's face was appallingly similar to that of Nick Weaver. Misery, horror, disbelief were all etched onto the childish features. She could not stop crying, blurting new realisations every mile or two. 'The *baby*,' she sobbed. 'The *farm*.' 'What about Ginny? And Joe? What's going to *happen*? Nick was so nice. He had so many great ideas. Plans.'

'Stop it,' ordered Thea eventually. 'None of it can be helped.'

'But was it *us*? Would everything have been all right if we'd never come?'

'I don't see how. Emmy would still have missed the knife and reached the same conclusion. We were entirely incidental to that.'

'No,' said Stephanie. 'She only looked for it because we needed another one for me. She said it was Nick's special one, that Alice gave him. She searched everywhere for it, for ages. Talking about the way he could peel an apple all in one piece, because it was so sharp and just a bit curved, and he'd really loved it. I think she knew right away where it had gone. But if there'd just been her, cutting the apples up, she'd have used the other one and might never have—' She subsided in another fit of crying.

'She'd have found out some other way. I think she had some worries about Abby and the way Nick seemed to go off with her such a lot. She would have known he was lying about the notebook. And Ginny would have backed her up.'

'I still don't understand most of it. Where does the notebook come in, anyway?'

'We might never know. I guess it was just a way of making us try harder to find Ginny. And I have a very nasty feeling he needed that to happen, in case she'd seen him and Abby as well. They took photos, remember? He might have worried that he and Abby were on them.'

'You think he would have murdered Ginny too?'

'Who knows?' sighed Thea.

'What's going to *happen*?' Stephanie wailed again.

In a desperate search for any sort of solace, Thea started talking about Emmy's skills and strengths. 'She'll keep the farm, I expect. She might go on with the courses. They're such a brilliant thing. I thought Dad might start doing something similar. You know – discussions about dying and funerals. Practical things like coffins and graves. He could even help Emmy, if she'd let him.' She found this diversion a big relief, and hoped Stephanie would be similarly distracted. A rosy vision was creeping up on her in which everyone rescued everyone else.

'That would be good,' said Stephanie slowly.

'If we could make it work. Do you think we could?'

There was no answer, but the idea acquired a life of its own in the hothouse atmosphere of the car. A new project for Emmy, who might well need the money; diversification for Drew; and a murky sense of reparation for the harm that Stephanie feared they had wrought. 'He's used to working with a baby beside him,' she said, having entertained a vision of Drew working alongside the new mother. It was oddly symmetrical and reassuring.

'Me? He told you about that, did he? I was there when he arranged funerals, when I was really small.'

'Oh yes.'

'What about you?'

'I could be there as well.' That part felt much more uncertain. 'Maybe.'

'We won't move, will we?'

'Darling – we're just dreaming. It probably won't happen. Look, we're almost there now.'

'Good. Because I don't think I ever want to go to Baunton again,' sniffed Stephanie.

* * *

Drew and Timmy were sitting down to a pizza lunch when the womenfolk got home. Hepzie greeted them with her usual excess and for a moment everything felt reassuringly normal. Then Drew saw his daughter's face and nothing was remotely normal for the next hour. Thea stepped back and let things unfold as they must. She accepted that she had done wrong, and was ready for the reproaches that Drew was sure to heap onto her head. But first she made a phone call.

'Vanessa? The police will probably contact you sometime today, but I thought I'd get in first. It was Nick Weaver.'

'Ah. Yes.'

'You're not surprised?'

'Everything did keep coming back to him, don't you think? Nobody else had such strong feelings about anything. Other people were far less exercised. Mild disapproval. Exasperation at times. Occasional bewilderment perhaps. Nothing strong enough to lead to murder. But Alice always talked about how *passionate* the Weaver man was. How that wife of his was his salvation and he should cherish her more than he did.'

'I'm not sure that's quite it. It's much simpler than that. It looks as if Alice must have seen him with his other woman. Abby, who lives right next to that shed.'

'Ah.'

'There might even be pictures on Ginny's phone – which she left with Alice last week. Ginny and Alice used it a lot, apparently, taking pictures out in the fields.' She gave this more thought. 'But I bet it's still in her house somewhere. Ginny was there for a few days after she ran away. If it is, the police'll find it and the photos will confirm my theory. Maybe they have already.'

'It's nice of you to tell me,' said Vanessa. 'I need to sit down and think it all through. It's absolutely certain, is it?'

'Oh yes,' sighed Thea.

'Then you probably need to sit quietly for a while, too,' said Vanessa gently. 'I imagine we've both had enough for one week.'

'More than enough,' said Thea, thinking of Stephanie. 'But it isn't over yet. Not by a long way.'

She had not expected any contact from the police, but Gladwin phoned while Drew was still talking to Stephanie. 'He's confessed the whole thing,' she reported. 'There was no satisfaction in it, I can tell you. I've never seen a man so broken. We'll have to keep him on suicide watch, he's in such a state.'

'So, you don't need to do any more investigating? The knife . . . Ginny's phone . . . Whether Abby knew what he'd done? None of that? And what about my part in it all?'

'Just enough investigating to confirm the confession and make sure he's not shielding anybody. There might be some issues around the Seldon woman, but nothing we can't handle. What do you mean about your role?'

'I must have been right there when he did it. Parked just around the corner. He probably knew that. He *used* me. I was a kind of alibi or smokescreen. Sending me down there and then stabbing poor Alice right under my nose, because he knew I had no idea how the fields and footpaths worked. Although . . .' she tried to think logically. 'He couldn't really have known where I'd be, could he? He just took the risk because he was so scared of Emmy leaving him.'

'Leave it for now, Thea. As far as you're concerned, it's over.'

'Drew's going to ban me from ever speaking to you again, you know.'

'Who can blame him? It was reckless, my friend, to take that girl into such a quagmire.'

'I know. But my main crime was not to foresee that it was going to be a quagmire from the start.'

'Hmm,' was all the detective had to say to that.

Drew had to go out for the afternoon, making it clear to Thea that he wanted to talk when the children were in bed. 'No problem,' she said, fighting a sense of being summoned to the headmaster's study.

Unexpectedly, Emmy phoned at half past three. 'How's Stephanie?' she began.

'Miserable.'

'Poor girl. She must be so confused. It's bad enough for the grown-ups.'

'It's good of you to think of her.'

'It's easier than thinking about myself. Then I just get to the point where everything's my fault.'

'How?'

'Nick got hopelessly dependent on me. He's really not very good at anything practical. It's some kind of defect in him – he doesn't follow things through, doesn't finish a job. He always has plenty of ideas and ambitions, and he's not *stupid*, but he was never cut out to be a farmer.'

'Ginny says you saved him.'

'I did. But I *wanted* to. I love this life. I know the courses and rewilding and all the plans for more along those lines is completely doable. We *were* doing it. But there were conditions, mostly unspoken. Like not having affairs with other women.' Thea could hear the words coming through gritted teeth. 'Such a ridiculous stereotype. Weeks ago now I made some joke about Abby seducing local landowners. I was thinking of Robinson-Finch, actually. He's got a wife, but they're separated. Nick went a bit pink, so I told him she'd better not set her cap at him, because I'd scratch both their eyes out. I never for a minute thought there was anything going on, at that point. But I suppose the possibility had lodged in my mind and I watched him more carefully. And I repeated my threats a few times, trying to convince him I was serious. I never saw anything definite, but I did hear two of the course people gossiping one day, when they didn't know I was there. I tackled him right away and told him I would leave him if it was true. He could carry on without me, and see where that would get him. I meant it, as well.'

'But he didn't stop?'

'Apparently. You saw what the wretched woman's like – all clinging and helpless. Honestly, if I wasn't so pregnant and flattened, I'd go down there now and shoot her.'

'Don't,' said Thea. 'Have you got a gun?'

'No, but I could borrow Robbers's.'

'Don't,' said Thea again.

'If it hadn't been the knife, it would probably have been something else. I keep wondering why he didn't just bring it home and put it back in the drawer.'

Thea had a faint insight into the man's thinking. 'He'd have been reminded of what he'd done every time he saw it.'

'So throw it away somewhere.'

'Things always get found, though, don't they? There's a certain sense to letting the police think it was Alice's. Nobody would ever think to ask you about it.'

'They might. If not me, then Ginny. She's blaming herself as well.'

'Why?'

'For drawing the police's attention to us. She's still in a muddle about the sequence of events. But she doesn't seem very surprised that it was Nick who killed Alice.'

'Nor does Vanessa. I expect they would have caught him in the end, one way or another.'

'Well tell Stephanie she didn't do anything at all to feel bad about. Tell her she can come and see the baby when it's born.'

'Thanks,' said Thea, feeling choked. 'And well done for being so strong. And . . . well, it's probably jumping the gun, but I have a feeling that Drew might be interested in getting involved with your courses. If you'll have him.'

'I'm not strong, Thea. I'm going to crawl away into

a corner now and let Ginny look after me. Tell Drew to come and see me in about a month.'

'Ginny's there?'

'Arriving any minute. I think she might be moving in, actually. We both need someone to love and we get along pretty well.'

And what about Joshua? Thea wanted to ask, but bit it back. She suspected she'd already said too much.

She went to tell Stephanie what Emmy and Gladwin had said, emphasising that nothing at all had been her fault. There didn't seem to be anything else she could safely or usefully say. The girl looked at her with bleary eyes. 'Thanks,' she muttered. 'Now please leave me alone.'

Finding Timmy in the kitchen, Thea made an effort to appear normal, moving things off the draining board and clattering cutlery into the drawer. 'You had quite an adventure, didn't you?' the child said.

'It was all a bit much for your sister, in the end.'

He nodded. 'I know. You never know what you're going to discover, do you? It makes life seem very dangerous sometimes.' He gave her a solemn little-boy look, and she pulled him to her in a tight hug.

'Oh, Tim – you say the wisest things, you know that?'

He wriggled free and grinned at her. 'Because I stay at home when you're out there being a detective.' He laughed. 'And make discoveries of my own.'

'Like what?'

'Like tomato soup tasting nothing like tomatoes.'

'Oh, Tim.' She wiped her eyes. 'That seems so long ago now.'

'Can we have it again for lunch on Sunday?'

'I don't see why not.'

Drew's reproaches were all the worse for being quiet and pained. 'She's much too young for this,' he repeated. 'I did my best to stop you. I can't let this ever happen again. I *told* you.'

'I know. I agree with you. I can't tell you how sorry I am.'

'Murder isn't a *game*, Thea. I'm not sure you've ever understood that properly. That's what Stephanie expected – some sort of puzzle, with an ending that wouldn't affect her much, if at all. Now she's seen the horrifying consequences for so many people. It's not the same as the ones she sees here. People die of old age, illness, accidents. None of that's at all like being violently killed for some mean selfish motive that spreads its taint over everyone involved. Do you see?'

'Yes,' she whispered. 'After all this time, I really do. I've been an absolute fool. A monster, I suppose. I've got no excuses – you never stopped trying to persuade me. It won't happen again.'

'Really?'

'I swear it. I'm going to sign up for a course in something, and get a qualification and find a job, and throw myself into something completely different. And let's start thinking about some really great family holiday, maybe next spring. We could go to the Lake District.'

314

Drew smiled at that. 'All we have to do, then, is to find something suitably absorbing for you to do. A law degree perhaps? Or psychotherapy? How about elder care? That's going to be in high demand in the coming years.'

She tried to smile back, while struggling to envisage herself in any of those roles. 'We'll have to see,' she said.

The quotation 'Death is nothing at all' on page 12 by Canon Henry Scott Holland, 1847–1918, Canon of St Paul's Cathedral, is part of a sermon on death delivered in St Paul's Cathedral on Whitsunday 1910, while the body of King Edward VII was lying in state at Westminster. The whole sermon carries the title *The King of Terrors*.

REBECCA TOPE is the author of three bestselling crime series, set in the Cotswolds, Lake District and West Country. She lives on a smallholding in rural Herefordshire, where she enjoys the silence and plants a lot of trees.

rebeccatope.com
@RebeccaTope